"Together with Greenwood's witty and fluid, elegant prose, Phryne Fisher is a sheer delight."

—*The Chronicle* (Toowoomba)

"Greenwood's strength lies in her ability to create characters that are wholly satisfying: the bad guys are bad, and the good guys are great."

—*Vogue*

Also by Kerry Greenwood

The LADY with the GUN ASKS the QUESTIONS

The LADY with the GUN ASKS the QUESTIONS

The ultimate
MISS PHRYNE FISHER
story collection

KERRY GREENWOOD

Poisoned Pen
PRESS

Published by Poisoned Pen Press, an imprint of Sourcebooks
P.O. Box 4410, Naperville, Illinois 60567-4410
(630) 961-3900
sourcebooks.com

Originally published in 2021 in Australia by Allen & Unwin.

Library of Congress Cataloging-in-Publication Data

Names: Greenwood, Kerry, author.
Title: The lady with the gun asks the questions : the ultimate Miss Phryne
   Fisher story collection / Kerry Greenwood.
Description: Naperville, Illinois : Poisoned Pen Press, [2022] | Series:
   Phyrne Fisher mysteries
Identifiers: LCCN 2021037061 (print) | LCCN 2021037062
(ebook) | (hardback) | (trade paperback) | (epub)
Subjects: LCSH: Fisher, Phryne (Fictitious character)--Fiction. | Women
   detectives--Fiction. | LCGFT: Detective and mystery fiction. | Short
   stories.
Classification: LCC PR9619.3.G725 L33 2022 (print) | LCC PR9619.3.G725
   (ebook) | DDC 813/.54--dc23
LC record available at https://lccn.loc.gov/2021037061
LC ebook record available at https://lccn.loc.gov/2021037062

Printed and bound in the United States of America.
VP 10 9 8 7 6 5 4 3 2 1

To all my faithful friends and colleagues at Sunshine Legal Aid, who have endured my extravagant irruptions into their ordered world with enviable patience.

* * *

With thanks to my forgiving friends, David and Dennis, Jeannie and Alan, Belladonna and Monsieur, and to three cafés, Alfamie, Delizia, and the Gravy Train, without whom we might all have starved…

CONTENTS

APOLOGIA

Dear Reader,

Thank you very much for buying this book (and if you haven't bought it yet, please do so—I have cats to feed. It would make an ideal present for anyone who likes history, clothes, fashion, food, or beautiful young men…have I left anyone out?).

No one was more surprised than me when Phryne was adopted into so many homes. She was a little taken aback as well. I trust that these stories will amuse you. They certainly amused me.

As you will see, sometimes I try out some of the cast of a novel in a short story to see if they like me enough to stay for a whole book, there being a great difference between 3,000 and 85,000 words, and an author needs to pick her company if she has to give house room to them for so long. If you like the Carnival people, you will meet them again in *Blood and Circuses*.

Oh, and by the way, please do not write to me and complain that the plot from 'Hotel Splendide' is stolen from a Hitchcock film, or a horror movie, or any other recent source. It is an urban myth, first written down by Alexander Woollcott in the 1920s, which is why I thought Phryne would like it. I had a really good idea for the Vanishing Hitchhiker, too, but there was such a fuss about 'Hotel Splendide' that I ditched the idea.

And go easy on the cocktails, is my advice. A green chartreuse hangover is as impossible to describe as it is to endure.

Why not email me on kgreenwood@netspace.net.au if you enjoyed this book? And if you didn't, give it to a charity shop at your earliest convenience.

Kerry Greenwood

ON PHRYNE FISHER

I began to write mysteries because I was trying to get published—a soul-destroying, painful process which I wish never to repeat. The novel I had to sell was not a mystery but an historical novel, and I had been hawking it around the publishers for four years. The only reason I did not give up is that I am a very obstinate person. I submitted it to the Australian/Vogel Literary Award, a competition for unpublished manuscripts. They did not give me the prize, but one of the Vogel judges asked me to come and see her, and told me that she didn't want the historical novel but could do with a couple of mysteries. I agreed so fast that the words echoed off the wall, and then sat on the tram going down Brunswick Street wondering what I had got myself into. I had never written a mystery before. I had been reading them since I learned to read, but I had never written one and didn't have the faintest idea how to begin. So I began with a character. If I had the protagonist, I reasoned, she could tell me what to do next. I had decided to place these mysteries in the 1920s—in 1928, in fact, because I had written a legal history essay on the 1928 wharf strike, my father being a wharf labourer, and had done extensive work on 1928 from newspapers and interviews.

I knew what she looked like. My sister Janet has a perfect 1920s face and figure; small, thin, elegant, with black hair and pale skin and green eyes. At that time Janet had a bobby-cut, too. She looked just like a flapper.

Then I needed a name. I had been looking at 1900 birth notices, for some reason, and a lot of them were Ancient Greek names—Psyche, Irene, Iris. These ladies (the naive Psyche, Irene the Goddess of Peace, and Iris the nymph of the rainbow) were far too respectable to be the sort of person I wanted my heroine to be, but then I remembered Phryne, a courtesan in Ancient Greece, so beautiful that the painter Apelles used her for his Aphrodite, and so rich and notorious that she offered to rebuild the walls of Thebes as long as she could put a sign on them reading: THE WALLS OF THEBES; RUINED BY TIME, REBUILT BY PHRYNE THE COURTESAN. My kind of woman.

Her last name is derived elaborately as a scholastic joke. She is a Fisher of Men, as all detectives are. Her name also reflects the Grail cycle Le Roi Pêcheur, the Sinner or Fisher King. I have always liked that absurd pun on Sin and Fish. And there was a street in Paris called rue du Chat qui Pêche, which was a good place to find a gigolo.

All of the information had come to me piecemeal from various sources. It was coagulating in my head as I sat on the tram, and when I got off the tram in Melbourne, I had the name of my heroine, Phryne Fisher, I knew what she looked like, and I was working on where she came from. I gave her a poor background to make her appreciate being rich, and a title so that she could not be overawed by Society.

Because I wanted her to be a female wish-fulfilment figure, I wanted her to be like James Bond, with better clothes and fewer gadgets. There was no female hero in the same vein as Leslie Charteris's Simon Templar, the Saint. In fact, as the Saint books were published in the same period of the 1920s, I wanted to make her Simon Templar's younger, more level-headed sister. All I really did was take a male hero of the time and allow her to be female. No one thinks it odd that James Bond has blondes and no regrets. I only ever thought I would have two books published, so I tried to pack everything I wanted to say about female heroes into them. The modern women detectives are afflicted with self-doubt, neglect their diets, worry about exercise, think they may be growing fat (as if fat was a disfigurement), and are generally burdened with low self-esteem and guilt. I wanted a character without guilt, with boundless self-esteem—as a role model, perhaps. She was no challenge to invent. All I really felt that I actually invented was the name and the background. She blossomed from the moment I wrote the first line of *Cocaine Blues*, and after the first five chapters, I had no further control over her. I feel like I discovered Phryne, rather than invented her.

She's a bold creature for the 1920s but not an impossible one. None of the things she does are out of the question for that brittle, revolutionary period. And, yes, Kerry Greenwood can fly a small plane (though I've only flown once in a Tiger Moth), and Kerry Greenwood can fire—or, rather, *has* fired for the purposes of research—a handgun such as Phryne carries. The research is essential to make the books convincing, and besides, I love original research. Historical novels walk a fine line. Too much detail and the reader is bored. Too little and it fails to convince. The ideal state for the reader is one where she trusts the writer to tell her everything she needs to know. Consider Maigret's Paris or Ellis Peters' Shrewsbury. And I find it essential for me to know what streets Phryne walks down. Fortunately, a lot of Melbourne is still much the same as it was in the 1920s. I use all the bits that are extant.

My favourite detective writer, Dorothy L. Sayers, always

included a slab of solid research in her books, and I decided, in homage, to do that too. In each of my novels you will find out something different about Melbourne in 1928, as well as the detective story. It is not so much a mission as a gift to the readers.

The process of writing one of these novels is odd. I choose a new aspect of Melbourne which I would like to research—the theatre, the circus, jazz, flying, the docks—and then spend six months finding out all I can about it. About one-hundredth of what I actually know about the subject ends up in the novel, but I need to know it to write the book. In fact, I worked out that for each novel I do as much work as a PhD student would for a thesis (but the novels are more fun to read than a thesis). After a while, the story starts to build up pressure, and finally it wakes me up at three in the morning and insists on being written. Other writers have a young and beautiful muse who descends in fire to inspire them. If I ever saw my muse she would be an old woman with a tight bun and spectacles poking me in the middle of the back and growling, 'Wake up and write the book!', and I always do. Because if I don't, the book gets vague and fades away. I do not plan the Phryne books at all. Once I have done the research, I just have to write fast enough to keep up. The actual writing takes about three weeks.

I have written many other novels with other heroines, but Phryne is my favourite, and I am delighted every time she drops in with a new book.

And now, about this book. Yes, it's a reissue from 2007, but with four brand-new adventures written in 2019 and 2020. The older stories have been lightly edited, since some things which didn't quite gel at the time are now gently poking me with the pointy end of an umbrella and saying—in the voice of my aged muse mentioned above—'Come on, girl! You left a few loose ends flapping about. Go and fix them!' So I did. The earlier stories are set in 1928. The very first Phryne short story was 'The Vanishing of Jock McHale's Hat,' for a long-vanished Christmas collection. I wanted something light and frivolous, yet with dark undertones. The abstraction of the infamously horrible greyish-green hat of the Collingwood Football Club's coach and tribal warlord fitted the bill admirably. And it was an opportunity to put Archbishop Mannix onstage. Nowadays he is all but forgotten, but he was a crucial figure in the life of Melbourne. I would not have liked Daniel Mannix, and find his association with the Magdalen Laundries reprehensible, but he was a figure of substance and integrity. I would have respected him, at the very least, as a formidable adversary.

I used some of the early stories—notably 'Marrying the Bookie's Daughter'—to explore further the theme of Phryne's personal independence. Lindsay Herbert importunes Phryne's hand in marriage; and yet not five minutes afterwards speaks slightingly of his friend being, as he indelicately puts it, 'shackled for life' in Holy Matrimony. You, my intelligent readers, will already know that Phryne will refuse him. Fortunately for her. Life as the Honourable Mrs Herbert would indeed be a serious clipping of her wings. And she has still to meet Lin Chung. It would be a great shame to miss out on him.

The four new stories are set in 1929, since the books have crossed into the New Year. The latest Phryne novel, *Death in Daylesford*, is set towards the end of summer; and I felt that the new adventures should reflect where we have reached in Phryne's world. Besides which, her sister, Eliza, does not appear in the novels until 1929; and since I wanted to include her in the first of my new stories, the change to 1929 was essential for continuity.

One thing which has not changed is that these stories are firmly set in the world of Book Phryne. I loved the TV series and the film *Crypt of Tears*, but they are set in a fundamentally different world. On TV and in movies you cannot have such a spacious cast. For those readers who have lamented the absence of Jane and Mrs Butler, for example, I can only point to the Rule of Eight, which is apparently a thing in television. I took their word for it. Every Cloud Productions is a thoroughly professional and successful company with whom it is a joy to work. But I don't tell them how to make films, just as they don't tell me how to write novels. Once they explained their ideas to me, I consented after some robust negotiations. I loved what they did with my books. I don't think anyone in the world could have done better. Even the most challenging moment—the romance between Phryne and Jack—was an essential component of their vision. We must have URST (unresolved sexual tension) or it won't work, they told me. I am still convinced that they were right.

To those readers who have told me they still prefer the books, I have agreed. So do I. Yet the TV series and the movie are a delight. Phryne remains Phryne. Essie Davis *IS* Phryne: magnificent in her sublime self-assurance. But my novels and these stories are firmly set in the world of Book Phryne, and this will continue to be the case.

Hotel Splendide

Desperate diseases demand desperate remedies.

—Proverb

'But please! You must know me! Oh, why won't you help me?'

Phryne Fisher, sitting in the lobby of her Paris hotel, laid down *The Times* (*Fog on Channel: Continent Isolated. Snow on Points at Haslemere. Plague in Bombay, Thousands Stricken. Test Team Defeated in Australia*) and turned at the sound of the plaintive, flat, Australian vowels. Born in Richmond to a cleaning lady and a drunken remittance man, christened Phryne the courtesan instead of Psyche the nymph, so poor that she had challenged the big boys for the old tomatoes from the pig bins of Victoria Market before being whisked to England, an Hon to her name and wealth, she had no reason to remember Australia with any favour. But the voice brought back hot sun, eucalyptus leaves, ice cream made of real cream. She folded the paper and listened.

'Phryne! We'll miss the first act of the *Nibelung*!' urged Alain Descourt. He was soigné, fascinating, and rich. The only flaw in his character that Phryne had so far discovered was a devotion to Wagner. He made the mistake of laying a hand on Phryne's arm. One did not try to compel Miss Fisher. She stood, quite deliberately, and went over to the desk.

'*Mais*, Madame… *je ne sais pas!*' protested the *patron* in the most arrogant, fast, slurred French at his disposal. Phryne knew that he prided himself on his perfect English. She had no time for Parisian games with what was evidently a distressed Australian.

'*Alors*, Jean-Paul?' she asked acidly. Phryne's French was very quick and accurate, and she was well known to the Hotel Splendide as an English milady with limitless wealth and nice taste in young men.

Jean-Paul threw out his arms in a wide gesture which almost, but not quite, toppled his coffee cup.

'This is Madame Johnson. Twice she has been here tonight! The lady is as mad as birds,' he said. '*Folle comme des oiseaux!* She says that she and her husband are staying here, but that is impossible: there is no signature in the register, and we do not have the passports, which is the law, as you know, milady.'

He showed Phryne the red-leather register in which there was no entry for Johnson. Phryne shoved the register over to Mrs Johnson.

'Hello,' she said, giving the woman her scented black-gloved hand. 'My name is Phryne Fisher. Can I help you?'

'Thank God!' exclaimed Mrs Johnson. 'They won't believe me. They've stolen my husband!' she said, and burst into tears. Again, by the look of her.

'Jean-Paul,' said Phryne quietly, 'if a large pot of coffee and a bottle of the good cognac is not placed in the blue withdrawing room within the next minute, I will be quite cross.'

Jean-Paul heaved a martyred sigh, snapped his fingers, gave the order to an underling, and exchanged a glance with Alain Descourt. *Women*, the glance said. *Nothing to be done about them.*

Phryne manoeuvred her charge to the small room, supplied her with a handkerchief, a soft chair, a glass of cognac, and a cup of coffee, and sat down to await coherence. Husbands, regrettably, did go astray in Paris. It was a very good city for going astray in. Usually they came back penniless from Montmartre, reeking of cheap perfume and guilt.

Mrs Johnson was young and would have been pretty before she had wept her face into sodden misery. She wore a good but colonial travelling costume, evidently purchased in Melbourne. Her favourite colour was pink. She had walked a long way in shoes not meant for distance. At some point she had fallen and landed heavily on both knees. She was certainly distraught, but she had spoken in sentences. Phryne reserved her decision as to her charge's actual mental state. And while Phryne dealt with this Distressed British Subject, *The Ring of the Nibelung* would be bellowing along, and perhaps she might only have to endure the last act.

Finally Mrs Johnson sniffed, gulped, gasped, and sipped some coffee.

'Can you tell me about it?' asked Phryne.

Mrs Johnson found that she was talking to a dazzling woman wearing an evening dress of scarlet brocade with black gloves and a diamond clip. There was a band of diamonds around one upper arm and around her throat. She had black hair cut in a cap and the most piercing green eyes. A young man hovered discontentedly in the background.

'I came here from the station,' she said. 'With my husband. Arthur. We came off the *Orient* and took the train to Paris.'

'Yes,' said Phryne. 'The Gare du Nord.'

'Then we took a taxi to this hotel. We registered—I'm sure I saw Arthur sign! They took our passports and showed us to Room 311a. We put down our things and had a bath—you get so filthy travelling on the train. Then Arthur said he felt sick. He was running a temperature. I asked that manager—that little rat who pretends he doesn't know me!—to get a doctor. The doctor came, a young man. He told me to go out and get some medicine from a pharmacy, so I went, and when I got to the pharmacy they didn't have it, and I didn't have any more money for another taxi, so I walked to another pharmacy and they didn't have it either, so I came back here. It was a long way. I must have been gone two hours.'

'Do you still have the prescription?' asked Phryne.

'No, the second chemist kept it. He said he'd send it on. Then I got lost. I've never been to Paris before. I got scared and … a man … spoke to me, and I ran and fell. But I found my way back here and then … all this has happened.'

'Are you sure that this is the right Hotel Splendide? It's a common hotel name in Paris.'

'Yes, of course! I know the clerk. And the furnishings.'

'Interesting,' murmured Phryne. She was full of admiration. This young woman, a total stranger in one of the most confusing cities in the world, had accomplished a fine feat of backtracking to return to her destination. Even now, under the influence of cognac, coffee, and a sympathetic listener, she was beginning to recover. They breed 'em tough in Australia. She deserved support. 'And when you returned, the clerk said …?' Phryne prompted, raising her voice over the sounds of a mutinous young man making 'we're missing the opera' noises at a side table.

'He said he never saw me before and there was no room 311a. He showed me. There isn't, either. Just a blank wall. No space for the key in the key board behind the clerk. No name in the register. This trip was our honeymoon,' said Mrs Johnson. 'It was wonderful—Egypt, India, and Ceylon, and all that. I never knew people could be so happy. I've never been apart from

Arthur from the day we were married. And now he's gone. Like he's never been.'

She started to cry again. The rodent Phryne detected had grown into a Sumatran beast such as Sherlock Holmes might have had to deal with.

'You will stay here,' she said gently. 'Alain will divert you with stories from the opera. I will go and interview the clerk. I will be back soon.' She rose gracefully and withdrew.

'Talk to me, Jean-Paul,' she murmured to the *patron*, leaning confidingly on the desk. 'The lady's story is very collected for a madwoman.'

'I will show you myself,' said the *patron*. 'Jacques! Mind the desk.'

While he was turned away, Phryne quickly flicked the register open at another page. 'Why, how curious,' she commented. 'This is a new register. And I could have sworn, when I came in, that there were pages and pages left in the old one. What a busy hotel this is, to be sure.'

'Indeed,' murmured Jean-Paul, giving her an uneasy glance. Still, she was only a woman, though a clever one. 'This way, milady.'

The third floor was reached by a hydraulic elevator and Jean-Paul opened the two sets of doors with a flourish. 'There is no room 311a,' he said. 'As milady can see.'

The Hotel Splendide ran to red plush wallpaper and Empire furnishings, picked out in gilt. Phryne paced the corridor until she came to the last room on the left, 310. Opposite it was 311. After that there was just an expanse of vermilion to the corner. Phryne, one hand against the wall, leaned down to adjust a stocking and rewarded Jean-Paul with a flash of pearly knee.

'I see,' she murmured. 'Yes. Well, let us go down by the stairs.' Jean-Paul offered the distinguished lady his arm and she accepted.

He glanced down at the composed face and saw her lips moving. She might have been counting. There was, he reflected, no understanding the nobility. When she smiled at him in the lobby, however, he was certain that he had convinced her. She had the innocent smile of a happy baby. He went back to his desk, whistling 'Auprès de ma blonde.'

Phryne returned to the withdrawing room. Alain was just concluding the plot of *Tristan und Isolde*. Mrs Johnson was looking rather glazed. Wagner had the same effect on Phryne. She sympathised.

'Then she sings her last song and dies,' he concluded.

'And not before time,' said Phryne. 'Now, Mrs Johnson—'

'Call me Beth,' said Mrs Johnson. She was much recovered: red-eyed but not likely to have hysterics. Phryne thanked providence for the healing gift of brandy.

'Beth, then. And I am Phryne. Did you catch the name of the doctor?'

'Dupont,' said Beth, biting her lower lip to aid concentration.

'The Paris equivalent of Smith. I thought so. And … what can you smell?'

She held the palm of her left glove to Beth's face. The woman sniffed.

'Jicky. Rice powder. And wallpaper paste.'

'Precisely. I have two more questions. Do you trust me? And will you do as I ask?'

'I have a question, too,' said Beth Johnson. 'Do you believe me?'

'Every word,' said Phryne.

The nail-bitten hand clutched the black glove in a firm grip. 'Then the answer is yes and yes.'

'Good. Alain, we need you.'

'We're already late,' fretted Alain.

'There are other nights,' said Phryne, in such a meaningful

voice that Beth Johnson blushed, and Alain rocked a little on his heels. 'I promise I will sit through the whole Ring Cycle with you in future. I am asking for your assistance as a true son of France with the aim of preventing a catastrophe to Paris. Will you help us?'

Alain, veteran of Verdun, patriotic to his cynical core, stood up straight and saluted. 'Your orders, my colonel?'

'You need to find the nearest doctor and bring him here. Don't waste time looking for this Dupont. The woods are full of them. Just the nearest.'

'That would be my old comrade, the army doctor Lestrange. He lives just off the Place de l'Opéra—where a fine production of Wagner is even now ending its first act,' he added with emphasis.

Phryne ignored this.

'Go get him, and speedily. Meanwhile, I am going to tell Jean-Paul that Madame has admitted the error of her ways and I am taking her to rest in my suite before we set out to find the real Hotel Splendide where her husband is doubtless waiting for her.'

'Hey!' objected Beth. She received a forty-watt glare and subsided. 'Very well, Phryne.'

'Come along,' said Phryne, and swept them away.

Beth Johnson had had such a strange evening that the rest of it could not have been odder. She was sure, however, that this elegant lady had the matter in hand and that, however confusing things might yet become, somewhere at the end of it she would find Arthur. So she obediently ate a small but delicious supper, allowed her feet to be bathed by a deferential maid, and snuggled into a sofa in Miss Fisher's palatial rooms. She was wrapped in a fleecy gown and was a little muzzy with cognac. But she did not feel like crying anymore, even though she had been provided with a new perfumed handkerchief.

In an hour, the tall young man was back with a scowling, black-bearded doctor. Mrs Johnson reflected that she would not like to meet him down a dark alley. But he bowed politely over her hand and bowed even more deeply over Phryne's.

'Milady,' said Dr Lestrange. 'Had my addle-pated friend told me that the summons came from you I should not have demurred. I have never forgotten that ambulance rocketing into our hospital under shellfire, and the shock I got when I saw that the driver was not only a lady, but a beautiful one.'

'Very pretty speech,' approved Phryne. 'Thank you for coming. Now, I am about to do something thoroughly unlawful, and if you do not want to watch I should stay here with Madame until I have done it.'

'What is this act of illegality?' asked Alain.

'I am going to set fire to the hotel,' said Phryne. 'Come to the third floor when you smell smoke.'

The door closed. The two men eyed each other uneasily. 'Does she mean what she says?' asked Lestrange.

'Invariably,' sighed Alain.

'And we are going to wait until we smell smoke?'

'Of course,' said Alain. 'Me, I am not clever. But milady—she is. She knew who was stealing from my father's vineyard seconds after I told her about it, and constructed a trap which caught the thief and freed an old servant of the estate from suspicion. So if she says she is going to burn the hotel down, then she will do as she says, and I will do as I am told.'

'Your lamb-like faith does you credit,' said Lestrange. 'And certainly she has no fear. She drove Toupie's ambulances through hell and around shell holes as cool as some cucumbers ... ah,' he added, as shouts of '*Fire!*' and the clanging of a big bell offended the quiet precincts of the Hotel Splendide. 'And now?'

'We go out,' said Alain. 'And up.'

Beth Johnson had not understood one word in ten of the fast, idiomatic French. She leaped to her feet and shucked her woolly gown. Alain offered his arm and they went out into smoke-filled corridors, threading their way up through the frightened throng to the third floor.

There they saw, in the thinning reek, Phryne Fisher in her scarlet brocade wielding a poker. She was attacking the blank wall beyond room 311.

'Come and help,' she yelled. 'We haven't got much time.' Galvanised, both men came to her side and found that she had peeled a swathe of wallpaper away from what was palpably a door. Beth Johnson attacked it with her fingernails.

'They did a remarkably good job in such a short time,' said Phryne dispassionately. 'New register, bit of coloured wax in the key board, fast work with the red plush. But it was still wet when I touched it.'

'Can you get the door open or shall I find a jemmy?' asked Lestrange.

'No need,' said Phryne, producing a key from her bosom. 'I pinched it out of Jean-Paul's drawer when his back was turned. Beth, perhaps you should stay here. We don't know what we are going to find.'

'We're going to find Arthur,' said Beth Johnson. 'And dead or alive, he is my husband.'

The door creaked open. A gust of stale air puffed out. Trunks were stacked against the far wall. The bed was occupied.

Beth screamed and flung herself on her husband's body. Lestrange pushed her gently aside and leaned down close to listen at the cracked lips.

'He's alive,' he said. 'Just. I need water, cold water.'

'Why did they do all this? What's wrong with him?' said Alain from the doorway.

'Ask your friend,' said Phryne. 'Beth, can you get that window open?'

'He's got a high fever,' said Lestrange.

'Check the armpits and groin for swelling,' instructed Phryne.

'You suspect...' began Alain. 'That is why you said it would be a catastrophe for Paris? You think it's...'

'There is plague in India,' replied Phryne. 'It was in the paper I was reading. The *Orient* calls at Bombay.'

'But we didn't land there.' Beth Johnson lost patience with the window latch and broke the pane with the heel of her mistreated shoe. 'We went on. We never stopped at Bombay.'

'Jean-Paul leaped to the wrong conclusion. Dr Lestrange? What's wrong with your patient?'

'Why, malaria, of course,' said Lestrange gruffly. 'Thousands of thunders! Is someone going to get me some water, or shall I go myself? And, please, Miss Fisher, is this hotel going to burn down around us?'

'No. I lit a wastepaper basket full of rags at each landing. They will be out by now. Any moment Jean-Paul will pound up the stairs and demand—'

'What is going on here?' came the *patron*'s voice from the corridor.

Phryne smiled seraphically, diamonds glittering as she moved. 'Such timing. Ah, Jean-Paul. This is going to be a very expensive evening's work for you.'

'Milady? What are you doing? Mad, like all the English.'

'Almost convincing, *patron*. This man has malaria, not the plague. His wife has almost been driven out of her mind, and how long were you going to leave Arthur Johnson in that sealed room?'

Phryne could see his various options flit across Jean-Paul's face. Stout denial? Not plausible. Outraged hotel owner? He could already hear the tone of milady's contemptuous laugh. Complete and utter submission and explanation? Nasty but feasible. His hotel, which he had striven all his life to expand and guard, was already lost. No travellers would ever come here again after milady told her tale.

'*Vae victis*,' he said, raising both hands. 'Woe to the conquered. Command me.'

'Move Mr Johnson into a suite and bring whatever Dr Lestrange orders, and do it with amazing speed.'

Phryne waited while a covey of attendants carried Arthur Johnson downstairs to the Royal Suite and scurried off in search of the potions Dr Lestrange required. Beth Johnson walked beside the stretcher, holding her husband's slack hot hand in her own. She had forgotten everyone else in the world. For the first time in her life Beth Johnson was beautiful. Phryne beckoned to the patron.

'Come with me, Jean-Paul.'

He sighed and followed with Alain. When Phryne had regained her own suite, she discarded her gloves, marred with paste and smoke. She sat down, poured a glass of cognac for each of them and said, 'Well?'

Jean-Paul gulped and filled his glass again. His voice was rough with remembered terror. The suave hotelier was gone. Here was a man frightened out of his wits.

'I was in India when the plague struck last time. My brother caught it. He died. It starts with a high fever. The buboes come later. I knew that the Australian had it. I had to save Paris.'

'And your hotel?'

'Yes, and my hotel. If anyone thought that a plague victim was here…'

'So you called a doctor?'

'No doctor, just my cousin. He sent Madame off to find a mare's nest, and we...'

'And you were going to remove Arthur Johnson? Or were you just doing an Edgar Allan Poe on him and walling him up alive?'

'He was nearly dead,' said Jean-Paul. 'If you saw how they died in India, in heaps, too great for the living to bury... I was going to bring a doctor in the morning. If he was still alive.'

Phryne examined Jean-Paul. He was shivering. His fear of the plague was real enough. He was as white as a swarthy man could get and still be conscious. His five o'clock shadow looked like an ink stain. His hands kneaded each other ceaselessly.

Phryne made up her mind. Justice, she had always thought, ought to be about compensation rather than retribution. Despite the delicious temptations of revenge.

'All right. I have a solution. I like your hotel and do not want to see it closed and you jailed. You do not have plague in the hotel, just malaria. That is not even notifiable. We will say nothing about it—provided that you allow the Johnsons to stay here free of charge until he is perfectly well. You will purchase suitable medical care and send a cousin or two to show Beth Johnson the sights of Paris, including a complete spring costume from a suitable fashion house. And listen closely, Jean-Paul: you will play no such tricks again or by God you will be sorry. I shall see to it personally. Also, you owe me a pair of gloves. Is it agreed?'

Jean-Paul, reprieved, fell on his knees and kissed milady's dainty feet.

'Now, is this all over?' asked Alain Descourt, helping Phryne up after Jean-Paul had gone and Dr Lestrange had reported his patient would recover.

'Yes, but it has been diverting, hasn't it?' She smiled her innocent smile again.

'Not as diverting as the Ring,' said Alain from the door. 'Come along. You promised. And we still have time to catch the last act. My favourite.'

Phryne Fisher swung her opera cloak around her shoulders and followed. Wagner was, regrettably, Wagner, but a promise was a promise.

The Voice Is Jacob's Voice

The voice is Jacob's voice,
but the hands are the hands of Esau.

—Genesis 27:22

'Do come in,' invited Death, and bowed.

Dr Elizabeth MacMillan, who had wrestled many a fall with this august personage, returned the bow and entered the Hon. Miss Phryne Fisher's elegant two-storey St Kilda house. There were lights, a buzz of conversation, and a tinkle suggesting filled glasses. Miss Fisher's Winter Solstice party, to which all her friends and everyone to whom she owed a favour had been invited, was evidently going well.

Death pushed his mask back onto his forehead, rumpling his fine blond hair, and revealed the ingenuous face of Lindsay Herbert. 'Mr Herbert,' Dr MacMillan exclaimed in her precise Edinburgh accent, 'you have chosen an unchancy disguise!'

'Always wanted to be macabre,' confessed Lindsay, smoothing down his robe and propping his sickle against the door. 'Dashed hot, these draperies! Ever since I read that thing of Poe's ... what was it called?'

'"The Masque of the Red Death," I believe. I hope that you are not a bad omen.'

'I don't think so—party's going swimmingly as far as I can see, though it's a crush. Who are you masqueradin' as, Doctor? You look forbiddin' in that sheet.'

'This is not a sheet, young man, it is a toga virilis, and I am Julius Caesar—observe my laurel crown.'

'Oh.' Lindsay could never remember who had won between Caesar and Pompey, even though he had been forced to study the civil war. He was about to offer '*Omnia Gallia in tres partes divisa est*,' which was all he could remember of the work in question, when Phryne swept into the hall, drew closer to Dr MacMillan, and whispered in her ear, 'You are mortal.'

'Correct,' said the doctor. 'And well guessed. Now who are you, I wonder? Magnificent, Phryne!'

Phryne stood back a little to allow the older woman to admire her. The black hair was drawn back under a red wig, and she had a crown bright with emeralds, a gold dress, and ropes of pearls.

Dr MacMillan made an Elizabethan bow. 'Your Majesty Queen Elizabeth, I am honoured.'

'I've even got the petticoat,' said Phryne, displaying it, a fine silk one with gold edging. 'Put me down in any part of my realm in my petticoat and I would be what I am. Lindsay, you can come in now and have a drink. Mr Butler has finished making his next batch of cocktails. Come along.' She laid a jewelled hand on each arm, and Julius Caesar and Death escorted her into the drawing room. It was full of people. Dr MacMillan was provided with a glass of good gin, and Lindsay collared two cocktails made to Mr Butler's own jealously guarded recipe. Jazz, provided by gramophone records, rose above the chatter of thirty guests.

'*Who,*' demanded the singer tinnily, '*stole my heart away? Who?*' He seemed destined to remain unanswered.

Dr MacMillan found herself next to a young woman whom she had previously seen as a patient.

'Well, Miss Gately'—she peered beneath a layer of make-up to confirm that this Columbine was indeed Miss Gately—'how are you?'

'Hellish, thank you,' muttered Miss Gately. 'What a press of people! I wonder that Phryne invited half of them.'

'Oh?' Dr MacMillan surveyed the room. 'Why?'

'Well, there's that policeman she's so fond of,' snapped Miss Gately, as a pirate in sea boots passed. 'Detective Inspector Robinson, isn't he? And I'm sure those three don't belong.'

She indicated a group of people dancing very close together: a cat in a skin-tight theatrical suit, head covered by a full mask; a carnival baby, plumped out with cushions, in lacy drawers; and a sleek and scarlet devil. They were all managing to eat some-how and, by the way they were giggling, had got at the cocktails fairly early. Dr MacMillan recognised in the devil a certain Klara, whom she had treated for venereal disease, and assumed that her companions were also ladies (or indeed gentlemen) of the night. She shrugged.

'They seem to be enjoying themselves.'

'Oh, I expect they are! They wouldn't often get into society like ours.' Miss Gately was generously including Dr MacMillan in this term, and Julius Caesar suppressed a grin. 'And I'm sure that she can't have known about Jacob and Esau Tipping, or she wouldn't have invited them both.'

'What is wrong with them?' asked the doctor, who had tired of Miss Gately's company some time before she met her.

Two gentlemen were standing at the buffet, which was laden with expensive treats, like champagne ices and smoked salmon sandwiches. One was dressed as a Doge, with the Phrygian cap in red leather and the scarlet robes. His hands were burdened with rings. The other, who resembled him closely, was clad in full Renaissance gear, jewelled chain and rings, flowing heavy, embossed velvet. Both had dark eyes and short black beards. Miss Gately was incandescent with scandal.

'They are brothers, you see, and their father made a most peculiar will—all the Tippings have been odd, though they are so rich. The grandfather made a killing on the goldfields, I believe, selling grog to the miners or something, and he only had one son, and that son only had two sons, twins, and they hate each other.'

'Oh yes?'

'Yes. Jacob is the Doge and Esau is Lorenzo de Medici. So over-done, but they never did have any taste. Their grandmother'—her voice sank—'was a gypsy, see? It's in the blood.'

Dr MacMillan, who had seen enough blood to fill a lake and had deep doubts about heredity, snorted.

'So their father, he was a friend of my mother's, horrible man, all tea and temperance, he died about two years ago and left this ridiculous will…'

Across the room, Jilly Henderson, attired as a Supreme Court judge, which she knew that she would never be, was telling Queen Elizabeth the same story.

'It was a mistake to invite them together, Phryne. Their father left all his property to the one who, by the time he was twenty-five, had never been drunk. They've had it in for each other since they were babies.'

'Oh? And when do they turn twenty-five?'

'Tomorrow—rather, tonight, at midnight. I only know about it because my firm represents the estate, and we had to get counsel's opinion as to whether Esau, who is the elder by one hour, would come into his inheritance before Jacob.'

'And does he?' Phryne settled her brocade skirts, a little taken aback. There were still things that she didn't know in the

Melbourne social scene, and she did think that someone might have warned her about the Tipping brothers. She did not want a quarrel to mar her party, which was going particularly well.

'No.' Jilly grinned. 'Counsel found it impossible to give an opinion based on precedent, but gave it as his view that the court would take judicial notice of the fact that each new day begins at one second past midnight. So tonight's their last chance. They have both been very good or very careful,' added Jilly, who was, after all, a lawyer. 'And the trustee hasn't managed to catch either of them tippling.'

'Who is the trustee?'

'Severe old gentleman in the Puritan garb. Just about suits him. And he's nicely named, too. Mr Crabbe. Temperance lecturer. Can't stand the man. Tried to stop us keeping port in the office. Said that Mr Latham's best crusty '86 was an alcoholic poison. You should have heard what old Latham said after Crabbe was gone! "My best port, alcohol!" he sputtered. "Alcohol is what they put in compasses!" Oh dear, he was wild, but we just close the door of the inner office when Crabbe inflicts his instruction on us, and warn all the clerks not to offer him a drop or breathe on him if they've been imbibing at lunch. He's been dogging the Tipping brothers' footsteps ever since the will was read.'

'What, is he paid to do this?'

'No, he's got a monomania about alcohol. In fact, talking about him makes me dry. Let's have another of those delicious cocktails.'

'Who are the women hovering around the brothers? The tall lady in that Pre-Raphaelite thing, and the short one in tights?'

'The tall one is Viola Tipping. She always comes to costume parties as the Shakespeare heroine, though I think that Viola in the play must have been more…well, boyish. You'd never take Viola Tipping for a boy, would you?'

'God's teeth,' said Phryne in character, 'never! Is she Jacob's wife?'

'Yes, and the beggar maid, as in "King Cophetua and the Beggar Maid," that's Tamar Tipping, Esau's wife. I can't say that I take to either of them, Phryne dear. Viola gushes and is as hard as nails, and Tamar is cool and distant and as hard as nails. Never mind. Why, by the way, are they here?'

'I owed them both an invitation. This party was to clear all my social debts before the beginning of spring, and of course I invited all my friends so that I should not be distracted with tedium.'

'Well, I do think that someone could have told you,' said Jilly, and summoned a server with a judicial wave.

Despite the Tipping brothers, the party was going well. Phryne drifted from conversation to conversation, smiling on social enemies and providing drinks for friends. She had edged quite close to the Tipping brothers and their guardian, and listened as she danced a foxtrot with the delectable Lindsay. He was wondering how difficult it was going to be to remove Miss Fisher from her armoury of clothes, if she allowed him to stay after the guests went home.

Lindsay looked for Dot, Phryne's companion, and sighted her, a Sèvres shepherdess, blushing like a poppy under the avalanche of compliments which a tall young Grenadier Guard was pouring into her ear. Dot would be able to help. She, presumably, had got Phryne into this mountain of a garment, and she would know how to get her out again.

Lindsay sighed. 'Can I stay tonight?'

The red wig and crown inclined; the green eyes, matching the emeralds on her head, cut through his mask.

'Perhaps, if you merit it,' she said.

Lindsay attempted to hold her closer, and was foiled by the density of the brocade gown, and painfully spiked by the stomacher.

'Perhaps?' he whispered.

Phryne smiled. 'Perhaps. Now hush, I'm eavesdropping.'

Esau Tipping as Lorenzo the Magnificent jutted a defiant beard at his brother and said, just above a whisper, 'You're contemptible.'

Jacob Tipping, as the Doge of Venice, swallowed an ice and snapped, 'So are you.'

'And no returns,' whispered Lindsay in Phryne's ear.

'You will never inherit!' said Jacob. 'My father meant the property to go to me!'

'You are wrong, brother,' snarled Esau. 'He loved me best and he meant it to go to me!'

'Loved you best!' sneered Jacob, forgetting to speak softly. 'Who was it looked after the old man? Who visited him every day? You never went near him! You and that wife of yours, you didn't care two straws for him!'

'What about that wife of yours, then?' Esau was also forgetting to keep his voice down. 'You set her on the old man, to flatter him and pat him and mother him, and it didn't work, did it, brother? He wasn't convinced by all that coaxing and petting. "Oh, Daddy dear, do leave your Viola something to remember you by."' The voice rose in a scathing imitation of his sister-in-law's gushing manner, and Jacob bristled.

'He wasn't taken in. He left her nothing but his pocket watch, and a few jewels that anyway would have gone to the eldest son's wife. No, my father was no easy touch,' concluded Esau admiringly.

Phryne, unashamedly listening, thought that the elder Mr Tipping sounded as if he had had a hard life between these brothers. Still, he had made them what they were. Both wives, Phryne noticed, were mortally offended. Viola was attempting to summon suitable tears for a wounded heart, and Tamar had frozen into a pillar of ice. Phryne wondered if, like an iceberg, she was about to sink a few ships.

'How dare you!' thundered Jacob. 'How dare you speak about my wife in that tone! At least I married a real woman, not an armful of granite.'

Phryne was about to intervene before the personalities became more general, but a dry voice cut in.

'You are quarrelling,' it observed. Mr Crabbe in Puritan collar, looking like he was about to order a witch to be burned, was not Phryne's ideal man, but he was effective.

'Yes, so we are. And tomorrow is our birthday,' said Jacob. 'A toast, brother! To our birthday!'

'Now, now,' said Mr Crabbe, in a voice that was probably meant to be soothing but sounded as though he had been told some time ago about the term and had never got around to practising. 'You are brothers and you should be friends.'

'I'd be friends if he would.' Jacob, smiling, put down his glass.

'Withdraw what you said about my wife,' Esau demanded, and Jacob smiled more widely, showing all his teeth.

'If you withdraw what you said about mine.'

'I withdraw.'

'I withdraw.'

There was an outraged breath behind both men as their wives realised that the insults were going to go unavenged. Phryne hushed Lindsay, who had been about to suggest that they move away from this uninteresting family quarrel. Both twins' glasses were on the table, in Phryne's line of sight. Mr Crabbe picked them up, refilled them from a water jug and handed one to each brother. They stared at each other.

'Change glasses,' said Esau, fumbling with his long sleeve. 'It's not that I don't trust you, brother, but I've known snakes with more integrity.'

Jacob grinned and handed over his glass.

'To our birthday!' they chorused, and drank.

Phryne was about to move away when Lorenzo suddenly clutched at his throat and choked. He fell towards the Doge, who was also giving at the knees, and then there was nothing of the Tipping brothers but a blur of scarlet and ermine as they collapsed onto the floor.

Odd things often happened at Phryne's parties, so no particular notice was taken, except by Dr MacMillan and a pirate who, in private life, was a detective inspector of police. The pirate and Julius Caesar inspected the fallen.

'Dead,' said Dr MacMillan.

'As doornails,' agreed Detective Inspector Jack Robinson. 'Poison?'

'Yes. In the alcohol.' The doctor sniffed at each glass. 'Very neat alcohol, at that.'

'Thus fall the unbelievers,' exclaimed Mr Crabbe, lifting his hands and his eyes to heaven. 'Look at the time!'

It was ten minutes to midnight.

Phryne detached Lindsay and said, 'Come along, now, we'll send all these people into the other room and close this door.'

She ushered her guests out of the room, gently shoving those who appeared to be incapacitated from surprise or gin. Lindsay shut the door and leaned on it, his robes swishing around his ankles, his mask over his face rendering him both antic and alarming. Behind him, the music began again, and a flood of talk. This was one of Miss Fisher's most interesting parties.

The Tipping wives, who appeared to have suffered the fate of Lot's spouse, began to speak.

'Do you mean that Jacob is dead?' exclaimed Viola, clasping her hands. 'My Jacob?'

'Esau, get up,' implored Tamar, descending to cradle his head in a flowing mass of draperies. 'Oh, Esau, just like you, to die before the time! Now what will become of me?'

Phryne, who was not very shockable, was shocked. She hoped that better obsequies would be spoken over her own corpse.

'Sit down, ladies, there, on the sofa. Mr Crabbe, could you sit down? I recommend this armchair.'

Mr Crabbe paid no attention. Tall and stiff, reminding Phryne of a statue of John Knox, he was denouncing the brothers.

'I told their father,' he said funereally, 'I told him! Bad seed, I said, they have gypsy blood in them, they are unreliable, and they will take to drink! Now look at the harvest of this wicked substance! Two brothers dead in their prime and their wives are widows. The hand of the Lord is upon them!'

'Yes, yes, I'm sure that it is,' agreed Phryne. 'Now you will sit down, please.'

Cold grey eyes glared into hers, alight with the red flare of fanaticism. Phryne stood up straight, set her crown in place, and glared haughtily back, in a manner befitting her disguise. Mr Crabbe, lowering his gaze, sat down as requested.

'Despite what Mr Crabbe says'—Jack Robinson had taken up the gentleman's dominant position in front of the fireplace—'they didn't die of drink.'

'But they took drink,' observed the doctor. 'Polish spirit, perhaps, or vodka. Pure alcohol, perhaps.'

Jack Robinson's eyes narrowed, surveying Dr McMillan's toga virilis. 'Where would one find pure alcohol?' he inquired.

'A hospital, a pharmacy... even a perfumery: they use it to make scent,' said the doctor. 'Had we not better call the police?'

Jack Robinson grinned at her. 'I am the police,' he reminded the company and stripped off his eye patch and scarf. In the pirate's breeches, loose shirt, and thigh-high sea boots, he was dramatically effective and oddly at home.

He searched in both brothers' pockets and placed his spoils in his scarf.

'Handkerchiefs, keys, cigarette case and lighter, nothing unusual.'

There was an imperious knock at the door. 'What's that?' asked Phryne. 'Keep everyone out, Lindsay.'

Lindsay had a brief conversation, and said over his shoulder, 'Miss Henderson wants to come in.'

'All right.'

Jilly Henderson was admitted and Lindsay shut the door again. 'What's up?'

Phryne answered, 'It looks like the two brothers should have been renamed.'

'Renamed?'

'Not Jacob and Esau, but Cain and Abel.'

This biblical reference woke Mr Crabbe from his trance. He had been sitting as ordered, but on the very edge of the chair, and now he half rose, his denouncing finger boring a hole in the air.

'I told their father!'

'Yes, yes, doubtless,' said Phryne crossly.

'Did they poison each other?' Jilly asked her.

'So it seems. What can you remember about the estate of their father? Was it land?'

'No, not that I recall. Shares, mostly, and quite a lot of money. It's in trust, of course.'

'I see.'

Both wives began to stir. The shock was wearing off.

'Oh, Jacob!' wailed Viola. 'I told you it was dangerous, and I said that we should just wait!'

'Esau, I knew it wouldn't work,' cried Tamar.

Both women stopped and stared at each other. Phryne held her breath. They were about to give her some useful information.

'What?' asked Tamar. 'Did your husband intend to make my husband drunk and get the money?'

'Did your snake of a husband intend to get my angel drunk and get the money?' echoed Viola.

'Well! I never heard of such a thing!'

'Well! I never heard of such a thing either. How?'

'How?' asked Tamar.

Viola sobbed aloud. 'How did that brute intend to cheat my poor Jacob?'

'The same way that dear Jacob intended to cheat poor silly Esau, I expect.' Tamar was recovering. It was possible that Esau would not be sorely missed.

'Well?'

Tamar, shaken, raised her glass to her lips. Phryne dived across the room and snatched it out of her hand.

'I don't think that the punch would agree with you, Mrs Tipping,' she said, sniffing at the glass. 'Bitter almond—now, I don't recall putting that in the punch or the water jug… Catch him, Lindsay!' she cried, as the black-clad figure broke for the door. There was a brief struggle, then the Puritan was down on his face, and Death was perched jauntily between his shoulder blades.

'Mrs Tipping, tell me how Jacob was going to spike Esau's drink.'

'I knew it wouldn't work, it was too simple,' wailed Viola, still not following the course of events and wondering why the pirate had removed her glass gently from her hand and stood it on the mantelpiece. 'He was going to supply the stuff—him!' She pointed to the fallen Puritan. 'He has pure alcohol for his temperance lectures, to demonstrate what happens when you dip an earthworm in it.'

'What does happen?' asked Lindsay, who was floating with events, as he always did, and had no idea why he had been asked to fell the elderly gentleman who was presently serving as his cushion. 'It shrivels up and dies,' said Phryne. 'Do belt up, Lindsay!'

Mrs Tipping,' she said to Tamar, 'how did Esau mean to get Jacob drunk?'

'The same way. That man came to my husband with an offer—to make the old man's will more fair—and Esau agreed. They were to change glasses, and the glass which was given to Jacob would be the one with the alcohol in it. Then Jacob was to drink, and Mr Crabbe would certify him drunk, and the money would go to—'

'I see.' Phryne would have found the situation amusing if not for the presence of two dead men on her parlour floor.

'So both brothers meant to do down the other and inherit under this ridiculous will. But Jacob did not mean to kill Esau, did he?' she asked Viola, who shook her head.

'And Esau did not mean to kill Jacob, did he?' she asked Tamar, who snapped, 'Of course not.'

'And John Knox here was to supply the booze.' Phryne was thinking aloud. 'He made the same offer to both brothers, and they both accepted, and if they were both found drunk they would not have inherited. What's the reversion of the estate, Jilly? Do you remember?'

'Oh, yes, the wives get five hundred pounds apiece and the rest goes to some temperance organisation. I forget the name… Sons of Water-Drinkers, something like that.'

'So you decided to kill them, Mr Crabbe. I wonder why? It was a risky thing to do, but you would have got the money, all of the estate, because I'll bet that you are the founder and sole member of the Sons of Wowsers.'

The black figure under Death squirmed.

'Oh, but wait a moment.' A thought had struck Phryne. She went to the buffet and found a bottle of gin, examined the cork and seal, then stripped it and poured herself a drink to assist cogitation.

'I see,' she said softly.

She strode over to the recumbent Puritan and hauled him to his feet. Glittering in the electric light, the shimmer of her gold dress was hard to look at, but Mr Crabbe seemed to have more difficulty with the furious green eyes.

'You don't have the money, do you?' she said with icy clarity. 'You spent it, didn't you? It wasn't enough just to disinherit the brothers, because then you would have had to pay the wives their husbands' share. You had to kill Jacob and Esau. I saw both glasses, half-filled with a clear liquid which I assumed was water. As did they.' Phryne had backed Mr Crabbe up against the mantelpiece. 'You monster; you nasty, wicked, hymn-singing hypocrite!'

'It was the Lord's work,' he insisted, though his voice faltered. 'The Lord told me to take the infidels' gold and spend it on a temple for the glory of his name and the cause of temperance!'

Mr Crabbe turned from her eyes, grabbed the glass standing on the mantelpiece and, before Phryne could stop him, gulped it down.

The tall man swayed and crumpled.

'Dead?' demanded Phryne, as pirate and Roman bent over the fallen murderer.

'He'll live to hang,' Dr MacMillan commented, taking off her laurel wreath and chuckling.

'Wasn't that glass poisoned?'

'Only with alcohol,' she said. 'He's drunk good gin for the first time in his life. That was my glass.'

~◠~

'Thank you, Phryne, it has been a very nice evening,' he said soberly. 'And a nice solution. Do ask me again when you haven't scheduled a double murder, won't you?'

He bowed, kissed Miss Fisher's hand, and turned to leave. There was someone at the door. Masked and cowled, Death bowed the detective inspector out of Miss Fisher's house.

Marrying the Bookie's Daughter

Rendering good for ill,
Smiling at ev'ry frown,
Yielding your own self-will,
Laughing your teardrops down;
Never a selfish whim,
Trouble, or pain to stir;
Everything for him,
Nothing at all for her!
Love that will aye endure,
Though the rewards be few,
That is the love that's pure,
That is the love that's true!

—W.S. Gilbert,
Patience; or, Bunthorne's Bride

'Phryne,' said Lindsay Herbert. 'Will you marry me?'

Phryne Fisher had been drowsing, lying naked on her moss-green sheets with the young man's head on her shoulder. Now she was shocked awake. She released Lindsay and slid down so that she could look into his face, and a highly inappropriate laugh was smothered at birth.

A golden boy, slim and beautiful, rising on one elbow to look at her earnestly, light hair curling away from a high forehead, round blue eyes, a sweet red mouth now drawn tight over white teeth. Her gaze left the face and slid down over the body. Lightly tanned skin lay smoothly over the slender musculature of a runner. Squared chest, flat belly, long legs.

'Why, Lindsay, I… I don't know what to say…' Phryne groped for a response, mightily puzzled. What had brought this on? 'I… I am very honoured, of course…'

'Well?' he demanded brusquely. 'Yes or no?'

She did not reply.

He sat up abruptly. 'It's time we got married,' he stated.

'Why?' asked Phryne, reaching for her long dressing-gown and pulling it on. It was patterned with green and scarlet macaws and suddenly seemed gaudy.

'Well, because… because we get on so well. I know I'm not very clever at law and things, but I've got excellent prospects… Father will give me a job in the firm… We could be very happy, Phryne.'

'I thought that we were very happy.' Phryne was finding it hard to keep her countenance. 'Get up, Lindsay, and we shall discuss it and have some tea. Look, it's five o'clock—perhaps a cocktail as well.'

'Yes or no?' demanded Lindsay, not moving.

'You can't expect an immediate answer to such an important question, Mr Herbert,' Phryne said coldly. 'I have said that we will talk about it.'

And she vanished into her dressing room to assume the usual habiliment of a lady going down to tea in her own house in 1928.

Lindsay was left alone. He swore explosively and scrabbled for his clothes.

~~~

Half an hour later Phryne found herself entangled in an argument which even Mr Butler's cocktails did not mitigate or unravel.

'But why, Lindsay dear? We are perfectly all right as we are,' she protested.

'Damnation, old thing, we don't need a reason for getting married! Everyone does it!' the young man spluttered into his ginger beer. 'I don't know why you won't say yes.'

'I don't know either,' said Phryne slowly.

'It's because I'm not clever, isn't it?' he asked suddenly, with a broad, generous gesture which distributed his drink over a considerable portion of the room. 'You only like clever chaps, that's what it is.'

'No, no, Lindsay dear, that isn't it,' objected Phryne. 'Not at all. I think you're lovely just as you are. And you are quite bright, sometimes—though not at the moment.'

'It can't be my prospects,' he mused as Mr Butler refilled his glass and began unobtrusively to mop ginger beer off the couch. 'It must be … it must be …' He stared piteously up into Phryne's eyes and whispered, 'Another man.'

'Lindsay, dear—'

'No, that's it, I see it all now,' he said feverishly. 'Another man: of course. A clever chap with lots of money—he's the one you want.'

Phryne sighed, leaned over, and took the glass firmly out of his hand. Lots of money indeed! Lindsay had plenty of his own, and access to a great deal more through his father's business, potentially. Those born to wealth—as she had most emphatically not been—always seemed to be looking over their shoulders, fearing to be replaced by someone richer. It was very tiresome. She was unable to account for this strange fervour, and was beginning to apprehend a scene. And she liked Lindsay, who was usually delightful, a good lover and an excellent and socially acceptable escort, but was rapidly rendering himself unfit for female company.

'Now listen.' Phryne planted herself on his knees to keep the young man still and took a fistful of the soft, light hair. 'You listen to me, Lindsay. I am what I am and I behave as I wish and I will not be dictated to by anyone. If I want lovers, I take them. If I do not want to be married, I will not be married, and there's nothing you can do to make me. Do you hear?'

There were tears in the eyes of the flushed face turned up to hers. She did not release her grip.

'Then the answer's no?'

'If it is?'

'Then I'll go away, Phryne. I'll walk out that door and you'll never see me again. I can't go on like this. I'm never sure of you.'

'And you'd be sure of me if I was married to you?' She could not stop her eyebrows from rising.

The young man drew a long breath and said earnestly, 'Yes, if we were married, then ...'

Phryne judged him calm enough for her to resume her seat. She did so.

'Then?' she prompted.

'If we were married, then you'd belong to me. I'd belong to you.'

'And?'

'Then we'd be happy.'

'Because I belonged to you?'

'Yes. You could sell this house and come and live with me. We could buy a big house in Toorak and have a country estate and a place near the sea and we'd have such larks, Phryne, just you and me, without a lot of people bothering us. I could finish law and go into Father's office. In the winter we could go skiing, and sailing in the summer, and—'

'And we could have a little cottage with roses around the door and Old Mister Moon peeping in through the window?'

'Yes. You don't have to say it in that tone of voice. It could be fun. Please, Phryne. I don't want to lose you. You could give up all this detective work and go to parties with me, and the opera, and all sorts of jolly things. And we could have...children? Two, perhaps, eh? Lindsay Junior and a pretty little girl like you must have been. Please say yes, Phryne. It came into my head because the pater is going on about being settled and the mater keeps introducing me to nice girls and...'

'Well, what's wrong with the nice girls?'

Phryne lit a cigarette. She didn't want to break Lindsay's ingenuous heart, so she was listening.

Lindsay reached out and ran a skilled hand down her breast and heard her gasp.

'That's what wrong with the nice girls,' he said simply. 'They're nice.'

'Of course they are. That's how they are trained to appear. You may be agreeably surprised to find out what they are really like. Lindsay, I can't decide something as important as this immediately. I have to think about it. Can you wait for an answer?'

'If I have to.'

'You have to.'

'Then I can wait,' he said miserably. He was not, however, altogether cast down. Phryne had not rejected his honourable proposal out of hand. There might still be a chance of securing her for his own.

'And in the meantime,' she said, taking another cocktail and returning his glass to the young man, 'I am going to a wedding on Saturday. The Sackville girl. Will you be my escort?'

'Of course. The Sackville wedding, eh? I didn't know you moved in those circles, Phryne.'

'Which circles?'

'Racing ones.'

'I don't, but the wretched girl is one of that pest Celia's protégés, so I really haven't a choice. You know how she takes up the petite bourgeoisie's ghastly daughters and launches them on what she fondly thinks is Society. Well, she launched Amelia Sackville, doubtless on the strength of her papa's fortune. All got from doing down the working punter, Bert says.'

'Stout fellow, Bert,' commented Lindsay.

'I see, so you propose to allow me to continue my friendship with the working class if we are married?' Phryne asked teasingly.

Lindsay took her seriously and pondered his reply. He said solemnly, 'Well, no, Phryne, you won't need them if you aren't detecting anymore.'

'Of course.'

Lindsay wondered what he had said to bring that metallic ring into her voice.

'So,' she continued, 'poor Amelia is to be sacrificed at the altar.'

'Good Lord, yes—old Fletch getting shackled for life. How are the mighty fallen.' Phryne gasped inwardly. Was this the same callow youth who had—not five minutes ago—proposed marriage himself? Not for the first time, Phryne wondered if Lindsay ever listened to himself. He continued with his schoolday reminiscences with an annoying smirk on his face. 'He was my house prefect at Grammar, you know. A fiend at rowing, captain of the football team. But a bit of a ladies' man. Nothing in skirts was safe from him. Cost his father a packet in breach of promise payments, I gather. Imagine him marrying the bookie's daughter.' Lindsay laughed. 'Well, and that's what one would expect, too.'

'Why?'

'Terrible gambling bug he had, old Fletch. Used to run a book himself, at school. On the Melbourne Cup, you know, not as a business or anything.'

'And what's he like?'

'Good chap, you know. Still plays for the OMs football team, does a bit of coaching of the fours.'

'Yes, but what is he like?'

Lindsay gaped. 'I've told you,' he said lamely.

Phryne gave it up. 'Never mind, dear boy. I'll pick you up at two; full soup and fish, we have to go to a very swish reception afterwards.'

'St Peter's, Eastern Hill, I assume?' he asked, accepting his coat from Mr Butler.

'St Peter's, Eastern Hill,' Phryne agreed.

'Marriage,' said Phryne, unaware that she had spoken aloud.

'Marriage, Miss Phryne?' echoed Dot. 'Are you thinking of getting married, Miss?'

Phryne looped a long necklace of amber beads around her neck and said to Dot's reflection in the mirror, 'I've been asked.'

'Oh, Miss, how exciting! Who is it?'

'Lindsay Herbert. What do you think?'

'Oh, Miss, they say he's ever so rich, and he's very well connected.'

'So you believe I should marry him?'

Dot was Phryne's maid and companion. She had always disapproved of detection as an occupation for a lady. Mirrored Dot clasped her hands.

'Well, Miss, you like him,' she said slowly, 'and you...er... know him.'

Phryne grinned, and Dot blushed. 'And, well, getting married means you'd have to give up all this dangerous detective work, Miss. You know how I worry about you.'

'Why would I give it up?'

Dot stared. Some things, she felt, were self-evident.

'Mr Herbert wouldn't like his wife to be doing something so…so…'

'Unladylike?' Phryne's smile now showed quite an array of teeth. 'What else would Mr Herbert not like his wife to do?'

'Well, Miss, it's to be expected. Gentlemen will have their house ordered the way they want, after all. Perhaps you could do some charity work. But married ladies don't work, everyone knows that.'

'No? What about you, Dot? Aren't you a lady?'

'That's different. I'm not married, and I've got myself to keep. But my husband won't like me to work. He'll keep me.'

'How sweet,' said Phryne without any inflection. 'The straw-coloured dress, please, Dot.'

A caller was announced at three the next afternoon. Mr Butler came into the drawing room where Phryne and Dot were examining the library catalogue.

'No, I don't think so, Dot dear, I really can't bear romances. One more heaving bosom, thunderstorm, and frilly white nightgown and I'll scream. Get me some thrillers. That new one, Charteris, he sounds good. Yes, Mr Butler?'

'Mr Aloysius Fletcher to see you, Miss.'

'Never heard of him. What does he want?'

Mr Butler came a little closer and said quietly, 'It's the racing gentleman, Miss Phryne, the one whose son is marrying the bookmaker's daughter.'

'Oh, yes. Well, I've finished with the catalogue, Dot dear, you can send it off—and you might stay, if you don't mind; I don't know how racing gentlemen behave. Wheel him in, Mr Butler.'

Mr Aloysius Fletcher was not alone. He strode into the room, large and magnificent, if a trifle past his prime, a big, stout, fleshy man in a quiet charcoal suit evidently chosen by his wife. His own taste announced itself in the shape of a violently patterned cravat and a horse-shaped gold stickpin with a diamond glaring from the middle. He had another diamond on his left hand, big enough to choke a parrot.

Scurrying behind him was a small, thin, plain woman of perhaps thirty. She was so self-effacing that she was hard to see. Her long blonde hair was scraped back into a migraine-inducing bun. She looked modestly down at the carpet. She was clutching a large black-bound diary in her arms and had a pencil behind her ear.

'Miss Fisher?' Aloysius Fletcher bellowed.

Phryne offered him her hand and he shook it hard, then let it go as though he had found himself holding a fish. Phryne judged him to be a severe man on china and invited him to sit down, hoping that he was reliable with chairs.

'I'm Aloysius Fletcher,' he said. 'Perhaps you have heard of me.'

Phryne inclined her head. 'I've heard of you.'

'You know my son's marrying Amelia Sackville on Saturday?'

'Yes, I'm coming to the wedding. And who is your companion?'

'Companion?' He started, and looked around. 'Oh, that's just Smithy, my secretary. Sit down, Smithy. She's a fool,' he confided in a ponderous undertone. 'But she'll do, if I watch her like a hawk. Yes, well, Tom's managed to snare the bookie's daughter. The family might get back the money the scoundrels have taken off me all these years!'

He laughed. Phryne watched politely. Mr Butler offered a drink and was sent for whisky and soda—'And don't drown the whisky!'

Phryne waited until Miss Smith had found a perch on the extreme edge of the sofa and then said, 'To what do I owe the honour of your acquaintance, Mr Fletcher?'

'Meaning, what do I want, eh?' He laughed again. 'Well, I want you to do something for me. Smithy! Show Miss Fisher the drawings!'

Smithy jumped, dropped the diary, and scrabbled for three scattered sheets of paper. She handed them to Phryne. They were watercolour drawings of jewellery done by an expert hand, showing a bridal set comprising High Victorian brooch, necklace, earrings, and tiara. They were heavy, solid, and respectably opulent.

'Yes?'

'They're the family heirlooms. The gift of the bridegroom, you know. Not that I expect a girl with pots of money like the bookie's daughter will care for them. But it's a tradition, y'know.'

'Yes?' Phryne was beginning to dislike her unwanted guest so much that she was hoping he would choke on his whisky, even though it was not the good whisky. Mr Butler had his own system of class determination.

'They're missing.'

'I see.'

'I went to the safe this morning—it's in Smithy's room, so that there is always someone in the way if burglars break in. The safe was open and the room had been torn apart, eh, Smithy?'

Miss Smith nodded.

'And the jewels were gone.'

'Have you called the police?'

'Of course, but they won't get quick results. I told my son about it, and his friend Herbert—you know him, apparently—said that you could find things faster than Sherlock Holmes. So here I am, Miss Fisher, asking you to help.'

'I'm afraid that I'm rather busy, Mr Fletcher.'

'Come along, girl!' barked Mr Fletcher. 'I came to get you, and get you I shall. And Herbert said you were a genius. Should have known better than to trust the little twerp.'

Phryne considered this. She detested Mr Fletcher, but Lindsay's good opinion of her was flattering and should be supported. She nodded, got up, and found her handbag.

'Very well. My fees, Mr Fletcher, are high. Can you pay them?'

'Fees?'

'Yes. This is my profession, you know.'

Mr Fletcher appeared to have been struck dumb. Smithy said in a soft, deep voice, 'There won't be any trouble with the fees, Miss Fisher. Can you come now?'

'Yes.'

Mr Fletcher was assisted to his feet and they left the house.

Phryne examined the room. It was a small, crowded bedchamber, where all the things in the house which were not immediately needed were stored. Smith's bed stood in front of a collection of walking sticks, golf clubs, and tennis racquets. Her clothes hung in a cupboard which also contained a vacuum cleaner and several boxes of illustrated racing papers. The only signs of her occupancy were hundreds of exquisite pen drawings pinned up all over the walls. Phryne exclaimed, 'They're beautiful! Who did them?'

'Smithy. She's always scribbling,' grunted Mr Fletcher. 'See, there's the safe, and it was open. They must have got in through the window.'

Smithy's only window was small but unbarred, and a smashed pane announced that the lock had been rendered useless.

'Hmm, yes. What was in the safe?'

'Nothing else of value. Papers—mainly deeds and so on.'

'Was the jewellery in a box?'

'Yes, about ten inches by ten inches square. Why?'

'Just wondered.' Phryne noticed that a tin trunk had also been forced open. From the female underclothes and drawing materials, she judged it to be Smithy's. A bottle of green ink had been smashed, and the trunk's contents appeared to have been tipped out and then roughly piled back inside.

'Hmm.'

'Well? Can you find them?' demanded Mr Fletcher.

Phryne smiled up into the beefy face. 'I'll try.'

'Good. Come up and see m'wife, will you? She's upset.'

It was possible to gauge the degree of upset from the sobbing and wailing which was apparent in the hall. Mr Fletcher muttered something about an appointment in the stables and fled. Smithy, unexpectedly, gave Phryne a sympathetic look, revealing that she had beautiful, large, expressive eyes the colour of forget-me-nots. She led Phryne into a sizeable room which contained a tall young man, a well-dressed young woman, and an older woman in the throes of what appeared to be inconsolable grief.

'Mama, please!' the young man begged. 'Smithy, can't you do something with her? Oh, I beg your pardon,' he added when he caught sight of Phryne. 'Hello! Are you Miss Fisher? I've heard all about you from Herbert. I'm delighted to meet you.'

He was a very good-looking young man, Phryne thought, with chestnut hair and brown eyes and a full red mouth. He held her hand a little longer than was necessary and the quality of the contact suggested that Lindsay had indeed told him all about Phryne. She smiled wickedly and released herself.

'This is Miss Sackville, my fiancée. Amelia, this is Miss Fisher. She's going to find the family jewels.' He grinned down at her and she shook her neat head.

'I told you, Tommy, I don't care about the family jewels. I've got jewels enough of my own.' The girl was taller than Phryne, offhandedly elegant, in a lapis lazuli suit with sapphires in her ears. Her dark hair was bobbed, her cosmetics reticent, and her manner unaffected. She was holding Tom Fletcher's hand to her breast as though she was cradling it. 'I just want you, old thing,' she said.

Tom Fletcher smiled and replied, 'And on Saturday you will be mine.'

Phryne caught her breath. This was the exclusive love which she had been thinking about; one creature claiming another, in complete indifference to the rest of humanity. For a moment, her heart ached. She wondered how it would feel to love like that, or trust like that, so perfectly and forever. Phryne had never before considered that there might be someone so close to her always, in whom she could have such single-minded faith.

Mrs Fletcher stopped sobbing. Smithy was fussing around her with salts and brandy, and a large gulp of spirit had temporarily taken her mistress's breath away.

Smithy introduced Phryne.

'I'll do my best,' Phryne promised, 'but the wedding is on Saturday, Mrs Fletcher. I think you'd be better leaving it to the police. It is their business, you know.'

'That's what I say,' agreed Tom vehemently. 'Leave it to the cops. That's what we pay taxes for, isn't it?'

But Mrs Fletcher looked like she was about to start wailing again, and Phryne, to keep the peace, agreed to continue her investigation.

Another inspection of Smithy's room revealed nothing positive, although Phryne did notice that folios of drawings had been emptied and rifled, and the contents replaced carelessly. She sat on the floor with Smithy to smooth the paper and stack it again.

'These are very fine,' said Phryne admiringly, leafing through life drawings of a nude young man, executed with loving care. The muscles were shaded with red chalk. The face was turned away.

Smithy snatched them from Phryne's hand and crumpled them into a ball. 'I'm not good on the figure,' she said hastily. 'I'm better at still life.'

Phryne admired flowers and fruit and asked, as she was leaving, 'Did you go to art school? You're very good.'

A painful blush burned Miss Smith's face. 'No. I couldn't afford it. I've been working here since my mother died, when I was sixteen. She was Mr Fletcher's cousin. He gave me a job and a place to live. It was…very kind of him.'

'Was it?' asked Phryne dryly.

One gleam of passionate emotion was allowed to escape from Smithy's blue eyes, and then it was veiled. 'Of course,' she muttered.

By the afternoon of the next day, which was Friday, the day before the wedding, Phryne had the solution to the mystery of the missing jewels and was at a loss as to what to do. She took a long walk, returning out of breath and with the problem still unresolved. She was also considering Lindsay's proposal. After all, Phryne was twenty-eight. She might never get another proposal so fitting. Yesterday's glimpse of the lovers, perfectly and passionately devoted to each other, had planted a splinter in her bosom. Tom and Amelia, smiling at each other with the kind of embracing, exclusive smile that forced all the world out past the boundaries of their magic circle and declared 'mine.' But Phryne and Lindsay, the sweet boy with the soft mouth, forsaking all others, alone with each other for the foreseeable future? She had never experienced perfect love; was it possible that it had never come because she had never tried hard enough? It could probably be accomplished, she thought, if she put her mind to it. She reached her own door still wondering and found the front hall full of flowers.

'What are these?' she asked, looking for a florist's label. Australian flowers, strange and spiky: waratahs, banksias, and sheaves of gum leaves. She inhaled the bush scent with delight.

'They're from Mr Herbert, Miss,' said Dot from behind a shrubbery of everlastings. 'He wants you to marry him.'

'Yes, I know.'

'Have you decided, Miss? 'Cos Mrs Butler was asking.'

'Mrs Butler? Why?'

'Because of the arrangements, Miss. They'll have to find another place.'

'Oh Lord!' Phryne dragged herself out of the scented haze. 'Tell Mrs B that I haven't made up my mind, but in any case I shall be keeping them on and this house, too. A fig for all this perfect love,' she snarled. 'I don't think I'm strong enough for marriage, Dot.'

Suppressing a private delight in muslin and wedding veils and orange blossom, Dot handed Phryne an armload of wax flowers and went off to the kitchen, leaving her mistress in possession of a magnificent fit of bad temper.

Phryne dressed for the wedding in a state of bemusement. She did not know what to do for the best, or even what to avoid for the worst. The state of the window, the folios, the reputation of Tom Fletcher, and Miss Smith's position in the house seemed to point to one conclusion, but the research undertaken by Dot had not confirmed it. Phryne got out of the bath, scented with Jicky, and allowed herself to be dressed in champagne-coloured stockings and underwear, and then sat in front of the mirror while Dot brushed her hair.

'Glass on the outside,' she said aloud.

'Miss?'

'Glass on the outside of the window,' she said, 'means that the window was broken from the inside. And no one would search flat cardboard folios for a box ten inches by ten inches. The burglar wasn't looking for jewels. There's only one solution, Dot, and I don't know what to do. Tom Fletcher and his Amelia, they really seem to love each other. At least, she loves him. Whatever that means. Oh, these society scandals are too, too enervating. One will have nothing to talk about for months and months but the disruption of the Fletcher boy's wedding. And it will not aid the lady... Ah, I have it. Stop brushing, Dot, and run down and get Lindsay on the telephone. He'll be at the Fletchers' if he's not at home—Tom Fletcher is an old friend of his.'

Phryne allowed Dot to drop her apricot and silver dress over her head and then found her bag and her cloche. As she descended the stairs, she watched Dot speaking into the telephone. Dot looked up and handed the receiver to her.

'Lindsay dear, it's Phryne. Can you give Tom Fletcher a message? It's important.'

'Yes,' Lindsay replied. 'I'm going there now to see the poor fish into his garments and help old Jack to keep custody of the ring. What's the message? Don't tell me you've fallen for Tom, like all those other swooning females?'

'Lindsay, have you ever known me to swoon?… Well, then. Tell him to bring the jewels to the ceremony with him. You can carry them. They're in a box, ten by ten.'

'But I thought that they were stolen!'

'They were. But Tom has them now, or my name's not Phryne Fisher. I'll meet you at the church. Will you do it?'

'Oh, of course, Phryne. If you say so,' he replied stiffly.

'It is offended—see, it stalks away,' quoted Phryne, hanging up the phone. Obviously Lindsay had taken offence at something she had said. Probably because she was showing no signs of incipient dependence upon him. 'Mr Butler! A cocktail, if you please. I am in need of strengthening. And I wonder,' she added to herself, 'now that Tom Fletcher knows that I know his secret, what he will do. This should be an interesting afternoon.'

Mr Butler supplied the cocktail, made with special care and to a secret recipe, and forbore from comment.

St Peter's, Eastern Hill, was crowded, and Phryne had some difficulty manoeuvring herself through the press of Melbourne's shrillest and most fashionable in order to sit next to Smithy outside the church. The secretary was unbecomingly attired in a charcoal suit evidently cut out with some agricultural implement, and a dark cloche was dragged brutally down over her high forehead.

Tom Fletcher was shifting from foot to foot, smoking like a chimney and, when he thought himself unobserved, taking little nips from a flask kept by his best man. Lindsay Herbert, in full elegant evening dress, sat next to Phryne nursing a box on his knee and looking bewildered.

'What did Tom say when he gave you the jewels, Lindsay?'

'He said he had to go through with it, whatever happened. He said he was sorry, to tell you that he was very sorry.'

'I see.'

'What is going to happen, Phryne?' begged Lindsay.

She kissed him on the cheek. 'I haven't the faintest. Hark, here comes the bride.'

There was a stir at the door. The groom threw away his cigarette, paled, and was escorted into the church. A carriage drew up and out of it the bride stepped, supported by a rubicund father bursting with pride. Amelia was draped in a Valenciennes lace veil so generous that it flowed over her and in careless folds to the ground. Her gown was of ice-pale silk, dipping down towards her heels, embroidered in silver with lilies and garlands. She carried a trailing bouquet of gardenias, and their sweet indecent scent reached Phryne and Smithy in their pew, stirring each of them in different ways. Smithy clutched her hands together and shut her mouth hard. Phryne breathed in the scent and remembered a certain hot night and the taste of salt on a young man's skin…

The organ pealed, a voluntary which slid into the full triumphal wedding march, and the bride was led towards the altar, leaning on her father's arm, to be given away to her husband.

Smithy began to shiver. Phryne took her arm.

'Are you feeling faint?' she asked. 'Why don't we go out? Very close in here.'

Smithy turned on Phryne eyes which reminded her of a mortally injured dog, and nodded.

They reached the church wall, which was low, and sat down. Phryne lit a gasper and said quietly, 'It wasn't like that at the registry office, was it?'

'No.'

'But Dot couldn't find anything in the records.'

Smithy groped in her bag and thrust a folded piece of paper into Phryne's hand. Phryne read it.

'That's why,' she commented. 'I didn't ask her to go back far enough. How old were you, for God's sake?'

'Sixteen,' muttered Smithy. Phryne realised that she was a lot younger than she looked. Life could not have been easy in Mr Fletcher's house, in possession of such a secret and despised by her employers, used like a domestic animal and mercilessly overworked.

'That's what Tom was looking for when he staged that break-in and searched your room. And the jewels were all part of his plot.' Phryne paused for a moment, staring at the names and dates and doing some mental arithmetic. No, this didn't add up. But what was she to do now? Her musings were interrupted by a mutinous quiver from the girl beside her.

'Yes. I loved him,' Smithy said through clenched teeth. 'I loved him so much! There was I, small and insignificant and plain and worthless, and he paid attention to me. He liked me—no one liked me—and... and...'

'And you slept with him?'

'Not until we were married. I held out for that. I was brought up well. If I'd wanted to be a whore I wouldn't have put up with old Fletcher all these years. Then Tom got tired of me. Years ago. And I stayed because... I still love him, I suppose. And I had nowhere else to go.'

'And what are you going to do now?' asked Phryne gently.

'There's a bit in the service—I looked it up—where they ask if anyone has just cause or impediment. I was going to...'

'Stand up and object? Well, you have just cause, all right; just cause indeed! You have been treated monstrously, Smithy... Smithy, what's your name?'

Smithy shook her head as though she could hardly remember. 'Chloë. My mother…liked…novels.'

She started to cry helplessly. Phryne cupped a hand under the small chin and forced Chloë to look at her.

'Listen, Chloë, I think I can deal more advantageously for you than just disrupting the wedding. I know that it will make you feel better for the moment, but what are you going to do after that? You can hardly expect to stay with the Fletchers. And I doubt if they'll give you a good character reference. And Tom… Tom is not likely to be much use to you, is he?'

The bowed shoulders shuddered, and Chloë Smith whispered, 'No.'

'Right. Give me that marriage certificate. Have you got old Fletcher's diary with you, as always? Has it got a chequebook in it? Good. Ah, Lindsay,' she added as the young man came up to them. 'Miss Smith is a bit overcome. Can you stay with her? Give her some brandy if you've got some. I'll be back in a moment, Chloë.'

Chloë stared at Phryne as she stalked back into the church. Lindsay sat down beside her and patted her gently. Emotional women did not worry or embarrass Lindsay.

'Mr Herbert—can I trust her?'

'Who, Miss Fisher? Of course. Have a little taste of this, now, just a sip. You can trust Phryne. If she says she'll fix it, then it will be fixed. I would trust her with my life,' said Lindsay, and Chloë Smith leaned against his tailored shoulder and sipped brandy and closed her eyes.

By the exercise of barefaced intimidation, Phryne managed to smuggle herself into the seat next to old Mr Fletcher as he opened a hymnbook with which he was evidently unfamiliar. Phryne laid the fatal certificate over the words of 'O Perfect Love' and watched his eyes bulge as he read it. He turned on her, about to demand an explanation, and she put a finger to his lips.

'Calm, Mr Fletcher,' she said. 'We don't want to cause a fuss, do we?'

'What do you want?' he choked. 'Where is Smithy? I'll tear her limb from—'

'No you won't. If you want this marriage to go ahead, then you'll have to pay up. Your son abandoned the poor little thing and you don't value her. She needs an independence or...'

'Or?'

Phryne was interested in the colour of his face—a glowing purple—but reflected that it clashed lamentably with her gown. She opened the order of service and laid a finger on one line. He read it. There was a smothered silence.

'Dearly beloved, we are gathered together here...' began the Bishop in a high, nasal, parsonical tone. Mrs Fletcher took out a lace handkerchief and began to cry decorously.

'Well? How much?'

'Five thousand. Invested, that should be enough.'

'Five thou—!' he began, then hushed as several people turned to look at him.

'It is a state which should be entered into reverently, discreetly, advisedly, soberly and in fear of God, duly considering the causes for which matrimony was ordained,' said the Bishop, with a reproving glance at the groom's father.

'All right. Later.'

'Now,' said Phryne, laying his own chequebook on the marriage service, and unscrewing his own fountain pen which she had somehow abstracted from his top pocket. For a moment she was worried that he would die of apoplexy before he could sign, but he filled in the cheque, and she took the book out of his grasp, waving it a little to dry the ink.

'I'll keep the certificate in case you try to stop the cheque,' she said coolly. Then she stood up as though her movement was part of the service and walked down the aisle and out of the church.

Smithy had cried out years of suppressed humiliation and pain onto Lindsay's shoulder, and was feeling a little better. Lindsay's closeness was comforting, and his perfect faith in Miss Fisher's effectiveness was infectious. She had also told him the whole story, and he had been considerably and gratifyingly shocked.

'I never would have thought it of old Fletch. How did it go, Phryne?' he asked.

'I've stung Papa Fletcher for five thousand of the best and brightest,' she said. 'Do you want to come back inside, Chloë?'

Chloë clung to Lindsay's arm in a way he found touching, and Phryne led them inside, along the side aisle to where Tom Fletcher could see them. He stood straighter when he saw Chloë Smith. Ever since Phryne's message about the jewels had arrived he had been waiting for this.

'Therefore, if any man can show any just cause or impediment why they may not lawfully be joined together, let him now speak, or else hereafter forever hold his peace.'

Tom Fletcher stiffened, his gaze on Smithy—the familiar and ill-used Smithy, who was in a position to ruin his life. Tom did not beg for mercy. He blinked once and Amelia's hand stole out to take his, divining that something was wrong. There was a silence thick enough to slash with a sabre.

Leaning on Lindsay, Chloë Smith smiled slightly, and in that smile released herself from Tom Fletcher. She nodded to him.

'I require and charge you both,' the Bishop continued, wondering what these three were doing standing in the side aisle and hoping that something socially unfortunate was not going to happen, 'as ye will answer at the dreadful day of judgment, when the secrets of all hearts shall be disclosed, that if either of you know any impediment why ye may not be lawfully joined together in matrimony, ye do now confess it.'

Amelia looked up at her soon-to-be husband. He looked at Chloë, who nodded again. Tom Fletcher gusted out a sigh of relief which caused the altar candles to flicker, and said nothing.

~⌒

Phryne saw Chloë Smith into and out of Mr Fletcher's house and into the car, with the trunk full of drawings. She drove her to a suitable boarding house, paying the first week's rent and seeing the young woman settled.

'I really couldn't do anything else, could I?' Miss Smith asked, sitting down on the bed and bouncing. 'This is a nice bed. It's got springs.'

'My dear girl, revenge is always sweet but it is not generally profitable. Now make sure that you bank that cheque first thing Monday morning. You can post the certificate to Mr Fletcher as soon as you have the money.'

'I've got nothing to do. I've worked for them all my life. I kept the household accounts and minded the dog and looked after Ma Fletcher when she had conniptions and dealt with the servants and paid the bills and they never appreciated me or noticed me and now I've got nothing to do.' Miss Smith seemed to have grown younger. She tore off the ugly hat and pulled her hair out of its bonds. Hairpins flew like fireflies. A cascade of corn-coloured hair tumbled down over the charcoal suit. 'What shall I do? What shall I do now?'

'Why, anything you like. Why not go to art school? Buy some nice clothes. And you may find another young man,' suggested Phryne.

Chloë thought about it, running her ink-stained fingers

through the silky strands. 'No. I don't know any young men. And I'm not a virgin. No one will marry me now. Oh, but what about Tom?

What if he has...children? Won't they be...'

'No, that was not a legal marriage, Chloë. Both of you were underage. Neither had you parental permission. You could have caused a massive scandal, though. So you can marry again, if you want to. You're in the same position as a widow.'

'I'll never forget him—Tom, I mean. Yes, I am a widow. It's like he's dead.' She wept for a few minutes, then tossed back her hair and wiped her red eyes. 'I think I'll have a cat. A house first, then a cat. I can afford a house, can't I? Oh dear, I'm going to cry again. Don't stay with me. I like being alone. I have to think. I haven't been able to think, not since Tom brought Miss Amelia home. But you must go back to the wedding, Miss Fisher. Tell Tom to be happy. And don't worry about me. I'm free,' said Chloë Smith, and laughed a little as she realised that it was true. 'I'm free of them all. At last.'

Phryne drove away, humming. After a while she found that she was singing Patience's song. *'Rendering good for ill / Smiling at ev'ry frown.'* Mr Gilbert had a satirical sense of humour, but it was hard to tell from the song whether he was exercising it or not. *'Everything for him, nothing at all for her!'* Phryne bit her tongue and found that she was unable to avoid the conclusion which had been forming in her mind since she had seen the lovers. Lindsay and Phryne were not like that. They could never be. Striving to place Lindsay in the position of Tom had forced her into the position of Amelia, and Phryne would not fit into the frame. She could not do it. She could not marry Lindsay Herbert.

She pulled the big car over and stopped to press both hands to her breast, sick with sudden loss. Beautiful Lindsay, so smooth and deft and loving. A hallucinogenic flash showed her the long body lying on her green sheets, the red mouth which would never again open under hers. Never. If she did not marry Lindsay, he would go away to find his own Amelia, and she would never touch him again, never see that turn of the head when the hair fell just so over his eyes, never kiss the nape of his neck.

Even so, she thought, putting the Hispano-Suiza into gear and resuming her journey. Even so, she could not marry Lindsay Herbert.

Phryne found a chair after dancing with a succession of rowers who had no use for tempo and no regard for her feet, and Lindsay brought her a glass of champagne and a water-ice. The moment could not be delayed any longer. She drew a deep breath. 'Thank you, Lindsay dear, and I won't marry you,' she said, gulping down the drink and beginning thirstily on the ice.

Lindsay gasped.

'I'm sorry, my dear, and I love you very much, Lindsay, but I have thought about it and I can't do it.'

'But…' protested Lindsay.

Phryne put down the dish and took his hand.

'You are lovely,' she said softly. 'Don't think that I don't love you.'

'I love you too, Phryne, old girl, listen—'

'I'll miss you,' she added, with tears springing to her eyes as she realised how much she would indeed miss him. 'But I can't, Lindsay dear, I really can't.'

'Phryne, please…'

'This has been a hard decision to make, Lindsay, so don't argue with me. Please don't make this more difficult than it is.' He had come closer and now kissed her cheek. The caress, so familiar and delightful, went through Phryne like a knife. He was saying something which she did not hear. Then he pulled away from her and dashed across the room to the wedding presents. Returning, he solemnly handed her a silver fish slice.

'What's this for?' she asked, wondering if he had taken leave of his senses. He sat down next to her, seeming rather jaunty for a man whose matrimonial plans had just been dashed.

'I had to get a word in edgewise somehow. I know you won't marry me. That's all right, Phryne, if we can go on as we have been. Seeing that poor Smith girl has rather turned me off matrimony, don't you know.'

'Oh? Get me another glass of champagne, will you?' Phryne felt rather faint with relief.

'Yes.' He collected two glasses from a passing waiter. 'Anyway, I told the pater that if I married I could only marry you, because I loved you like billy-o, and he turned red and choked and went off the idea completely. Not such a good idea, marriage, eh? What do you think?'

Phryne looked at the bride and groom, enthroned at the high table. Amelia, glittering in Victorian garnets, was laughing as her spouse kissed her hand. Whatever explanation Tom had produced about that strange pause in the ceremony, he had clearly been believed, accepted, and forgiven. The lace was thrown back to reveal the pure line of the bride's head and the groom's profile, dark against the white wall behind. They were engrossed in each other, elevated with relief and wine, and as beautiful as they would ever be.

'Not for me, thank you,' said Phryne, and kissed Lindsay Herbert hard on the mouth.

The Vanishing of Jock McHale's Hat

God defend me from my friends.

—Proverb

'Miss! Miss Phryne!' screamed Dot, belting up the stairs as though bears were after her. It was a measure of her social progress that six months had allowed her to call the Hon. Miss Phryne Fisher 'Miss Phryne'. She rounded the corner to Phryne's boudoir and hurtled through the open door. She knew that beyond, in the leaf-green bedroom, her mistress was at least partially awake, for she had ordered Greek coffee half an hour before.

Phryne rubbed both hands through her short black hair and yawned, dragged on a silk dressing-gown, and hauled herself upright. Her current beautiful young man was sound asleep and she drew a corner of the quilt over his delectably smooth shoulder after kissing it lightly, and went out to see what the matter was. Her maid Dot was usually a model of decorum and order.

'I almost hope that the house is afire, Dot, or you have some fairly devastating news, because otherwise I shall be miffed. What's up? What time is it?'

'Miss, the Archbishop's secretary is on the telephone. He wants to see you!'

'What, the secretary? And is that a reason to wake me?'

'No, Miss,' puffed Dot indignantly. 'The Archbishop! A professional matter, he says!'

'Well, it would hardly be a religious one,' murmured Phryne. 'I feel absolutely foul. I must have a bath and some breakfast. Say, ten o'clock?'

'Miss, it's eleven now!'

'Oh dear, I have overslept.' Phryne smiled reminiscently. 'Well, say twelve thirty, and ask him if he would like to stay to lunch. Then tell Mrs Butler if he is, and come back and find me some clothes. And aspirin.'

Dot sped off, and Phryne called after her, 'Which Archbishop?'

'Mine,' replied Dot and ran down the stairs.

Phryne mixed herself a fizzy powder, supposed to be sovereign for an overindulgence in alcohol, and made a mental note that cocktails concocted of gin, Cointreau, and vermouth should be crossed off her list of potables. She ran a sumptuous bath, liberally laced with Nuit d'Amour salts, and soaked herself comprehensively, trying to remember how one addressed an archbishop. Was it my Lord Mannix? His Excellency Mannix? Dot would know.

It appeared that a Catholic archbishop was 'Your Excellency.' Phryne, clothed in neat and modest dark blue against her wishes for a bright scarlet wool dress that Dot considered was much too short and tight, was sitting by the fire in her sea-green parlour, sipping coffee. The young man had gone, much to Phryne's regret, though she was sure that he would be back. The tea table was set and decorated, as His Excellency could not stay for lunch. Dot, in a clean uniform, fussed about the room until Phryne lost patience.

'Sit down, Dot, do! You shall stay while he is here, if you please. I can't imagine what a Prince of the Church wants with me! Did the secretary give you a clue?'

'No, Miss.' Under direct orders, Dot was constrained to sit down on the very edge of a chair. 'But it must be important.'

'Important to him, I suppose, or he would not be consulting me. I'd have thought an archbishop would have better methods of finding things out and enforcing his will than by employing a heathen such as myself! There must be something he wants found, or someone, that he can't do by respectable channels. Have you seen him before, Dot?'

'Me, Miss? When would I see an archbishop? But he's well thought of. The priest at St Mary's thinks he's wonderful.'

'And who am I to argue with the priest at St Mary's?' Then, as a commotion at the door carried to them, 'That will be him, Dot. Take a deep breath and don't be so nervous. He's only a man, you know.'

Dot's protest at this blasphemy was stifled as Mr Butler showed two men into the parlour. One was tall and distinguished, not as old as Phryne expected, with sharp eyes and a bony, intelligent face. The other was middle-sized, dressed in threadbare best, with a ruined Celtic complexion and the piercing hazel eyes of a wedge-tailed eagle. He raised those eyes to take in the parlour and Phryne herself with extreme dislike, then lowered them again. The Archbishop allowed Dot to kiss his ring without any haste or embarrassment, and blessed her. Phryne stood up to greet him and held out her hand, which he took and released with no discernible pressure.

'Your Excellency,' said Phryne. 'Do sit down.'

'May I introduce my companion? This is Mr McHale, who is the coach of the Collingwood football team.'

Mr McHale muttered something and sat down gingerly. His hands seemed to grope for each other in a wringing gesture, as though he was used to holding something that was no longer there. He looked down in surprise and locked both hands together lest he betray himself. The Archbishop accepted tea. Mr McHale wanted nothing.

'Well, Your Excellency, to what do I owe the honour of your company?'

'You undertake discreet enquiries, do you not, Miss Fisher?'

'I do.'

'I am faced with a problem which could be crucial to the success of Mr McHale's team, in which I am of course interested, but more importantly involves the credit of my church,' said the Archbishop, taking a sip and putting down his cup. 'And I cannot invoke any of the people who usually help me, because they may be involved. Will you help?'

'What can a sheila do?' snarled Jock McHale suddenly, and with frightening hostility. 'What use is she?'

Phryne was filled with fury, but not a flicker showed on her face.

'Mr McHale, if you please!' said the Archbishop sternly. 'Please overlook this outburst, Miss Fisher, he is a rough fellow. It's like this. McHale, a devout man, came to the service in my cathedral on Sunday. After mass, he was kind enough to talk to some of my young men about football. At some juncture, while he was in my church, someone stole his hat.'

Both men looked at Phryne solemnly. She repressed a laugh. The Archbishop continued.

'I gather that you do not follow football? Obviously not, or you would have known about it. That hat has been Mr McHale's companion, I might say talisman, for many years. He feels lost without it, and there is an important game this week, against

Richmond. Collingwood must win to make sure of being in the finals and their coach has lost his principal lucky token. It is vital that it be returned. Vital for Mr McHale and his team; vital also for me, because it was stolen in my church. You have less than a week, Miss Fisher, but I will double your usual fee, and I will give you all the help I can. I feel very strongly about this,' said the Archbishop, and Phryne could see that he did, and respected him for it. She also had something to prove to Jock McHale. Sheila, eh! Phryne poured herself some tea.

'I will try,' she said. 'Describe the hat.'

'Grey felt, though now it is a little greenish; battered, because of Mr McHale's habit of twisting it between his hands.'

Phryne stood up. 'I will come to early mass tomorrow, Your Excellency, and have a look at the scene of the crime.'

The Archbishop winced a little, took his leave affably, and swept Jock McHale along in his wake. Phryne sat down to think, reached for the telephone, and called up her minions.

~~~

Bert and Cec were more at home in Phryne's parlour than her earlier visitors had been, and knew a lot about football.

'Me, I don't follow the VFL, my team is Port,' said Bert. He was short and stout, and Cec, his mate, was tall and thin; together there were very few things they could not do. Cec smiled his spaniel smile and accepted tea—black and syrupy, as he liked it.

'Well, you see, Miss,' said Cec, who did follow the VFL, it seemed, 'Collingwood won the last premiership—that is, '27— and there's every chance they'll win again this year. They've got a lot of money and some hard men supporting them, and they can buy players, and rough! Street fighting's nothing compared to a match against the Magpies. But everyone knows about Jock

McHale's hat. You see him at every game, wringing it, bashing it—even wearing it, sometimes. It's an old battered grey thing, like a pot, with the brim turned up at the front. And someone's pinched it! The poor old bloke must be having heart failure.'

'He seemed to be very upset,' agreed Phryne. 'Why would anyone take it?'

'To put the mozz on the Pies,' stated Bert, taking a cake. 'Good cakes, these. No one could want the old relic.'

'Why take it in church?'

Bert and Cec looked at her. 'Why, Miss, I don't reckon he ever takes it off if he's not holding it. They say he sleeps in it. And seein' it, I could believe it. But every man takes his hat off—'

'In a church. Of course, how silly of me. Put the word out, Bert. I want that hat, and I'll pay for it. I don't want to know who took it. The Archbishop's probably excommunicating him now; divine vengeance should be enough for him.'

'All right, Miss. But a man with a real down on Collingwood might think it was worth it,' said Bert, and took his leave.

~~~

The next morning, Phryne—up and dressed at what she considered to be daybreak—sat at the back of St Patrick's and observed. It was a beautiful building, though a touch overdecorated for Phryne's taste, and the statue of the Sacred Heart near which she was seated gave her cold shudders. The pew which Jock McHale inhabited was in the middle, near the nave, and Phryne had already searched around it. Her veil scratched her face, the Latin service was incomprehensible, and she dared not yawn. There were no corners in this church for a hat-stealer to hide; he would have had to be in the congregation.

The service ended. '*Ite, missa est,*' announced the priest, and the people started to shuffle out. Phryne put back her veil and walked boldly up to the priest, who was emerging from his robing room. 'Good morning, Father. I'm Phryne Fisher, and the Archbishop has given me leave to speak to you.'

'Ah yes,' said the young man, blushing. 'Miss Fisher. Nice to meet you.' He pumped her hand with vigour; a strong young man.

'You were celebrating mass last Sunday, were you not? I gather that you know what has happened.'

'Oh yes, His Excellency told us. A terrible thing. The Archbishop is furious.'

'Us?'

'Me and the altar boys, and the seminarians. Mr McHale was talking to them about football.'

'Where?'

'In the forecourt.'

'You were there?'

'Yes, Miss Fisher.'

'Did Mr McHale have his hat then?'

The young man thought deeply, scratching his head. Then he blushed again.

'No! He didn't! It's such a horrible old hat, Miss Fisher, so battered, that he often folds it up and shoves it in his pocket. No, he didn't have it in the forecourt. Oh, I am glad!'

'Why should that make you glad?'

'It means that it went missing in the church. The boys and the students couldn't have taken it.'

'But that means the thief was in the church itself, and the theft took place during the service!'

The fresh face blanched. This was a transparent young man.

'Oh Lord, so it does.'

'Never mind. Now, come and show me how your service works. What's your name, by the way?'

'Father Kelly. The Archbishop told me to help you all I could, Miss Fisher.'

'Now, you are a member of the congregation, coming in from outside. Where do you take off your hat?'

'At the door, Miss Fisher.'

Father Kelly wondered that so much intelligence and drive were contained in this small, fashionable, Dutch-doll woman. Her green eyes were as bright as pins.

'Then you sit down.'

Father Kelly murmured his way through the mass, sitting down, kneeling, and rising in the right places. It had by now dawned upon him that Miss Fisher was not a daughter of the Holy Church.

'Does anyone pass along the aisle while the service is going on?' Phryne asked.

'Yes, of course. I mean, yes. The communicants go up to the altar and come back, and the collection is taken.'

'By whom?'

'Members of the congregation, usually. Last Sunday there were four, all respectable men—Mr Davis, Mr McLaren, Mr O'Reilly and Mr Flynn.'

'What's this?' asked Phryne, and dived for a scrap of paper poking out from under the hassock. It was torn from a larger sheet, and in stern script bore the words: *Thou shalt have no other gods before Me.* Father Kelly examined it.

'Out of one of the schoolbooks,' he said dismissively. Phryne folded the paper and obtained the address of the respectable member of the congregation who had borne the plate to Mr McHale.

Mr Flynn was not at home. The bedraggled maid who answered the door said he was at his work, and directed her to the office of John Playford and Sons, religious publishers, where her master worked as a clerk. It was still too early in the morning for the man to have lunch, so Phryne telephoned her own house to see if there were any messages.

'Two, Miss Fisher,' said Mr Butler's magisterial voice. 'One from Mr Bert, who was calling from the Royal Melbourne Hospital. He said that neither he nor Mr Cec was much hurt, and he would call on you at two this afternoon. The other from an unknown person, who attempted to be threatening. I informed him that his conversation would be reported to Detective Inspector Robinson and he rang off. I gather that the person was concerned for his football team, and seemed to think that you were a threat to it.'

'What has happened to Bert and Cec?'

'A small contretemps, Mr Bert says, Miss Fisher.'

'I knew I shouldn't have got involved with religion,' muttered Phryne darkly. 'Call the Archbishop's secretary, Mr Butler, and tell him of the threat. I think I know who made it and I will be surprised if I get another. And disappointed. I should be back by two. If I'm held up, ask Bert and Cec to wait.'

She rang off, seething. It was known that organised crime had something to do with this football game—thousands of pounds were wagered on it every week down every back lane in Melbourne. Phryne was fairly sure that she knew where the hat was, if it was still in existence, and had half a mind to retrieve it and burn it herself. The adulation that men gave to football was quite beyond Phryne. It seemed to equal and surpass the delight she herself took in food, sleep, intellectual puzzles, clothes, and beautiful young men. Odd. But she had Jock McHale to astound, and that was not a revenge to be passed up lightly.

She drank real coffee in a bohemian haunt in Russell Street until it was time to go and beard Mr Flynn.

The boy at the reception desk of John Playford and Sons gave her a fast and impudent once-over before he freed his mouth from a corned beef sandwich and called into an inner office, 'Mr Flynn! Someone to see you!'

A gaunt and elderly man stalked out to the desk. He took in Phryne's figure, hat, silk stockings, and smile, and stepped back half a pace.

'Why, Uncle, don't you recognise me?' she cried, taking him by the arm. 'I have come to take you to lunch because I'm only up in the city for the day. Come along, we'll be late.'

Mr Flynn, utterly astounded, allowed himself to be led to the front door. The office boy ran after him with his hat, which he took and put on, still staring.

'There's a teashop not far from here,' said Phryne brightly. 'Come along, and there won't be a fuss.'

Mr Flynn was seated and supplied with tea before he found his voice.

'Young woman, who are you, and what do you want with me?'

'I'm Phryne Fisher, and I want Jock McHale's hat. I know you pinched it. I know how, too, and when. Do you think it was fair to the church to commit such an offence during the service? But I don't want to get you into trouble. I just want the hat, then it can all be forgotten.'

Pale blue fanatic's eyes stared into hers. 'No.'

'What do you mean "no"?'

'I will not give it to you.'

'Aha. So you did steal it?'

'I took it, yes.'

'While the poor man was rummaging for a penny to put in the plate, and you were leaning over him?'

'Yes. You are very astute,' he said with distaste. 'Very clever, Miss … Fisher, was it?'

'Miss Fisher is me. Why did you take it?'

'Because that man has created in that miserable scrap of felt one of the false idols, like the Golden Calf. He could have a holy medal of a saint's image, with all a saint's power, but he chooses to invest his faith in a hat! Such a thing is blasphemous. It was an affront to the altar to bring it into the church. I have watched him for years, at matches, wringing that hat, fondling it, even crying into it. It was indecent.'

'Granted that it was indecent, have you the right to judge other men's sins? Has Jock McHale no free will? Can he not be allowed for his salvation to turn away from the hat, and have you not, by stealing it, removed every chance of such renunciation from him? Is that just?'

Mr Flynn gulped some tea. Phryne tasted hers; it was as hot as molten metal. It seemed Mr Flynn had a mouth of pure leather, to go with his heart and his religious convictions.

'I … do not know.'

'And another thing. Your own Archbishop has asked me to find this … this artefact. If the Prince of your own Church doesn't see anything wrong with it, why should you?'

'The Archbishop!' gasped Mr Flynn, greying around the mouth. 'Lord help me! How shall I amend my sin?'

'Simple. You give me the hat and I'll return it. Then you go to confession and purge your soul.'

Mr Flynn reached into his coat pocket and laid on the tea table a flattened bundle of greyish felt. The brim was bent out of shape. They both stared at it.

'Thank you, Mr Flynn,' said Phryne, stuffing the relic into her handbag. 'Don't worry. I'll fix it.'

She rose, paid the bill, and left. Mr Flynn stared into his tea and began to cry.

~~~)

Phryne arrived home in a state of high excitement to find her parlour inhabited by Bert, Cec, and Dot. Bert had a black eye and Cec a bandaged hand.

'What happened to you two?' demanded Phryne, tossing her handbag aside and shedding her coat.

Bert grinned. 'We were putting the word about and met a few of the Collingwood men. We had some words and there was a bit of a barney, but you shoulda seen them. There's no sign of the hat, though, Miss. They was searchin' for it too, and we had a chat about it once we stopped belting each other. They ain't found a trace of it, and neither have we.'

'Ah,' said Phryne with deep satisfaction. 'But I have. I can't say it suits me, though,' and she straightened out and donned Jock McHale's hat, grinning up at them from under the sad, drooping brim.

~~~)

The Archbishop's residence was grand enough. Two storeys' worth of red brick, with a tower that might have done justice to an Irish castle. Phryne could easily imagine Mannix rallying his troops from the battlements. Perhaps he already had. The Archbishop saw himself very much as the defender of his flock, and his scorching contempt for Protestant clergymen was a periodic feature of the morning papers. Yet Phryne had noted that he rarely opened hostilities. He certainly finished them.

She was ushered in by an Irish-looking maid in spotless black and white, and presently His Excellency appeared in a plain black cassock with just a hint of purple about the collar. With an imperious gesture he beckoned through an open side door and McHale emerged, saw Phryne, and gaped. 'But who took it?' asked the Archbishop, marvelling as Jock McHale turned the hat around in his hands suspiciously, as if it might have been an impostor.

'Ah well, one of your congregation who will shortly be confessing to one of your priests. His motives were odd and I'm not going to discuss them. But I think that you are satisfied with the outcome?'

The Archbishop smiled. 'Most impressive, Miss Fisher. Name your fee.'

'Twenty pounds,' said Phryne promptly. 'Damages for two of my men, who were a little battered in your service.'

'I trust that you suffered no more...er...harassment, Miss Fisher? I was very concerned to hear of the telephone call.'

'No, I haven't heard a peep out of whoever it was. Football produces strange passions.'

'And your agents were not seriously hurt?'

'Nothing that ten quid apiece won't cure.'

'But your own fee, Miss Fisher?'

'I would not think of taking one, Your Excellency. I look on it as sixpences tinkling into my heavenly money box.'

Phryne got up to leave. Jock McHale jammed the defeated grey hat onto his bullet head and shook her hand.

'Thanks,' he muttered. 'You're a very clever sheila.'

Phryne took the compliment as it was meant. After all, she was a very clever sheila.

Puttin' on the Ritz

Or where the gorgeous east with richest hand
Showers on her Kings barbaric pearl and gold

—John Milton, *Paradise Lost*

Phryne Fisher removed herself with difficulty from the Austin's front seat. The makers had obviously decided that cars were to be worn tight about the hips that year. The road was quite busy, so she allowed her escort, William Barlow, to take her hand. Fully three cars passed while they waited on the kerb. Light rain drifted down, rendering the streets slick and shiny.

Situated next to the Princess Margaret Club, the Ritz was an unobtrusive two-storey building entered through a wine cellar. Phryne negotiated the steps without difficulty and listened with interest to the barrels gurgling. An ambrosial scent overwhelmed them as they came up into the restaurant to be greeted by Antoine, the maître d'hôtel.

Antoine was as perfect, Phryne thought, as the icing sugar groom on a wedding cake. He was, unusually for Melbourne, genuinely French, from Lorraine.

'M'sieur Barlow, 'ow delightful. I 'ave your reservation. Madame,' he added, his eyes widening a flattering half-inch at the sight of Phryne.

Phryne took this as her due. She was arrayed in a claret-coloured evening dress by Patou, tunic-cut, loose and gorgeous. It had golden and black grapes embroidered around the hem and it had cost her, if not a king's, at least a crown prince's ransom. With it she wore gold slippers and a very fetching cap of the same purple as the dress, decorated with a bunch of golden grapes. She was pleasantly conscious of being quite, quite stunning.

'If you will be seated,' suggested Antoine. 'Here we 'ave a nice table. The menu I shall bring directly.' He snapped his fingers and another dinner-jacketed worthy floated towards him. ''Ere is the wine steward.'

William and Phryne sat down at a table by the wall, where the lights were subdued and it was possible to converse. The wine steward approached with what looked like Volume I of the wine list and William said hurriedly, 'You order the wine, Phryne, there's a good fellow. I don't know anything about it and this chap always makes me feel like a squib.'

Phryne smiled at the wine steward, waving away his list. 'I want a bottle of burgundy, the '08 if you still have some. Then a bottle of Veuve Clicquot, the '23, with dessert. We will discuss liqueurs later.'

The wine steward, crushed, wrote this on his little pad and went away.

'Splendid.' William leaned back in his chair. 'Thank you so much.'

He was a tall and rather rumpled young man, with thick curly chestnut hair which would not stay back despite liberal applications of Floris tonic. He had earnest brown eyes like a Jersey cow. (Phryne had once spent a week on Jersey and eaten herself sick on cream. They were, however, quite her favourite cows.)

William Barlow was also a lawyer, working with the small

firm that employed her friend Jilly. The Barlow family, Phryne recalled, included two brothers, both lawyers—William and his brother John. William was affable and generous. Phryne had only met John once and had been unfavourably impressed by his only topic of conversation, which was money. Phryne did not find money, per se, at all interesting.

With Albert, the father of the Barlows, she was all too familiar. He had been pursuing her relentlessly since her arrival in Australia. The spectacle of a red-faced, overfed, and arrogant industrialist going down on one knee had not amused her at all and she had instructed her staff that she was never at home to Mr Barlow Senior. 'For entrée?' asked Antoine's voice, snapping her out of her reverie. 'Madame would like hors d'oeuvres *variés*? Quiche Lorraine? Perhaps the terrine maison?'

'Quiche Lorraine,' said William. 'That's that sort of egg-and-bacon pie thing? Yes. I'll have that.'

Antoine was a professional maître d'hôtel, so he did not respond visibly to this graceless description of the chef's masterpiece, but he blinked and under his breath said something actionable in French. Phryne intervened before he combusted.

'I would like the terrine, please,' she said sweetly. 'Is it chicken liver?'

'No, Madame, it is canard *à l'orange.*'

'*Bon,*' said Phryne. She was hungry and wanted something solid to eat while William revealed whatever it was that he had brought her here to learn.

She sipped her glass of burgundy and said, 'Will, old thing, I am enjoying myself and all that, but what do you want to tell me? Can we get it over with, so that we can devote all of our attention to the food?'

'Oh well, yes, of course—but it's not a nice tale, Phryne. You know that my mama died ten years ago?'

'Yes. I'm sorry.'

'She wasn't,' said Will frankly. 'She was sick of being in pain, poor old girl, and it came as a relief to all of us. But since then my papa has been…er…misbehaving himself.'

'Yes,' agreed Phryne gently.

'And—the thing is—I don't know…'

'Have some more wine, draw a deep breath and tell me from the beginning.'

The young man did as instructed and said clearly, 'He's lost Mama's pearls.'

At this inauspicious moment, the waiter arrived with their entrées.

Phryne watched her companion tuck into the quiche as though he was starving while she daintily but thoroughly demolished the terrine, which was remarkable.

'The pearls were left to me,' William continued, dusting crumbs off his ear. 'I was going to sell them to set up a Poor Persons' Defence Fund with Jilly. You know how the defendants in *forma pauperis* just get a court-appointed barrister, sometimes not the best or the most experienced. Jilly feels that this bears particularly heavily on women. They seldom have any money behind them and no support, because they've usually killed their husband or their kids. I agree with her—in fact, we were thinking of setting up a partnership. She's a cracking good solicitor, Jilly is, and she's right when she says that the firm isn't giving her a chance at the big cases. She says the closest she came to a murder trial was foiled when you went and found the real murderer, Phryne.'

Phryne laughed. 'That is true, she was very cross with me. Will, this sounds like a good idea. Do you want me to supply some funds? A loan, perhaps?'

'No, no, Phryne, not at all.' The young man made a sweeping

negative gesture and Phryne removed his glass of wine from its path. 'No, I didn't ask you here for that, not at all.'

'All right, Will, you have adequately demonstrated that you don't want money from me. Here, take your glass back and tell me what you do want—preferably in words of one syllable, there's a dear.'

Will gulped some wine and spluttered, 'I want you to retrieve Mama's pearls for me.'

'You mean you know where they are?'

'Well…yes. I mean, I think I do. My papa is—well, you know what Papa is like. He'll be dining here tonight, I think. He usually does on a Wednesday. With Mrs Priscilla Veale.'

'Priscilla Veale?' Phryne coughed on a laugh.

'Yes, his…er…friend.'

'English really is an amazing language,' commented Phryne. 'What sort of friend, Will? Do you mean a lover?'

The young man blushed. 'Yes, I think so. He wants to marry her. She's a seamstress, so all the family is up in arms. They say she's a designing hussy. But Papa is not precisely a catch, either. Look, here they come. That's Mrs Veale.'

A gaudy woman fluttered in, accompanied by the red-faced Mr Barlow. Antoine seated them considerately out of the public eye, near the wall, three tables away from Phryne and her companion.

'Well,' said Phryne, considering Mrs Veale. She wore an extravagant gown of blue and green veined like a butterfly's wings, and was suspiciously blonde for her years, with an appliquéd chocolate box prettiness. If not mutton dressed as lamb, she was definitely shin of ox dressed as Veale. Nonetheless, she was expensive. Her corset alone must have required ten yards of industrial-quality elastic, and pearls gleamed at her neck. The face that Phryne caught sight of as Mrs Veale responded to Antoine's flattery was overly made-up and powdered to the pallor of death.

'Gosh, Phryne, she's wearing them!' said Will despondently. 'If my papa has actually given her the pearls already, there isn't a chance that she'll hand them over.'

'Can't you ask your father for the money instead?' Phryne suggested.

'I have but he just temporises. John's all right. He snaffled the ruby and diamond set Mama left for him as soon as she died—took it out of the safe. I don't think Papa has much remaining money these days. He has been flinging it about rather.'

'Have you tried explaining to the lady that they were your mother's pearls and asking her to give them back to you?'

'No, of course I haven't!' The young man seemed shocked. 'And I really can't sue her for them. That would be washing the dirty family linen in public with a vengeance. I'm afraid that it's all up with our scheme for the Poor Persons, Phryne, unless you can think of something.'

'I still consider there's no harm in asking,' Phryne suggested, and the young man went purple with embarrassment.

'I couldn't,' he confessed.

'Well then, we'll work out some sort of plan. Here comes Antoine. What do you want for a main course?'

'I don't know,' said William glumly. 'You order.'

'Madame?' Antoine had overheard the last comment. 'What would please you? The *boeuf à la Bourguignonne* is excellent and le chef 'as made a truly delicious *filet en cochonailles*. Or perhaps you would prefer tournedos? We 'ave zem à la Béarnaise, à Rossini, or à la Beauharnais.'

'*Le filet*,' decided Phryne. '*Avec pommes de terre à la Lyonnaise et salade verte—vinaigrette. Merci*, Antoine. There, my dear, this will be delicious, I promise. What is your papa ordering?'

A loud voice could be heard demanding a decent plate of brown Windsor soup and a cut off the joint. Antoine winced.

'Oh dear,' murmured Phryne. 'A cut off the joint, when he could be ordering *filet en cochonailles*. I'm afraid that your papa is a truly wicked man.'

When their main courses arrived, Phryne bit into the delicate flesh of the filet and listened to Mr Barlow making an idiot of himself. He had risen to his roughshod feet and was waving his arms as though conducting an inferior chamber orchestra. She was profoundly glad that she was not his companion. It seemed to be getting to Mrs Priscilla Veale, too.

'Do sit down,' she said shrilly, pulling at his coat-tails. 'Herbie! Everyone's looking.'

'I want roast beef,' demanded Mr Barlow. 'And I can pay for it too.'

'A chic boulevardier the old pater isn't, is he?' murmured his son. Then, 'By Jove, Phryne, I think that this is the best beef I've ever tasted.'

'Indeed it is.'

They ate in silence, while Mr Barlow was placated with the offer of *roti de boeuf* and Mrs Veale ordered *boeuf en daube*. Phryne remembered idly that this dish was made with red wine. It gave her an idea.

'Antoine, that was absolutely superb,' William Barlow was enthusing to the maître d'hôtel. 'I never tasted anything like it.'

'I will convey your compliments to ze chef, m'sieur. Some dessert, perhaps?'

'In a moment. I must go over and say hello to my father.'

Antoine expressed, verbally and through his stance and his raised eyebrow, how very surprised he was to find that such an appreciative young man—accompanied moreover by such a soignée woman—was related in any way to the *cochon* (or pig) currently occupying the nearby table. He murmured, 'As you wish,' and left William to finish his Lyonnaise potatoes.

Phryne rose as Mrs Priscilla Veale passed her on the way to the ladies', while William pushed his plate aside and went to exchange hearty inconsequentialities with his father.

'You're looking well, Father.'

'Feeling well, too, my boy. Amazing what a good effect a woman's company has on a man.'

William winced. He endured a powerful handshake and then saw with relief that Phryne had returned, after a brief discussion with Antoine. He retreated to his own table, where Miss Fisher appeared to be elated.

'I think it is time for the champagne,' said Phryne. 'Yes, here it comes—my favourite vintage. Apart from that, Antoine, *mon brave*, just some cheese—Camembert, perhaps—with fruit. And coffee, of course—*café noir*, if you please.'

At that moment, a shriek came from the other table. Antoine muttered, 'Zis is too much!' and all the diners turned to attend to the fuss.

Mrs Veale was holding in her hand a string, hook, and clasp. 'My pearls! They must have fallen off into the stew!' she cried.

'*Vache* Espagnol,' Antoine muttered. 'Zat is not stew. Zat is *boeuf en daube*.'

Phryne and William hurried over to Mr Barlow's table. 'Well, well, that was an expensive dish,' commented Phryne.

'The *daube*, it contains much wine,' observed Antoine, for the benefit of all the bystanders. 'And pearls, zey are dissolved by wine. Zere was Cleopatra, madame—she wished to give Caesar, 'er lover, ze most expensive drink in ze world. She dropped 'er earring, which contained a priceless pearl, into ze glass and pouf! It was gone.'

'You're right,' agreed Phryne. 'Jilly told me about some sailor clients of hers who were hiding smuggled pearls. There was no evidence against them because they had shoved the loose pearls into a bottle of vinegar and they dissolved. Jilly said that the police were quite cross about it, though not as cross as the smugglers at losing their precious cargo. I'm afraid your necklace is gone, Mrs Veale.'

'I told you not to eat that Frenchified stuff,' snapped Mr Barlow.

'Now, Herbie, don't fuss. You really ought to learn some manners,' said Mrs Veale sternly. 'Heaven knows, you're old enough. You gave them pearls to me and I lost them—well, what's to fuss about? I just got a shock when I found the string in my plate—thought it was a mouse's tail. You sit down and have some more of that red plonk and don't worry about it.'

Mr Barlow, considerably amazed, did as ordered. Antoine stood rooted to the spot with horror at the idea of anyone's expecting to find mice in his *boeuf en daube*. Meanwhile, Phryne steered William back to their table. She raised her glass to the other woman and was answered with a brief nod of the head.

The Camembert arrived, accompanied by little water biscuits, and Phryne nibbled. Her escort still looked dazed.

'What happened?' he asked. 'I say, this is top-hole cheese.'

'You heard Mrs Veale. Her pearls fell into the wine of the *daube* and dissolved,' said Phryne artlessly.

William was not a lawyer with a large criminal practice for nothing. He knew that tone of voice.

'Phryne, what did you do?'

'I'll tell you in a moment. They're leaving.'

Mr Barlow, shepherded by Mrs Veale, was collecting his coat and hat. The blonde woman gave him a brisk pat, said, 'Off we go, dearie,' and left the Ritz, pink-faced with righteousness and fluttering with butterfly wings.

'Well,' said Phryne. 'Hold out your hands, William.'

Into his cupped palms she poured thirty-five perfectly matched pearls.

'I told you that you only had to ask,' she said triumphantly. 'I spoke to her when we were in the ladies'. We had to find a way of doing this without arousing your sainted papa's cupidity. Antoine went along with the joke—he is an old friend of mine. I think she'll make a rather good mama, William.'

'You do?' said the flabbergasted solicitor.

'And I think the pearls'll make a rather nice contribution to the Poor Persons' Defence Fund. Your father really is a pig, as Antoine said, which gives a new twist to the old proverb. But we can still use it.'

'Phryne! Explain!'

'It's the first time,' said that young woman ruminatively, 'that I've ever stolen the pearls from the swine.'

The Body in the Library

They say there is divinity in odd numbers,
either in nativity, chance or death.

—William Shakespeare, *The*
Merry Wives of Windsor

'Bloody hell!' said Detective Inspector Jack Robinson, who never swore, and certainly not in the presence of ladies. There were two ladies present. One dead, and one alive.

'Quite,' agreed Phryne Fisher absently. The body was sprawled on the hearthrug. She was very dead. Her face was congested and her red dress had been ripped to rags. She was an incongruous addition to the tasteful atmosphere of the library of Robert Sanderson MP, and Phryne caught her errant mind commenting that the red dress clashed quite frightfully with the tiled Dutch-blue hearth, whereas the corpse's cyanosed skin matched. She pulled herself together.

Jack Robinson said, 'She's been dead for hours. Rigor's set in. Could have been here all day. Room's been closed while the chimneys were swept. How she got here's another matter.'

'Couldn't have walked,' said Phryne, examining a small bare foot. 'Her feet are clean. And soft. She didn't spend all summer running around with no shoes on, and you haven't found any shoes. What does the doctor say?'

'Indeterminate cause of death,' groaned Robinson. 'Recent sexual activity. There's going to be a scandal, you know. That's why I asked you in.'

'I had been wondering.' Phryne saw with a pang that the dead girl had a corn plaster on one toe.

'Mr Sanderson is trying to pass a private member's bill to regulate brothels—you know, to legalise prostitution. I think it's a good idea—we both know how the girls are exploited by the pimps—but he's got a lot of enemies.'

'Who particularly?'

'Worst one—well, the loudest one—is the Reverend Josiah Blackroot. You've probably read one of his pamphlets? The wages of sin is death, he reckons.'

'So is the salary of virtue,' murmured Phryne. 'And at least the wicked have a good time.'

'Yair, well, the nicest thing that the Rev. has called Mr Sanderson is a whoremonger. And what he could do with a dead prostitute on the hearthrug—well, you can imagine.'

'Easily. That's strange,' commented Phryne. 'Look at this, Jack.'

'Glass bracelet,' said Robinson, examining it.

'Odd,' said Phryne, sitting back on her heels. 'This dress would be expensive at seventeen and six. It's cheap art silk and ready-made. Such as remains of her underwear is fine Chinese washing silk with hand embroidery and the remnants of Valenciennes lace edging. Last time I priced it, it was three guineas the inch. On that hand is a brass wedding ring. On this wrist is a diamond bracelet with some really very nice stones. She doesn't match, Jack. It's mostly safe to assume that underwear expresses the real woman.

Perhaps she's a lady's maid who has robbed her mistress's underwear drawer or a lady of light repute with a very rich protector. So what is she doing wearing a shop-bought dress and a brass ring?'

'Dunno. She ain't been doing any hard work,' said Robinson, examining the fingers. 'No pinpricks, no calluses.'

'Not a lady's maid, then. About twenty-five,' said Phryne, trying to mentally reduce the swollen contours of the face. 'Any ideas?'

'She's probably called Alice. This was stuck on her back.' He handed over a card which said: *For a good time call Alice MW 421.* 'Otherwise she's just a well-nourished female with blonde hair.'

'It *is* blonde, too,' mused Phryne, rubbing a tress between her fingers. 'I mean, she was born blonde, not decided to be blonde. This hair is gritty. Fetch me that *Table Talk,* will you, Jack dear?'

Phryne combed out the hair over the open magazine, clamping down firmly on her inexplicable tendency to shudder. 'Well, we know how she got here. Look at this. It's coal dust. The sweep brought her in in a sack. There's a smear on her shoulder, too, and on her knees. That gives us the time. Now, we need a name—I don't believe in Alice.'

'No handbag,' said Jack Robinson gloomily. 'No tags in the clothes. You stay here, and I'll see about arresting that sweep. He might be able to tell us more.'

The inspector departed. Phryne shook the coal dust out of *Table Talk* and found that the issue contained an interview with the Reverend Blackroot. A good-looking man. *'REPENT!'* screamed the banner headline. Phryne kept reading, addressing the dead girl.

'Did you repent at last, then?' she asked, skimming down the page. 'Did someone object to your repentance? And did the Rev. Josiah Blackroot promise you heaven? That is not an unusual male promise, though it seldom comes off...by God,' said Phryne, flattening the magazine under the lamp and staring at the picture and then at the corpse. 'By God, Jane Trellis-Smythe, how did you come to this?' Phryne looked at the picture. Then she looked at the sweep's card again. Then she stared into space for some minutes, biting her lip.

Phryne shoved the picture at Robinson when he returned from instructing his sergeant. He read, *'Mrs Trellis-Smythe is active in Church work and frequently helps the Reverend at his home for fallen women.* That's her all right. But what's she doing here?'

'Not much. Tell me, Jack, has she been reported missing?'

'No. Her hubby's away in Japan, I think. I know because he's a friend of the Commissioner. Oh Lord, this gets worse and worse!'

'It isn't a lot of fun for Mrs Trellis-Smythe, either,' Phryne reminded him tartly. 'I have a story to tell you, Jack dear. Are you sitting comfortably? Then I'll begin. A rather foolish, bored young woman whose husband is often away takes up with a reverend who is doing Good Works among the fallen women. So exciting for a nice, well-brought-up gel. Then matters advance. She may be the Reverend's lover. So deliciously wicked.'

'So he kills her when she threatens to tell all to her husband?'

'Not so simple. Have you ever wondered about that home for fallen women? Here it says that there is a terrible lot of recidivism there. Did it occur to you, as it might have to Mrs Trellis-Smythe, that—'

'You don't mean that the Reverend is running a brothel?'

'What could be a better cover than a home for fallen women? He can even keep them all together. Anyone listening to the women would have worked it out. So when poor silly Mrs Trellis-Smythe wondered what it would be like to be a fallen woman, she put on the dress and the brass ring. Then—what? Perhaps she was smothered with the skirts of that dress, perhaps she died of a heart attack or shock. So the Reverend Josiah realises that he now risks exposure not only as an adulterer, but a brothel-keeper. Seeing her dressed in some of his fallen women's attire, he knows that his other guilty secret is known to her. So he killed her.'

Jack Robinson held up a warning finger. 'But then—what did he do with the body? He wouldn't have brought it here, would he?'

Phryne shook her head. 'I'm not sure. Perhaps Josiah had her brought here to embarrass Mr Sanderson and put paid to all that nonsense about legal brothels, which would ruin his business. Or perhaps he panicked and asked the sweep to dispose of the body, and the latter had the same thought.'

Jack Robinson stared at Phryne. 'What has the sweep got to do with it?'

'This article has his telephone number,' said Phryne. 'I found this card on the hall stand, and of course we found this stuck to her back.'

'*Chimneys swept,*' Jack Robinson read, and put down the first card. '*The Reverend Blackroot's Home for Fallen Women,* and *For a good time ring Alice*... MW 421. They're all MW 421.'

'It was safe enough,' commented Phryne. 'The various clients would never speak to each other. They simply wouldn't know what to say.'

'Neither do I,' said Jack Robinson.

'It was stupid to dump it here, even so. Far better to have stripped her body of everything identifiable and thrown it in the river at midnight. But he (or possibly the sweep as well) couldn't resist using the occasion to try to incriminate his bitterest enemy. Well, Jack, I don't know if you'll be able to find enough evidence to hang the Reverend Josiah, but you can have fun trying.'

Jack Robinson inclined his chin forward and straightened his hat. 'I intend to give it my best endeavours.'

The Miracle of St Mungo

Venus, wounded, rightly takes up arms,
gives dart for dart to the aggressor
and makes him suffer
in his turn the hurt he has caused.

—Ovid, *The Art of Love*

Phryne Fisher sipped. The cocktail might well be the hit of 1928. A dazzle of golden light from the Derwent shone on a shaker of gin and an elaborate ashtray-and-cigarette-box full of Balkan Sobranies. Hobart might be regarded as the veriest antipodes of fashionable society, but its hospitality left nothing to be desired and was well worth the journey thus far. The ferry trip across Bass Strait was notoriously productive of seasickness; but Phryne had taken the opportunity instead to hitch a lift with Bunji Ross in the latter's two-seater.

'All right, Lucy dear,' said Phryne evenly, sitting down on her bed. 'What do you want me to do?'

'Phryne!' protested Lucy, Lady Wessex. 'The pleasure of your company…'

'Out with it, old thing,' said Phryne.

'Thank you for coming,' Lucy began, biting a thumbnail. 'I have got into a…difficulty. Everyone says you're horribly clever. It seemed like providence when I heard you'd flown down here. And it's James, you see, I do love him, and he'd never understand, he's so upright and Scottish and…'

'A young man?' asked Phryne, blowing a smoke ring into the light.

'How did you guess? I really thought he loved me. It was madness, *madness*, and now he's got my locket.'

'Tell him to give it back.'

'You don't understand, he took it when we were… when I was in his rooms in Montpellier Retreat, and now he wants a hundred pounds, Phryne, and I can't ask James.'

'And if you don't pay?'

'He'll give James the locket, and it has a picture in it of the two of us together.'

'That could be explained,' commented Phryne.

Lucy wailed and tore her hair, an act which Phryne had never actually seen before. 'But the picture's got a quotation from Ovid on the back!'

'Oh,' said Phryne. Ovid was known for his carnal poetry.

'I tried selling some jewellery. I took that ugly great tiara into Jamieson's and they told me it was paste! Great-Grandmama must have had it made. She was rather extravagant.'

Phryne examined the portrait on the wall. A face very similar to Lucy's—heart-shaped, dimpled, with a milk-and-roses complexion—and blonde curls which covered a head entirely devoid, as far as Phryne could tell, of brains.

'I could lend you the money, but that's encouraging a blackmailer. What have you told James about the locket?'

'I said it fell overboard when I was out in the yacht. He was cross—the locket was my wedding present and it's been in his family since they came out from Glasgow.'

'Glasgow, eh? That could account for the alarming saint I saw on the wall downstairs, next to the flag of St Andrew and over the crossed claymores.'

'That's St Mungo, patron saint of Glasgow. He's rather a dear. St Mungo found a lady walking by the river, weeping, because her husband had found out that she gave her marriage ring to her lover. The husband threw the ring into the river, then ordered his wife to present herself, wearing the ring, that night at dinner or he'd kill her. He knew she couldn't do that. St Mungo called up a salmon and took the ring out of its mouth and gave it back to the lady. Isn't that a nice miracle? He resurrected a robin, too. Oh, Phryne, what am I to do?'

Lucy sobbed. Phryne tugged on one golden curl.

'Pull yourself together, Lucy. Tell me about this young man.'

'His name's Percy Fellowes. He's a medical student. I met him when my brother brought his friends home. James quite approved of them, though they did sit up all night playing cards and the housekeeper complained about the mess. Then I met him crossing Arthur's Circle in Battery Point and … somehow I went home with him. I don't know how it happened! For three months I was so happy. But he grew cross and wanted me to leave my husband, and I'd never leave my dear old James, and then one morning I got a note demanding money.'

'I've got an idea,' said Phryne. 'Leave it to me. Now, let's dress for dinner. What would be suitable for Hobart, Lucy?'

'Something with more back in it than this,' said Lucy, examining the dresses Phryne had brought. 'And more front than that. This one, Phryne. It will go beautifully with all that polished wood and starched linen.'

Phryne donned the scarlet tunic and watched as her maid

threaded a scarlet panache into her perfectly straight, perfectly black hair. A pale, oval face with penetrating green eyes, a firm mouth, a decided chin, and eyebrows like thin black wings. She blew herself a slightly tipsy kiss and went down to dinner.

~~)

She retreated several hours later, exhausted by trying to make conversation over a crowd of Gay Young Things who reminded her that she was no longer as Gay or Young as she had once been. Phryne's dinner partner had been an elderly and partially deaf bishop, which had not made the task easier. But the food had been excellent. Phryne had eaten sole with lemon, roast beef with potatoes, carrots, Yorkshire pudding and gravy, raspberries and clotted cream, and a savoury of cheese and biscuits. With the meal she had drunk burgundy (imported, French) and after it a positively ancient port (laid down for Sir James when he was born by his wistful, gout-afflicted father).

A Gay Young Thing caught at her scarlet hem as she mounted the stairs.

'I say, pretty lady, don't desert us! We're going to dance!'

'Nice for you,' said Phryne.

'Dance with me?' he pleaded.

'Not even if you dance like a dervish, my dear,' she said gently, for he was very good-looking and excessively young. 'But if you fetch me an ashtray and a glass of water, I'll talk to you for a while,' she conceded, sinking down onto a carpeted step.

The young man vanished with a whirring noise and returned with a smoker's stand and a tray on which reposed two glasses and a jug of iced water.

'You,' Phryne told him, allowing him to light her gasper, 'will go far—possibly too far. I'm Phryne Fisher. What's your name?'

'Gerald. I'm Lucy's brother. Gosh, are you the famous Miss Fisher? The detective? You're not at all what I thought. I thought you'd be…'

'Yes?' Phryne leaned back.

'Not like you are,' he said clumsily. 'I mean, beautiful, poised, like a bird, an exotic bird, among these Tasmanian chickens.'

'Your compliments are good,' said Phryne judiciously, 'but you should practise the delivery. Surely not all your contemporaries are plain?'

'Well, no, there are some fine girls here, I'm sure, but Hobart's a small place. I've known them all since we were children. Everyone knows everyone. Lucy's never brought anyone like you to the house. Only her dowdy school friends… There, I've done it again, haven't I?' He laughed as Phryne laughed. Blond to the brain stem, both siblings, Phryne thought, dismissing any idea that this ingenuous young man could be in league with Percy Fellowes to gouge money out of Sir James. Not a single malicious thought had ever taken refuge under those absurdly fluffy curls.

'Are you at university?' she asked.

'Yes, I'm studying arts. No need for a profession, you know. The pater's rich as Croesus. Says if I want to spend my life writing Latin verse I can. Lots of my friends aren't—rich, you know. People like poor Tommy and Percy Fellowes have to do all sorts of jobs to pay the fees. Tommy's a chucker-out at the Montpellier. Lots of the chaps go there to play cards. Waste of time, in my opinion.'

'Could you take me to play cards at the Montpellier?' asked Phryne, lowering one finger to touch the glowing cheek very gently.

'Not a place for ladies…' sighed the boy, enraptured. 'But if you say so… tomorrow night?'

'Tomorrow night.' Phryne dropped a kiss on the unlined

forehead and resumed her climb. She turned at the landing and saw the upturned, cherubic face still gazing aloft, like a visionary drinking in his favourite saint.

~~⁓~~

The Montpellier was much as Phryne had expected. It stank of beer and men. The main pub was closed, but the side bar was kept open for the refreshment of seamen who came wandering along Salamanca Place in search of the usual maritime amusements. The unswept pavement was clotted with old horse dung and tar and dust. The unswept bar was lined with unclean sawdust in which reposed rat droppings, drunken sailors, and human debris too revolting to contemplate.

'Charming,' said Phryne. She found squalor interesting, once in a while, and so far the Montpellier had not produced the bladed Apache who could be expected in the equivalent Marseilles bar. It seemed astounded almost to the point of silence by the entry of a real, live lady, dressed in red satin and loaded with jewellery. Several voices called out suggestions. Phryne replied so indelicately that there was another silence. Not even the dock women swore like that.

Wisely, the pub decided that she was none of their business and the proprietors turned back to their own concerns: robbing sailors, watering beer, and calculating exactly how much turpentine could be added to the Montpellier gin without the customers actually expiring on the premises.

'They're in here,' said Gerald, leading Phryne to another side bar. This one contained a large, scarred table, an overhead electric light, ten chairs, a lot of bottles, and an assortment of dissipated young men. One caught her attention immediately. A smooth, glossy young man with patent-leather hair, a shirt collar which was still white and a full red mouth. A vampire, thought Phryne, a bloodsucker—just the sort to attract that little goose Lucy. She smiled on the gathering. Gerald tipped a friend off his chair, dusted it, and set it down. Phryne sat.

'Cut me in?' she asked.

'We're playing poker,' said the glossy young man.

'Good,' said Phryne. 'You're Percy Fellowes, aren't you?' she added, putting a purse on the table. 'Florins?'

'Florins,' said Percy Fellowes. 'Have we met?'

'No,' said Phryne, smiling warmly upon the young snake, 'but I've heard all about you.'

'Nothing good, I hope.' Even his voice was smooth.

'Oh no,' Phryne assured him. 'Nothing good.'

For her plan to work Phryne had to lose consistently, and since luck was running her way she had to start cheating much earlier than she ordinarily would have. The cards were old and the players noticed that the lady's rings appeared to be tight. She was forever fiddling with them, especially a rose-cut diamond with sharp facets. She handled the cards clumsily, too, almost dropping them. And she managed to lose, first all her coins, and then all her notes.

'Come home with me, Phryne,' Gerald urged, shocked at the amount of money she had lost. 'It's late.'

'No,' said Phryne. 'One more game. With you,' she said loudly to Percy Fellowes. The forefinger she pointed at him trembled. 'For a certain piece of jewellery,' she said.

The glossy head shook. 'You've nothing left to stake,' he sneered.

'I have myself,' said Phryne.

The table gasped. The other players drew away. Gerald's hand fell from Phryne's arm. His sister's guest was drunk, unsteady, and about to stake her virtue on the turn of a card. And Gerald had no idea what a gentleman was supposed to do under these circumstances.

'Out you go,' said Phryne to the others. 'This is between him and me.'

Gratefully, they left the room. Such a force of hatred was building up between the scarlet-dressed woman and their old friend—a good bloke, really, Percy Fellowes—that they didn't want to watch. But they couldn't completely tear themselves away. Phryne heard them breathing outside the door and grinned, very privately.

She chose her chair. The mirror was not behind her shoulder. The light did not fall on her face. She shuffled the cards and laid the deck down. 'Cut for dealer,' she said. 'Stake on the table.'

'Why should I be carrying the thing with me?' he asked.

'Where would you leave it? Nothing's safe in this rat hole. Come along. I'm wagering my body on this. Show me your stake.'

Reluctantly Percy Fellowes reached into a side pocket and extracted a heavy gold chain and locket. Phryne picked it up, took out the loose picture and read the inscription on the back of the photograph. 'Yes, that would be rather hard to explain,' she murmured. She clapped the locket closed and replaced it on the table. Then she cut the cards, revealed a red king against Percy's five of clubs, and took the deck.

'Why are you doing this?' he asked, accepting two cards. 'Because I want that locket,' said Phryne.

'Why do you want the locket? Another card, please.'

'A whim,' said Phryne.

The young man examined his cards with mounting concern. Then he threw them down on the table. 'Two more,' he demanded.

Phryne, who knew perfectly well what two cards he was going to draw, passed them over.

Percy noticed two things. One was that the woman opposite him, who had earlier seemed hysterical, desperate, and more than a little drunk, was now collected and smiling. The other was that he had drawn the two of clubs and the nine of diamonds from a deck which he had personally stacked.

Phryne gave herself another card. She could not raise her stake any higher. She returned the puzzled stare with a cool smile.

Percy requested more cards. He was beginning to sweat. His patent-leather hair looked tarnished.

Then Phryne laid down her hand. 'Ten, jack, queen, king, ace,' she said calmly.

'Can't be!' Percy grabbed the pack and scattered the cards. He ran his fingertips gently along the backs and turned to Phryne a blanched, shocked face.

'You cheated!' he whispered.

'Of course,' said Phryne. Then she added, as Percy leaped to his feet, 'And so did you, my boy. You only noticed the dents from my ring because they are in different places from your own. I use the French system,' she said with detached interest. 'Easier and faster. If you are good I may teach it to you. Don't do anything rash,' she advised as he reached across the table for her.

The young man froze. He was looking down the barrel of a small but serviceable pearl-handled pistol. He growled.

'Think,' Phryne urged, secreting the locket in her garments. 'Let me get out of here without a fuss and I won't tell your friends that you are a cheat. I will also refrain from enlightening that engaging boy, Lucy's brother, as to the nature of your relations with her. Make a scene and I'll shoot you where you stand—no one in this pub is going to notice. You've won ten pounds from me. Keep it. Now, Percy, are you going to be good?'

If looks killed, Phryne would have been not only dead but carbonised.

'She broke my heart,' he muttered, slumping into his chair.

'You should never entrust your heart, or other important organs, to anyone with that shade of hair or those blue eyes,' said Phryne unsympathetically. 'If you were married to her you'd be homicidal in a month. Nice girl, but a butterfly. Be thankful you got out of this with a whole skin. Nice playing with you,' she said, passing behind him and opening the door. 'Gerald? It's late. I think I'd like to go home now.'

~

'Lucy, I want you to tell me two things. One, when is your fish delivered? And two, can you get the cook out of the kitchen for about two minutes?'

'But, Phryne, have you got it? What happened? You came in terribly late.'

'Lucy, do as I say and we shall get out of this with your reputation intact,' promised Phryne.

'All right, all right. The fish should be here by now; they bring it up from the harbour about eight. And I can always ask Mrs McGregor about last night's carrots. They were as hard as wood.'

'Good. Come along, I want to get this fixed before breakfast and I'm starving.'

Phryne found the tray of fresh, gleaming fish, a sharp knife and the required two minutes. She completed some minor oral surgery on a large sea bass, cleaned her hands, replaced the knife, and was staring out the window when the cook passed her on the way back to the kitchen, having delivered herself of a refreshing tirade about the greengrocer. Phryne went in to breakfast—scrambled eggs with cream, fresh toast with local butter, kedgeree with crispy edges and a whole pot of coffee—with the sense of a job well done.

They were in the middle of morning tea when Phryne heard a shriek from the kitchen. Sir James put down his cup testily. 'What's the matter with the woman?' he demanded.

'I'll go and see,' offered Lucy. She flickered out of the morning room in a tumble of curls and lavender cotton. Phryne continued talking about Scotland with Sir James. She liked him. A nice, steady old buffer, just the thing for a flibbertigibbet like Lucy. Phryne was just extolling the glories of the Highlands when a procession came in. Lucy, looking amazed. The butler, carrying a dish. The cook, clutching her fish-gutting knife.

On the salver was a large sea bass. It looked surprised, as well it might. Spilling from its belly were innards and the gleam of gold. Sir James drew it forth. Lucy sat down abruptly and fanned herself. 'Whoever heard of such a thing?' demanded the cook. 'I was just cleaning the fish for dinner and the knife jarred on something and there it was. That'll be milady's locket what she lost overboard, I said to Mr Hughes, I said, and I was right.'

'We have been particularly blessed, Mrs McGregor,' said Sir James, looking up at the picture of St Mungo on the wall. 'Have the locket washed, will you. I would like to see it where it belongs again.'

'Oh, James!' Lucy flung herself into her husband's tolerant embrace and burst into tears.

Phryne caught Sir James's eye. He was looking straight at her over his wife's bent head as he spoke.

'Indeed, we have been particularly blessed. And I have not forgotten the stories of St Mungo, either,' he said gently, and winked.

Phryne raised her coffee cup to him and drank a silent toast. To St Mungo, of course.

Overheard on a Balcony

This was a good dinner enough, to be sure,
but not a dinner to ask a man to.

—Dr Samuel Johnson in
Boswell's *Life of Johnson*

Phryne Fisher surveyed the ranked waiters with the slightly doubtful air of a head of state taking the salute from a very well-dressed, well-trained army.

My, she thought, they do look spruce. Each white shirt front gleamed like a pedigreed cat's fur, glossy with grooming. The black trousers were of stygian hue, and each bow tie perched at an exact angle on each neat starched collar, as though twenty black butterflies had alighted north of the waistcoats and frozen in some sudden frost. The Queenscliff Hotel's staff was under constant, quasi-military discipline.

It was 25 June 1928 and Phryne was invited to celebrate Antipodean Christmas. Tom Adams, the publisher, liked Australia. He liked Miss Jane, his fiancée. He approved of the beaches, the beer, the people, and the writers. However, he was willing to consider any offer for the dust and the flies, and he still longed for a white Christmas. He yearned for snow, plum pudding, robins, and roast turkey. He felt that decorating a Christmas tree and eating a Christmas dinner in temperatures above 100 degrees Fahrenheit was ridiculous.

So he had arranged to put on a proper Country House Christmas feast at a time when the weather might cooperate. He had chosen for his setting an establishment so sure of itself that it had no other title but 'The Queenscliff Hotel.' Tom Adams admired arrogance, particularly when it was justified.

Phryne had motored down from Melbourne in the Hispano-Suiza with her maid Dot, a plain young woman dressed entirely in brown: a chocolate-coloured coat, hat, gloves, and scarf over an ochre woollen costume. She was shivering. Dot did not like winter.

'Oh, Miss, I'm that cold!'

'One moment, Dot dear, I'll just sign the register and we shall go and sit in front of that nice fire in the salon.' She scrawled her name with a characteristic flourish and saw her baggage borne up the red-carpeted stairs by marching minions to the best room in the hotel.

Dot sat down on the edge of a leather armchair, directly in front of a blazing fire. Phryne, who did not feel the cold, leaned on the mantelpiece between the Chelsea spaniels and a huge vase of cotoneaster berries and ferns, and surveyed the room.

Tom Adams was not there. Huddled to one side of the fire was a thin, nervous blonde girl, who was staring at the open pages of a romance as though she had forgotten how to read. She was so pale as to be almost transparent. In response to Phryne's greeting, she whispered, 'Emmy Harbottle.' Her fingers were icy cold. A large, red-faced, bluff military gentleman bellowed, 'General Harbottle—call me Alex,' from the chessboard. A buxom red-headed woman wearing very few garments, considering the weather, gave Phryne a languishing glance and murmured, 'Lilith Johnson.' Phryne had heard of her. She wrote convoluted novels of what would have been shocking indelicacy if they had been less obscure to the general reader. As it was, no one, including the censor, was quite certain that she could have meant what they thought she meant. Her novels enjoyed considerable sales and wide acclaim.

The General's opponent was immediately recognisable. He had long dark hair, curiously dead-looking, which hung down over his disordered collar, four big silver rings on his left hand, and thick glasses. Zechariah Silk, the cubist poet. Phryne had tried to read some of his work and found it so dense with depressing imagery that she sent the book back to the library. She had it in for him, especially for a fetid little offering called 'Dead Foxgloves,' the first line of which had burned itself into her memory: 'Slimy-green, envenomed, desiccate-petalled, the death of foxgloves.'

The poet got up, observed, 'Check and mate,' to the General in a heavily accented voice, and took Phryne's hand to kiss it. His smile was sweet and rather shy, and his mouth was warm on her wrist. 'Merry Christmas,' he said. 'I am delighted to meet you, Miss Fisher.'

She could not identify the accent—it was a rich, plummy Middle European, maybe Hungarian, perhaps Russian.

'Mr Adams has telephoned,' the waiter informed the General. 'He and the Smythe and Brenton parties will be here directly.'

'I should think so. Been waiting for the feller for an hour,' grunted the General. Losing at chess had not improved his temper.

'But you have not been bored,' observed the poet. 'You have learned not to underestimate an opponent and also a valuable lesson about the queen's side defence.'

The General snarled. Phryne sauntered away from the fire to

look at the board. A very pretty attack had decimated the General's men and trapped his beleaguered king behind his remaining pawns. She recalled that General Harbottle had conducted at least one large battle—was it the Gallipoli campaign?—and hoped that he was more skilful with real men than he was with chess pieces. She said as much to the poet, who shrugged.

'It is a game of strategy and intelligence, Miss Fisher. You would not expect a soldier to have any knowledge of it.'

Mrs General Harbottle had got to her feet, one hand on the back of her chair. 'Where are you off to, Emmy?' demanded her husband.

'I thought I'd go and lie down,' she faltered. She looked ill.

The General barked, 'I didn't bring you all this way for you to hide from company. I'm a crock, ticker's gone bad'—he looked around the room for sympathy—'but I'm sticking it out. You're all right, Emmy. Sit.'

'But, Alexander...' she protested faintly.

He swelled and turned purple. He grabbed his wife's arm and forced her down, pinching her upper arm so that she winced. With his other hand he felt in his pocket and produced a letter. His wife blanched at the sight of it.

His manner nettled Phryne, who did not like bullies. She slid between the General and his spouse and said, 'Come along, Mrs Harbottle, we'll go up together. Travel is so fatiguing, isn't it?'

The General, scowling, had no choice but to allow his wife to take Miss Fisher's hand.

Phryne and Dot took Emmy to her room. Dot assisted her to remove her shoes and lie down, covered with a patchwork comforter. 'I'll order some tea for her, Miss, and perhaps I'd better stay.'

'All right, Dot dear, that is kind of you. If you have any trouble with the General give me a shout. Wife-beaters are scared of women. Do you want to dine with the company?'

'Oh no, Miss, not unless you need me. The staff dinner's sup-posed to be really good and… that might be more fun.' Dot, who had been brought up not to criticise her social superiors, blushed a little.

'Yes, I see your point. Though the presence of those Bright Young Things will mitigate the atmosphere a little, I expect. Come and get me dressed at about seven thirty. I think I'll take a walk.'

Phryne took herself off to stroll along the pier, where she encountered the promised Bright Young Smythe girls and Brenton boys and spent an agreeable afternoon travelling to Portsea and back on the ferry *Hygeia* among a festive crowd, breathing in the scent of ozone and brass polish and steam.

~

Tom Adams watched her sail down the grand staircase, dressed in an Erté original. She flowed from step to step in the loose folds of the heavy red satin gown. Phryne gleamed with the expensive gloss of famille-rose china, from her close-cut cap of shining black hair to her red brocade shoes.

She extended a scented hand for him to kiss and observed, 'Tom dear, how lovely to see you. I was hoping to meet your fiancée. Is she not here?'

Tom grimaced. 'Her mother is ill, and Jane's doing the angel of the hearth thing. It's a shame. I wanted her here for Christmas. Good of you to come.'

'Thank you for inviting me. Tom, I don't wish to be rude, but what on earth possessed you to inflict that brute of a general upon us? I don't recall doing you any harm.'

Tom Adams seemed ill-at-ease. His ordinarily rubicund com-plexion was pale and he had been biting his fingernails.

'I owe him… a favour,' he said with an unconvincing smile.

'Anyway, his wife's my cousin and you'll enjoy the others. Lilith is always good value and so is Silk. They should make up for one irritating general.'

'Very well, if you wish to dine with a bounder it is your business,' said Phryne, and allowed him to conduct her into the dining room.

It was a high-ceilinged, wood-panelled chamber with more polished plate than the collective annual output of the Peruvian mines, and damask tablecloths starched to the rigidity of paper. Holly wreathed every table and the epergnes were full of bright berries. Tom was seated at the head of the long table with Phryne at the foot.

The guests smiled at each other. Phryne had a Brenton boy to her right and the poet to her left. He had added to the usual gentleman's evening dress a bright red cummerbund and a ribbon of some foreign order. Phryne resolved on being as bright as possible under the circumstances.

Silk was engaged in animated converse with Lilith Johnson, so she engaged John Brenton on the subject of skiing, in which she had minimal interest but upon which both Brentons could be relied to converse until whole herds of dairy cows came home.

'Last year at Baw Baw we were skiing on rocks but this year…' He closed his eyes in rapture. 'There is powder down to five hundred feet.'

'Oh, good,' murmured Phryne, wishing she were elsewhere. The waiters served the soup. It was a delicate flavourful julienne of vegetables and its excellence moderated Brenton's snowy discourse. Beside her, the underfed poet laid his thick glasses down on the menu and slurped. Phryne looked idly, then with increasing interest, at the glasses and the menu beneath them. How curious! she thought.

A political argument was developing, the storm centring

around the General. Now Lilith was amusing herself by attracting one of the Brenton boys in direct competition with one of the Smythe girls—Lilith was winning—the military man was proclaiming, 'These trade union chappies, disgusting, holding the country to ransom. Ought to join the army, there's no bolshie stuff there—soon beat it out of them, few years' military discipline, straighten their ideas up.'

'A lot of them were soldiers,' observed the poet quietly.

'Not in my war.'

'Oh yes, many of them,' said Zechariah Silk.

The General swallowed a huge mouthful of turkey and chestnut stuffing and slapped his wife's hand off his arm. 'Leave me alone, Emmy. Remember the letter!' Emmy shrank back with a little cry. 'Consider your place. You came from the gutter and you can easily go back there.'

Tom Adams said, 'Here, I say, Alex,' and an adroit waiter poured the General more wine, which he gulped. Lilith removed her gaze from the Brenton boy and directed at the General a glance so full of malice that it should have stung.

'You, Silk,' bellowed General Harbottle. 'You were a conchie, I'll bet; a yellow, lily-livered, white-feathered conchie. I had one in my regiment. We sent him into the front line pretty smartish. That's what I do with cowards!'

The poet leaped to his feet, tipping over his chair, and left the room without a word, his hair flopping across his face, his shoulders bowed.

Tom Adams protested, 'Really, General,' and the older man bared his teeth at his host in return. 'I know about you, too, Adams. I know your secret. And that slut down there—I know about her.'

'But you do not know anything about me,' observed Phryne in a clear, carrying voice as cold as one of Brenton's blizzards. 'Moderate your tone and mind your manners.'

Perhaps General Harbottle had had a governess. The ice cut through his bluster and he harrumphed and gulped more wine.

'Shall I go after the poet chappie?' offered a Brenton boy, and Tom Adams sighed. 'No, he'll have taken offence, and who can blame him?'

A waiter came to the table to remove the plates. Even the indefatigable John Brenton had run out of conversation. In silence, they waited as a huge and perfect plum pudding was brought to the table. The waiter sliced it and Phryne nibbled a fragment or so, wishing that she had not come.

The General bolted his serving, choked, and fell balletically from his chair, which crashed to the floor on top of him. It was the most interesting thing he had done all evening.

It took some time to disentangle the chair from the General, take the patient to his room and summon a doctor from the township. And when he arrived, the General was perfectly dead.

~

Phryne perched on the arm of a chair and smoked and thought. Everyone wanted to kill the General, except possibly the Brentons and Smythes. Phryne observed sardonically that Amelia Smythe had collapsed into Tom Adams' arms and that Lilith had captured the Brenton of her choice and was reclining on his manly bosom. Mrs Harbottle was sitting on one corner of a sofa with Dot in attendance. She was not crying. In fact, she seemed to be relieved. Her suppressed hair was fluffing out from its band.

Clearly Tom Adams was being blackmailed, and so was Lilith—what dread secret was that notorious flapper hiding? Phryne wondered. It must have been something fairly choice. Of course, the old pest might simply have had an apoplexy and died from the enormous dinner he had just eaten. She reflected that her thoughts were turning too frequently to murder. She took up a magazine and glanced through it.

Ten minutes of *Table Talk* were enough to drive her into inviting an unattached Brenton to walk along the pier with her. She was on her way out when a large policeman politely asked her to return once again to the salon to await the arrival of his sergeant. Phryne smiled at the brass buttons and asked sweetly, 'What killed the General?'

'Doctor says it was an overdose of his heart pills,' said the policeman, dazzled. 'I think it will be all right, Miss.'

The salon contained a large jigsaw puzzle which was half completed, and Phryne and her attendant Brenton sat down to fit the remaining bits together.

The guests were dismissed an hour later and allowed to go to bed. Phryne reached her own room, undressed herself, and sat on the pearl-coloured loveseat in the bay window, staring into the night.

There was no way that anyone could have poisoned General Harbottle at dinner. She ran through the courses one by one— the soup, the entrée, the turkey, and the pudding had all been shared between the diners. Tom Adams had been sitting beside the General, and might have been able to sprinkle something onto his plate. Phryne was restless and unable to sleep. She wondered if Tom Adams felt the same.

Phryne found him on the upstairs balcony. He was leaning on the rail and she saw the glow of his cigar.

'Can't sleep? Neither can I,' he greeted her. 'What a thing, Phryne.'

'Indeed, though if I had to choose a victim, he would be high on my list. Tom, you know my profession. I can help you. Did you poison him?'

'No, by God, Phryne, what a question!' he said loudly, and she laid a hand on his arm.

'Hush, idiot, four rooms abut onto this balcony, speak quietly. What did he have on you, anyway?'

Tom Adams stared, summed up his acquaintance with Miss Fisher, and said rapidly, 'A marriage, Phryne. It's a relief to tell someone. When I was a student I married a girl in London. Recently I've been courting...'

'So you have. Does Miss Jane know about this?'

'Of course not. I'm pretty sure that the woman's dead anyway. I've got people finding out for me. But Jane... Jane's the one; amazing girl. I want to spend the rest of my life with her. And her father doesn't approve of me above half, so...'

'Was the old beast blackmailing you? The General, I mean?'

'Well, yes, but only for things like this invitation. He wanted to go about in society. Can't imagine why. Needed new people to insult, I suppose. Well, he's gone and I didn't do it, but the relief is profound, let me tell you.'

'Then who did it?'

'It might have been an accident. Perhaps he just gulped a handful of heart pills. But I'm afraid... the person he treated worst...'

'Yes. His wife. But I don't think she'd have the nerve. What did he have on Lilith?'

Tom Adams laughed softly. 'You promise not to tell?'

'I promise,' said Phryne promptly.

'Her blameless private life.'

'Oh, Tom, don't be silly.'

'No, really.' Tom drew Phryne close so he could whisper. 'She has a husband who is a clerk in the public service and two very nice children. But half her stock in trade is her femme fatale act and the General knew she couldn't afford to lose it. Who wants to read shocking novels written by a bourgeois housewife? It was a serious threat. But I can't see how she could have done it. She was too far away and, moreover, she was vamping the Brenton boy.'

'True. Has anyone seen Zechariah Silk since he flounced out?'

'Yes, he went into the small salon and was playing chess with himself. I saw him later in the evening. I'm going for a walk along the beach. Want to accompany me?'

'No thanks, Tom dear. I'll go down and see if someone can make me a cocktail.'

The next morning brought orders to stay in the hotel, which was no hardship, and a police surgeon who announced that the patient had died of an overdose of digitalin. The guests were searched and no one had any supply of the drug. Phryne idled the day away, dressed for dinner, and sat down to another excellent supper, irritated at her inability to solve this puzzle. She could not see the General killing himself, and he did not seem to have been a careless man.

'Perhaps he realised what a bounder he was and removed himself to spare us his company,' said Lilith from across the table, echoing Phryne's thought.

'No such luck,' rejoined Tom Adams, as the waiter reached past him to ladle a delicate chicken soup into his bowl. Phryne sipped at the fragrant broth, possessed of the edges of a memory which slipped away as she tried to grasp it. Her unease lasted through two courses and coffee, and persisted as she went upstairs.

There had been something about the waiter's hand as he sliced the plum pudding. Not rings or scars. Just some oddness about the colour of the skin... She stopped abruptly and Zechariah Silk, who was behind her, stood on the hem of her red satin dress and muttered an apology. She grabbed his arm, proceeding up the carpeted stairs and through the little door onto the balcony, where she turned and faced him, her arms around his neck.

'If anyone sees us they will think we are spooning and look away,' she said into his shirt front. 'Mr Silk, you are a fraud.'

'Fraud, ma'mselle?' said the liquid, heavily accented voice, and Phryne tugged at the long hair. It came off in her hand. She pulled off the glasses. A young man with cropped black hair stared uncertainly into her green eyes.

'Yes. This party is full of them. Tom Adams has a secret wife, Miss Johnson has a hidden husband and children, and you, my dear, have a secret identity.'

'How did you know?' The voice was lighter than it had been and had a pronounced Eton accent. 'I thought I did a dashed good Zechariah Silk.'

'You did.' Phryne was enjoying his closeness. 'It was superb. But you put your glasses down on the menu and they did not magnify it. And your hair looked dead; it is not a very good wig.'

'Second-hand,' confessed the young man.

'And you murdered the General.' The body flexed in her arms and she held tight. 'It's all right, my dear, I just want to know why. And how would be nice. You took all your rings off when you doffed the wig, cummerbund, and glasses and impersonated a waiter, but I saw his hand and he had patches of lighter skin on all four fingers. Unusual.'

The young man sighed heavily and said into her hair, 'All right. Are you going to turn me in, Phryne?'

'Depends,' said Phryne. 'Tell me how and why.'

'I read about the method in a book of notable British trials when I was imprisoned by the Turks.'

'So you were a soldier.'

'I was, and that old bastard was our commander. He sent us

over the top at Gallipoli. They all died, all my friends, but the Turks found me alive and kept me as a slave for two years.'

He released Phryne and unbuttoned his soft white shirt. A bullet had carved a track across his chest.

'I spent a lot of time thinking about him—the General. He had sent us up an unclimbable hill to take an untakeable machine gun. I saw them die, Phryne, cut down around me, all my mates—that's what the Aussies called them: mates. Fellows I'd known since I was a child. Well, I was released when the war ended, then I met the old devil in London. I was quite alone, you know—everyone I knew had been killed. I took to being Zechariah Silk, partly because no one would publish my poems if I didn't look right, and good old Silk looked perfect. I had quite a success. Then there was Emmy—we were engaged, you know, before the war. I did nothing for a long time, just watched. But the fellow kept intruding into my world, seemed to positively seek my society. I couldn't bear the way he treated her. That letter he kept talking about—it was my letter, one I'd written her before the war.'

'So you decided to poison him—how?'

'Easy. I just left the table, ran into the gents, took off the disguise and took in the pudding. I had a knife smeared on one side with the poison, and the greedy blighter gulped the stuff down. But now, Phryne, tell me how you knew.'

'About the poison? Your poem—that ghastly one about the death of foxgloves. That's where you get digitalin. Foxgloves. What's your real name?'

'Ian. Ian Roberts.' He stared out to sea, one hand on Phryne's silk-clad shoulder.

'What are you going to do now?' she asked.

'Go away. I can't tell Emmy what I did—that wouldn't be right. She's free now, though—he can't torture her anymore. I've got an offer of a job in Africa; I used to be a medical student. Lot of disease to be treated in Africa. Promise you won't tell Emmy. She must never know.'

Phryne considered the face in the half-light. It was determined, sober, beautifully made. The lips were set and the jaw firm. She moved away.

'What are you going to do?' whispered Ian Roberts, and Phryne said, 'Nothing. I am going to do nothing. Unless someone else is charged, and that doesn't seem likely.'

A figure shot past her in a whirl of white draperies. Mrs Harbottle, freed of her appalling husband, ran straight into Ian's arms and clung to him as though she would never let go.

'Oh dear,' observed Phryne. 'I forgot about the bedrooms opening onto the balcony.'

'I heard it all,' Emmy said into Ian's shirt front. 'I thought you were dead! Oh, my dear, my dear.' She kissed him, tears running down her face. 'Oh, Ian darling.'

'Emmy, no—I never meant you to know...' he protested, but she stopped his mouth with another kiss.

'I'm terribly sorry, Ian,' she babbled. 'I got married when they said you were dead—missing, believed dead, they said. I dreamed about you dead on that cliff, then Father died and Mother was ill and I didn't have any money, and the General was nice at first, he brought me flowers, and everyone was dead, Ian, all our friends...'

'Oh, my dear.' The erstwhile Zechariah Silk's head bent over the disordered hair. 'Emmy, think. We can't start our life together with such a weight on our consciences—it would drive us apart. Oh, my dear.' He held her close, the pale hair crushed against his white shirt. 'Oh, Emmy, I love you so much.'

'I love you too, Ian. Do you forgive me for marrying the General?'

'Of course,' he said fondly.

Emmy drew herself partly out of his embrace and scolded,

'Why didn't you come back to me? You made me think you were dead and then I didn't care what happened to me! How could you? How could you watch while that beast of a man tortured me all this time?'

'I… I didn't believe that you still wanted me,' he said helplessly. 'I thought that I wasn't good enough for you. I thought… damn it, Em, you had a house and a car and servants. I haven't a bean in the world—you don't make a living out of poetry. Forgive me,' he said, and Emmy subsided into his arms again.

'But it won't do, Em,' he said, gently pushing her away from himself with wincing effort. 'You can see it won't do, my girl. We might be happy for a few months, but then as soon as we had a quarrel—and we will have quarrels, everyone does—you would think of how I killed your husband, and I would think that you might be afraid of me, and even if we didn't think like that there would always be the shadow of a dead man to poison our love. You can see, can't you, Emmy, that it won't do?'

Emmy gave a stricken cry and burrowed into his embrace.

Phryne looked at the agony on Ian Roberts' face, backed by stoic resolution, and felt a pang of pity. What he said was true. A relationship based on murder could not succeed. It might have been all right in the old days, when knights were bold, but even then that did not include the deliberate poisoning of a rival.

She was about to withdraw when a quiet voice observed, 'There is something you should know.'

Lilith Johnson stepped through her open window. She was draped in an expensive silk negligee and had a piece of paper in her hand. 'Before you make any hasty decisions, lovebirds, have a look at this,' she said.

Ian took the note and Phryne came close as he angled it towards the moon to read. In black letters it read:

I know you don't love me, Emmy. You are still hankering after that Roberts chap, but he's dead. You can't compete with the dead. The quack tells me that my ticker is so dicey that I may go anytime. So I'm taking the easy way out. If you marry again, you won't have a penny. The money will all go to my brother. Goodbye. I did love you, Emmy. I really did love you.

It was signed with a bold military signature.

'It's his writing,' observed Emmy, not letting go of Ian Roberts for a moment. 'It's the General's writing.'

'Where did you get this, Miss Johnson?' asked Phryne.

Lilith Johnson lit a gasper. She looked out to sea as she spoke. 'That monster of a man was pursuing me. He thought I was an easy touch—fallen women excited him.' She puffed on her cigarette. 'He slid this under the door, with a note demanding an assignation. So you didn't kill the loathsome old beast, Mr Silk, or whoever you are. How much digitalin do you think you can get by boiling foxgloves? You just get foxglove soup. He killed himself and good riddance. Tomorrow I will give the note to the police and we will all go home.'

Emmy vanished into a rapturous embrace. Then she sagged. The so-called Zechariah Silk swept her up into his arms and carried her triumphantly from the balcony into her own room.

'That's not all there is to it, is it?' asked Phryne very quietly, as she leaned on the balcony with Miss Johnson. The woman smiled, her red mouth a sidelong slash in the moonlight.

'And what if...' she said deliberately, lighting another gasper and blowing a plume of smoke at the moths. 'What if I told you that a woman with a dearly loved husband and two lovely children was being blackmailed by a military ape? If I said that all her happiness was being threatened by that bounder's knowledge of a moment of madness with a pretty boy? If I mentioned that the woman's husband is worthy but dull and very jealous, and that the soldier in question was offering her the choice between disclosure of this brief affair and a lifelong affair with him? And perhaps she felt desperate—perhaps she invited him to her room and talked to him and gave him a glass of wine in which a lot of heart pills were dissolved? She might have known that he was a self-pitying bastard and had a habit of writing suicide notes, and she might have stolen one for use at a suitable juncture. She might have been quite mad with fear. If you had overheard that story on this balcony, Miss Fisher, what would you do?'

The woman's face was set and she turned her blue eyes on Phryne. She looked haggard and resolute and one hand crushed the silken nightdress into creases. There was a pause in which the sea sounded, wash and crash, and a night bird cried with unbearable loneliness.

'I don't know what you think you can overhear on this balcony,' said Phryne, walking away from Lilith and pausing with her hand on the doorknob, 'but I didn't hear a thing.'

The Hours of
Juana the Mad

Memorial from the soul's eternity
To one dead deathless hour.

—D.G. Rossetti, *The House of Life*

The academic cocktail party was not Phryne's idea of a good time. She had been enticed to enter the solemn portals of Melbourne University by the charms of a rather spiffing young associate professor upon whom she had designs. Jeoffrey Bisset had pleased Phryne on first acquaintance by pronouncing her name correctly (Phryne to rhyme with briny) and displayed an unacademic interest in her matchless person and her Hispano-Suiza racing car, both things of which she was fond. He had promised, in addition, to show her the department's treasure. It was a Book of Hours made for Mad Queen Juana of Spain, purchased in that country by a graduate of the university and found among his effects after he had succumbed to a random bullet in the mountains of Catalonia. The university had not tried to remove his blood from the binding, in case cleaning should injure the gilding. It had a macabre interest, as well as that intrinsic to a medieval work of art.

Phryne sipped some sour, new sherry and surveyed the crowd. The wood-panelled room was full of academics, packed in so close that they could hardly move. This did not in any way inhibit their flow of discourse, though the parts that Phryne could catch did not sound very scholarly.

'They say that poor Bradbury is completely broke,' shrilled one bird-like woman, pecking up peanuts from the palm of her hand. 'Not a penny left, and all his goods to be sold...'

'I shall bid for the Catullus,' said a pale young man, slicking his hair back cautiously, as though it might bite. 'He found it in the Charing Cross Road, apparently...'

'And the two of them, out taking the air, bold as brass!' whickered a horsy man in a checked coat evidently made from a blanket. 'I said, "Good morning, sir, nice morning, is this the wife?" and he bellowed at me, "Mind your own bloody business, Hoskins!" In Lygon Street, I'll have you know, on a Saturday morning!'

'Too, too distasteful,' worried a small, bald man. 'Such a nice man, frightfully good family, and takes Holy Orders even though we all said that it was not, really not, a good idea, and now there are all these wretched choirboys!'

Jeoffrey interrupted Phryne's eavesdropping just when it was getting interesting. He smiled a sweet and guileless smile down at her from his six-four height and asked, 'You don't want any more of that revolting fluid, do you?'

'I do not. If I want vinegar, I'll buy vinegar.'

'I've mentioned to the committee that the sherry is terrible, but they are all teetotallers except for Connors, and with those foul cigars he smokes he can't taste anything anyway. Never mind. Come and see the Book.'

Phryne tucked her hand between his elbow and his side, and they tacked across the room, sliding through scandalous conversations, the tall blond man linked to the small Dutch-doll Phryne, who followed in his wake.

'And then he had the nerve to say that my work was derivative. Me! Derivative!'

'Everyone knows that you are a most original writer, dear boy. If you weren't so original I might be able to understand you,' murmured a beautiful, dark brown voice, soft and malicious. It belonged to a short, gnome-like man with sharp eyes. 'Ah! A vision!' he cried.

Phryne replied, 'Not a vision, but Phryne Fisher, and I think I'm stuck.'

'Phryne who offered to rebuild the walls of Thebes?' asked the man, edging a little sideways to allow her to pass.

'The citizens wouldn't agree,' she said, slipping out of his grip. 'And I hope they enjoyed their ruins. Goodbye.'

She caught up with Jeoffrey, who had just noticed that she was no longer with him.

'Who is that small man—there—talking to the poet?'

'Gerald Street. Anglo-Saxon and Old Norse. He's a very kind chap—pays out most of his salary to indigent students. Anyone who shows an interest in his subject is family, but he has a tongue like a viper. Here we are. This is the library, and it might be a bit quieter. Kitty? I've brought a visitor.'

A plump and smiling middle-aged man crawled out from under a desk, removing spider webs from his hair and holding a very indignant cat.

'I do beg your pardon, Bisset, but I had to find Pussy. I just saw a mouse in the tutors' room and I want to lock her in there tonight. You've come to see the Book? Wait just a moment. I shall return directly.'

'Kitty?' asked Phryne.

Jeoffrey smiled. 'His name is Katz—K-A-T-Z—and he's very

fond of the library cats, so he was almost guaranteed to be called Kitty. The Book is in the safe. You see, we look after it well.'

Phryne examined the green-painted safe and curled a lip. It had a very impressive front with a huge lock, and a back made of a sheet of tin which was peeling away from its rivets. It was the same mentality which provided a front door which could not be opened with a battering ram and a back door protected only by a Keep Out notice. But she did not want to offend the young man.

Kitty returned, dragged out of his pocket a chain with at least seventy keys on it, and opened the safe door. There were many things in the safe, including examination papers and the dean's wife's pearls, but the Book of Hours of Juana of Castile was not one of them.

⁓

Phryne had been introduced to the emergency meeting called by a frantic dean and was now on her knees beside the open safe.

Gerald Street lounged in his chair, smoking a cigarette. Mr Katz hovered in the foreground, squeaking with dismay. The dean, Mr Connors, was pouring departmental whisky with distracted generosity for the Classics professor, John Hoskins, who was slumped over the library table, his ruddy face paled to the colour of tallow.

'This is a disaster!' he moaned. 'The Book of Hours stolen! And we were so careful with it!'

'Ha,' commented Phryne. 'I could crack this safe with a hairpin. What are these? I can't read Latin.'

'They are the half-term examination papers,' answered Jeoffrey, taking the bundle out of Phryne's hands and leafing through them. 'Hang on, though. This doesn't seem to belong.' He exhibited a leaf of parchment, with a couplet lettered on it in a beautiful flowing script.

'*Hac in hora sine mora corde pulsum tangite*. Anyone recognise it?'

'You should know it yourself,' snapped Hoskins. '*Carmina Burana*, part of the 'O Fortuna'. We read them this term.'

'Excuse me, gentlemen, but what does it mean?' asked Phryne, getting up and dusting her knees. 'It seems to be the only thing in the safe that doesn't belong there, so it may be a clue.'

Hoskins gulped his whisky and his lecture-room manner began to return.

'*Hac in hora*... in this hour... *sine mora*... without delay... *corde pulsum tangite*... touch the beat of the heart. A broad translation would be, "I submit, pluck the strings of the heart," wouldn't you agree, Dean?'

'Yes, though "touch" is more correct, Hoskins. But what leads our distinguished guest to believe that it might be a clue, as she puts it?'

'What does *hora* mean?' asked Phryne, collaring the whisky bottle.

The Dean blinked. 'Hour.'

'And what are we looking for?'

'A Book of Hours, yes. But is it not more likely that the Book has been stolen by a common thief?'

'A very comforting thought, no doubt, but there are two problems with it.' Phryne sipped her drink. Unlike the sherry, the whisky was quite good. 'One is that a common thief would not have left those pearls and the petty cash.'

'Perhaps he did not notice them.'

'Perhaps. The other is that a common thief could not possibly sell a Book of Hours. Art theft is a highly skilled profession. Usually the buyer is arranged in advance. Your local tea-leaf is not going to try to sell a Book of Hours to the boys down the Collingwood pubs, is he? But if you think that someone crept in and stole it, gentlemen, you should send for the police.'

A shudder ran through the gathering. Phryne eyed them cynically.

'No? So you do think that one of you pinched it. Who else can walk into the library without Mr Katz watching their every move? Well then. Who needs money, and has contacts in … say, America?'

There was a silence. Finally Gerald Street butted out his gasper as though he had a personal grudge against it and laughed.

'I'd better say what we are all thinking. Our colleague Bradbury has been bankrupted. He had a system for picking horses, poor fool, and it succeeded as such systems always succeed. He is a mad gambler and … well, he has extensive debts, a wife and two little girls, and as Fine Arts professor he certainly knows people who would buy it.'

'And the Carmina couplet?' asked Phryne.

Gerald smiled a razor-edged smile at her. 'I'd say that you are suffering from an overactive imagination, Miss Fisher.'

'Very well, you solve this your way, and I'll solve it mine, and we'll see who finds the Book. And if I find it I want to dine at the High Table.'

'Miss Fisher! No lady can dine at the High Table!' objected the Dean, shocked.

'This lady shall, indeed, if I find your Book.'

'It's a bet, Miss Fisher,' said Mr Street. 'I shall escort you myself. If you find the Book.' He grinned maliciously at Connors. 'The least we can do, eh, Dean?'

Mr Connors muttered an agreement, and Phryne took her leave.

Outside the red-brick wall of the English Department building was a courtyard in which grew a huge Cussonia tree. Phryne stood for a moment under the gnarled branches, one hand resting on the trunk, relishing the age and strength of the tree and the shade of the abundant dark green leaves. This tree had been a sapling when the university was built, but it was not as venerable as the Hours of Juana the Mad. Pinned to the tree was a piece of parchment and on it was written in the same beautiful hand and in very black ink, *Tempora a lapsa volant, fugitivis fallimur horis.* Although Phryne could not read Latin easily, a sweating teacher had hammered the rudiments of the language into her head. She recognised *horis* as 'hours' and she laughed. 'The game's afoot, Watson!' she said softly. She rummaged in her bag for a pencil and wrote underneath the couplet, *Quare?*, which she recalled from a tedious lesson involving the Latin for 'why.'

Then she left the university, walking with her usual enjoyment through the Gothic arches of the Law Quadrangle and into Carlton for a bite to eat and some real coffee.

~~~

Jeoffrey Bisset translated the couplet, which she had copied into her notebook, at dinner that night in the Café Royale.

'"Time that is fallen is flying, we are deceived by the passing hours"—it's a medieval Latin song, from one of the *vagantes*, I think, the wandering scholars. Such good verse. Do you think that you can solve this, Phryne?'

'I don't know. But it's a game, and I love games. Have some more wine and tell me what you do at the university.'

'I'm an Associate Professor of English Literature and a tutor in Classics. Latin, you know, and Greek.'

'Oh. Do you like it?'

'Well, yes, it gives me time to work on my book. I'm studying the poems of Alcuin. I don't think that they are sufficiently appreciated.'

'Indeed, I've never heard of him.'

'In translation they lose their magic. I am preparing new translations, attempting to keep the freshness of the verse … the dawn light now upon the sea … Such good poems—perhaps you might like to see some of them?'

'I would,' agreed Phryne. This was a very attractive man indeed, now that his enthusiasm was aroused. His blue eyes shone and his pale cheeks pinkened and his beautiful hands made broad gestures. 'I saw one of the original manuscripts, you know, in the Bodders. They say that there is a manuscript in Tours, but it belongs to a local family and they will not let it be studied.' His face was now flushed with rage. Phryne was fascinated.

'Well, it is their manuscript, you know. I suppose that they can keep it secret as long as they don't harm it.'

'Knowledge should be free!' exclaimed Jeoffrey. 'There is no excuse for keeping a work of art locked up, hidden, just for the private satisfaction of one person. It's … it's … immoral!'

'And that's what will happen to the Hours of Juana, you know, if it is sold in America. Some collector will gloat over it or keep it in his safe and no one will see it, until he dies. A strange passion, collecting,' commented Phryne. 'Have some more osso bucco, it's delicious.'

'In Florence and Venice there are works by Titian and Raphael which are hidden away for hundreds of years, until some family goes broke and all their stuff is sold,' exclaimed the young man, helping himself to more of the rich, oniony stew. 'Dreadful! I only got into the Scuola di Farnese by bribing the doorkeeper. There were spider webs all over the face of the Raphael virgin.'

'Appalling,' agreed Phryne.

Jeoffrey Bisset took a huge mouthful of hot osso bucco and calmed down as he choked.

'Who do you think stole the Book of Hours?' asked Phryne, patting him on the back and administering water.

'I can't believe that it was Bradbury—but he is a gambler, and gamblers cannot be trusted. They are addicts, like alcoholics. But I can't see him doing it; I've always found him a very honourable man.'

'I will find the book, Jeoffrey,' said Phryne idly, 'because I will dine at the High Table. I am determined,' she said, and passed the wine.

The Cussonia tree bore a new leaf, white and fluttering, when Phryne came back to it the next day. Phryne snatched it down, as she could not read it from the ground. It had been pinned high up on the trunk. This time it was not in script, but Gothic capitals, and Phryne could puzzle it out: *QUIS LEGEM DAT AMANTIBUS?* 'What law for lovers?' she translated. 'Or something like that. Now what does he mean? I wonder how the faculty are getting on. Time for a threat, I think.'

She printed under the capitals, *Render unto me, Monmouth*, pinned it to the trunk, and walked into the faculty office, where Gerald Street was draped over the secretary's desk, blowing smoke in her face and proofreading her typescript.

'That *d* is a *th*, Beryl,' he snapped. 'Get it right, or the abysmal stupidity of my students will be rendered even more deep. Ah, Miss Fisher. How is the Sherlockery?'

'I will dine with you yet. How is yours?'

'Come over here.' He drew her aside, aware of Beryl's outstretched ears. 'Bradbury denies it, but that is what one would expect. He was alone in the library for a good couple of hours, too, when Kitty was busy with the new books. And can you open that safe with a hairpin?'

'Yes.'

'Show me,' requested Gerald Street, grinning, and Phryne was conducted into the misused library where Kitty was still fussing over the mice in the tutors' room.

'You will note that the front is secure,' said Phryne, feeling in her handbag and finding her strong German nailfile, 'but the back is tin and rivets. Watch.'

With little effort, she lifted the sheet of tin off its rivets with the nailfile and removed the whole back of the safe.

'Remarkable!' exclaimed Professor Street. 'Can you put it back?'

Phryne twisted the nailfile, re-socketed the holes in the tin over their rivets, gave the safe a sharp tap with the flat of her hand and removed the lever.

'See?'

'Yes, I see. Very impressive. And I also see that the scratches produced by your operation on the safe are duplicated on the other side.'

'Yes, I saw that at once. He used a chisel, I think. Not as neat, but then he probably hasn't as much experience as I have. Is that all, Professor?'

'Yes, Miss Fisher, thank you. And I look forward to dining with you,' he added.

Phryne left the room, and walked back to the tree.

There was a new parchment on the branch. She pulled it down and shivered. He must have been watching me, she thought— now what?

Dolorous Gard, said the paper cryptically.

'Arthurian legends,' Phryne mused while she delved for her

pencil. 'Two castles, Dolorous Gard and Joyous Gard, and I don't remember anything else about it. I shall have to go home and read Malory, not something a woman wants to do lightly. Now what shall I write?'

She thought deeply, trying to remember all the Latin she had been so laboriously taught.

Ubi est liber? she wrote, pinned back the notice and went home to read Malory, a prospect which did not please.

~~~

Extended study of medieval verse, thought Phryne at breakfast, produces a hangover almost as bad as that obtained by drinking absinthe cocktails. She tossed the crust of her toast onto the floor for her black cat to play with, dressed in a regrettable temper, and returned to the university and the Cussonia tree, which bore the usual banner of white paper.

'Not Latin again! I wish I had paid more attention to poor Miss White; how she would laugh if she saw me now! Oh. English. In fact, Chaucer. But not helpful. *A Knight there was, and that a worthy man… he loved chivalry, truth and honour, freedom and curteseye…* What can he mean?'

She scribbled on the paper, *Give me back that book or else!*, pinned it to the tree, and sat down on a nearby bench, looking over the south lawn down to Grattan Street.

Several students were lying at ease on the grass, and some hardy souls were reading, though most appeared to be absorbing literature by the osmosis method, which involved resting one's head on the text and hoping that some of the knowledge would seep through into the sleeping skull. It was a breezy, gusty, reckless day, but Phryne could not relax and enjoy the sun. The unknown game player had given her sufficient clues to find the Book—he was now alarmed, and wanted to return it, wanted her to be able to find it. The rules of the game, however, did not allow him to tell her in plain words where it was, but they also did not allow him to cheat. Therefore with 'Dolorous Gard' and 'A Knight there was' she should be able to guess where the Book was, and she had not the faintest idea.

She lit a gasper and allowed her mind to wander. She noticed that the red-brick English building had a clock tower. She looked at the stately grey pile of the Law Quadrangle. It was built in a Gothic manner, like a castle, though a small castle—rather, a Norman keep. She wondered idly why the builders had put in capitals with faces on them and what foes they expected the Law School to have to fight that they needed battlements. She mused delightedly on a mental picture of capped and gowned lawyers pouring boiling oil on the attacking working class, dropped the cigarette into her silk-clad lap, and did not even swear as she brushed it off and stamped it out.

Phryne entered the English faculty office at a run, skidded into Professor Hoskins, and grabbed his arm.

'Come along, Professor, I have something to show you. Is Professor Street in? Good, bring him too. I'll meet you in the Law cloisters in ten minutes. Where is Jeoffrey? I must have a ladder!'

She found Jeoffrey finishing a tutorial on Boethius, and he found a maintenance man who provided a ladder. Then they sped across the courtyard and into the Law Quadrangle, where a disturbed and puzzled group of professors awaited them.

'Miss Fisher, what is this all about?' demanded Hoskins, who had never approved of women as a sex and particularly disliked excitable ones. 'Why the ladder?'

'You shall see.' Phryne placed the ladder against the inner battlements and climbed up several rungs to deliver her lecture.

'I was given two clues to the whereabouts of your book,' she said, balancing easily. 'One was "Dolorous Gard" and one was the beginning of the description of the Knight in the *Canterbury* prologue. If one takes the English building as Joyous Gard—'

'An attribution which can only have been the product of a diseased mind,' commented Professor Street.

'Then the Law cloisters are Dolorous Gard, aren't they?'

'Possibly,' agreed Hoskins. 'But why the ladder?'

'Wait. Have a look at the capital of the pillar directly in front of me.'

The assembled professors looked. Carved into the soft grey stone was the stern face of a helmeted knight.

'Where, then, is the Book of Hours?' asked Mr Katz, trembling with eagerness.

In answer, Phryne scaled the ladder, heedless of the fine display of expensive undergarments which she was giving, and peered over the battlements.

'I can't reach it, damn it. It's wrapped in oilskin... Jeoffrey, come up and give me a boost.'

The tutor climbed uncertainly up the ladder and hoisted Miss Fisher on his shoulder. Phryne reached for the parcel, slipped and almost fell, and found herself with one arm hooked around Jeoffrey Bisset's neck and the parcel in the other hand. With a certain difficulty and a further flourish of French knickers, Phryne climbed down and Jeoffrey Bisset descended without hurt, shaken by such close proximity to Phryne's strong arms and her Nuit d'Amour scent.

'There's another note,' she said, pleased, as Kitty dropped to his knees to unwrap what seemed like miles of oilcloth and string and an inner layer of tissue paper. 'What does it say?'

'*Ave, formosissima*,' read Gerald Street. 'Hail, most beautiful Lady! It's an invocation to Venus,' he added with a sly grin. 'And very fitting.'

'It isn't even damp,' cried Kitty, clutching the Book to his bosom. 'Look, Miss Fisher!'

He laid it down. Open on the lush green of the Law School's grass was an illuminated manuscript of such colour and delicacy that Phryne's breath was taken. She knelt down next to it as Kitty turned the pages with a reverent hand. Monkeys and cats danced down the side of black-lettered pages; bright birds which had been dust for centuries sang loud and shrill from branches of thorns, a bunch of spring flowers which Chaucer might have picked lay dewy and complete across a windowsill through which angels were peeping, and the gentle ass ate the hay in the Christ Child's manger as the baby clutched at his mother's lapis lazuli gown. It was beautiful beyond words, perfect, enamelled, the colours as fresh as yesterday and as bright as jewels.

'How could you lock this in a safe?' cried Phryne.

Hoskins said portentously: 'We won't lock it up again. I had forgotten how beautiful it is. We shall have a secure glass case and Kitty shall turn a page every day. Pick it up now, Kitty, we don't want it getting wet.'

Kitty scurried away to his library to search every page for damage. He was almost weeping with relief, and Phryne was touched. There was a man who really loved books. To have his Book of Hours out of his loving custody had nearly broken his heart.

'Well, Miss Phryne, we have to thank you, and ask you to explain who stole it,' the dean said gravely.

'I shan't tell you,' Phryne replied, ordering her clothes, which had been ruffled during the climb, 'because I don't know. I played a long-distance game with the thief and he gave me the Book, and that will have to be enough for you.' She put back her perfectly straight black hair from green eyes as sharp as pins.

The faculty members stared at her, and sighed.

'Well, if that is your decision, Miss Fisher...' The Dean was looking on the bright side. 'Now, Hoskins, if you will give me a few moments of your time, we shall decide about the glass case. Thank you, Miss Fisher. A very precise demonstration.'

Phryne bowed and smiled, and took Jeoffrey Bisset's arm. 'Naughton's,' she commented. 'I need a drink.'

'You shouldn't have stolen it, Jeoffrey,' she said over a gin and tonic in the crowded pub. 'It was a huge risk. If they had called in the police your academic career would have been shot.'

'The Book cried out to me,' he said plaintively. 'All that beauty, locked in that green iron prison. I never meant to steal it, you know. I would have given it back. But I would never have found so…delicate a way to do it. My congratulations, Phryne. Are you going to turn me in?'

'No. When did you decide to give it back?'

'When you announced that you knew me. Who is the Monmouth that everyone knows? Geoffrey of Monmouth. I decided then that you had penetrated my game and… I put it on the roof, which is easy if you go out of a window on the second storey.'

'I see. Order me another drink, will you? It was a fine game, my dear.'

'How did you decide it was me?'

'I shall tell you later. And you have done me a favour, dear boy, because now I shall definitely dine at the High Table.'

'The food is awful, and don't touch the table wines. The port is drinkable. Dear Phryne, won't you tell me how you knew it was me?'

'There were only three people it could have been—Kitty, you, or Gerald Street.'

'Yes, but how did you decide between us?'

'You are the only one that is tall. You pinned the parchment high up on the tree. The others are all not much bigger than me. Simple, eh? Like all mysteries when you know the solution.'

'Ave, formosissima,' said Jeoffrey Bisset.

Death Shall Be Dead

Death shal be deade, if we canne hym finde!

—Geoffrey Chaucer, *The Pardoner's Tale*

'He says that someone is trying to murder him,' chuckled Detective Inspector Jack Robinson, as the waiter refilled his glass.

He was dining with Miss Phryne Fisher, which was notable, and he was at the Café Royale, which was surprising. Phryne liked the Café Royale because it was raffish and bohemian. Jack Robinson had never been there and considered it luxurious, slightly dubious, and far above his touch. Miss Fisher had invited him and was at present engaged in deftly twirling flat green spaghetti around her fork. Jack, who had no taste for foreign food, was dissecting the best steak he had ever eaten. The lights were low, obscured with charcoal and the pungent, unfiltered cigarettes which the Café Royale's clients smoked. The tables were wooden, the waiters Italian, and the noise subdued, except around the big log fire where three artists were arguing about Modernism.

'And is someone trying to murder him?'

'I don't know. He said he was shot at, but we couldn't find the slug. He's a cantankerous old cuss, lives all alone with his dog, and his neighbours don't like him, but why would anyone want to kill him? He hasn't got any money—at least, I don't think so. He also says that someone is trying to buy his house, but he won't sell.'

'That's interesting, Jack, do go on.' Miss Fisher's green eyes gleamed and she laid down her fork and smoothed back her perfectly black, perfectly straight hair. Although Robinson knew that she was a powerful young woman, possessed of courage and a very bad temper, she looked elegant and harmless in wine-coloured wool and a close-fitting cloche decorated with green and black flowers.

'That's about all I know. He lives in Austin Street, Footscray, in a worker's cottage, and he's been there five years. It's an ordinary place, a bit rundown. Apparently someone offered him hundreds of pounds for it, but that's not likely. I reckon he's loopy—it happens to old men who live alone.'

'What's his name? And how is your steak?'

'Jackson, Albie Jackson, and the steak is the best I've ever eaten. Did I tell you I've taken up poetry?'

'Poetry, Jack?'

'Yes. Always liked it at school. Mechanics' Institute has a night class. We're beginning at the beginning. Chaucer, you know. I'd never heard of him before.'

'Good stuff,' commented Phryne, a fresh mouthful of fettucine neatly poised before her. 'How are you managing the language?'

'Oh, it's all right, once you work out that you have to say it out loud. We're reading *The Canterbury Tales*. Sharp tongue he had, old Chaucer. Bring him to the attention of the censor if it wasn't so long ago. What about that Wyf of Bath with all those husbands?'

'She only had them one at a time,' objected Phryne. 'Have some more wine.'

'If I have any more I'll be drunk in charge of feet,' objected Jack Robinson, then conceded to the hovering waiter: 'Well, one more glass, perhaps.'

The sweet red Lambrusco from the Po Valley was much to his taste.

'And what have you been doing, Phryne?'

'Nothing much. Things are quiet. I traced a missing son for a very old family last week—no wonder he went away, his father kept locking him in the coal cellar, and you can't do that to an eighteen-year-old for too long. And I exposed a nice little fraud being worked in a shop. The owner was creaming off the profits and blaming the bookkeeper, intending to sack her and tell his partner that she had taken the money—nasty, wicked little man. Nothing else. I might go and see the snow if the weather holds.'

Outside, the wind howled through the alleys. Jack Robinson leaned back with the added contentment that bad weather gives to being inside, fully fed, and near a fire.

'I suppose that you didn't send us the gen on the shopkeeper?'

'No, Jack, worse—I told his wife.'

As she was bidding her guest farewell some time later, Phryne said, 'About Albie Jackson—why not find out who owned the house before?'

Jack Robinson did not get her drift, but her ideas were usually good. He nodded, buttoned his greatcoat closely, and stepped out into the storm, running with Miss Fisher to her indecently big and red Hispano-Suiza racing car.

She dropped him at his respectable cottage in Collingwood, declined an invitation to see his orchids, and drove home to St Kilda.

The next morning dawned colder than a tomb and, as no cases were pending, Phryne decided to stay in, taking to the parlour a few books, a box of Hillier's chocolates, and a glass or two of a dry Barossa vintage which she was trying for a vintner friend. It was young but sprightly and she passed the morning pleasantly before the fire, the red light washing the sea-green walls.

The phone rang.

'Jack Robinson here. You remember that case we were talking about last night? Albie Jackson? Well, things have happened at old Albie's place. It caught fire last night. What with the rain and the local fire brigade, they put it out fast enough. But…'

'But?'

'There are three dead people in the house,' said Jack glumly. Unlike Miss Fisher, he hated mysteries. 'I don't know what to think.'

'How odd!'

'Odd isn't the word I'd use, Miss Fisher.'

A bad sign. Last night, Robinson had called her Phryne. 'One of 'em's a client of yours,' he continued. 'Thomas Mason.'

'What, that creep? His wife was my client, Jack; she wanted a divorce and we had to get it through while he was still in jail. She was afraid that he'd kill her. Oh no… don't tell me…'

'Yeah. One of the dead 'uns is his wife. You want to have a look? We got no one else to confirm her identity.'

'Very well. What number Austin Street? I'll be there directly.'

Jack Robinson told her the number. Phryne ran upstairs to dress for the weather and found garments suitable for clambering around a half-burned house in the rain: boots, trousers, and a big woolly jumper decorated with multi-coloured parrots. She dragged on a black cloche and pulled on an airman's sheepskin-lined leather jacket.

Who could have wanted to kill poor downtrodden Mary Mason except her revolting bank robber of a husband? She gunned the

Hispano-Suiza down Footscray Road, with the railway yards and the clutter of hovels on Dudley Flats miserable under the rain.

Austin Street had trees, bare and sad, and she parked next to a black maria and an ambulance. Jack Robinson was at the sagging, paintless door.

'Mind the verandah, it's burned through. In the kitchen, Miss Fisher. Things are bad.'

'Bad?' Phryne picked her way from beam to beam through to the kitchen, taking the policeman's hand. It was a gardener's hand, calloused and hard.

'The damage is worst here. And it's burned all along the hall.'

'The door must have been open. What a dump! I mean, even before it was burned. No one's painted the place since it was built.'

Visible and soaked with water from the firemen's hoses were piles of old newspapers, opened and mouldy cans of soup and beans, unwashed dishes caked with old meals, rags, and broken chairs—the detritus of friendless old age. It smelled of fire, now, and cold, and burning, with the musky aftertaste of squalor. Phryne walked carefully down the hall into the parlour.

Three people were sitting at a dining table, on which was a teapot, several mismatched cups, an ashtray filled with butts, a bottle of whisky and three glasses, and a flat iron which had been put down hot and had burned the table. The three were dead. One had fallen forward, his face a carnival horror, a grinning mask. Mary Mason had slumped sideways from her chair, prevented from falling by the wall, and grinned at death as though she had at last seen the joke.

'God help us, Jack!' Phryne stepped back a pace. 'What has happened to them?'

'Is that Mary Mason?'

'Yes, yes, of course. She got her decree nisi last week. When did her husband get out of prison?'

'Yesterday. He collected her from her boarding house. Landlady said that she was terrified, but went with him.'

'Yes, she was terrified all right. And with good reason. Who is the other... the other dead man?'

'Foxy Harris. Old mate and accomplice of Mason's.'

'Bank robbers, weren't they?'

'Yes. We never found the last lot they pinched—eight hundred quid. Now I don't suppose that we ever shall! Ah, here's the doctor.'

A small and fussy GP was escorted in over the burnt beams and made a brief examination, tutting under his breath.

'Cyanide,' he concluded. 'They were all poisoned. You observe the *risus sardonicus*, the deathly grin? Well marked, very well marked. Probably in the whisky. I wouldn't advise you to have a tot. Dear me no, wouldn't advise it at all.'

'How long would they have taken to die?' asked Jack.

The small doctor shrugged. 'Five minutes—less, perhaps. Nasty death, cyanide, but quick, undeniably quick. Rigor is holding them in place. I'd say, with the weather as it is, time of death was last night, twelve hours or so. Not less. Hard as stone.' He tapped Mary Mason's horrifying face with a casual finger. 'If you want to move the bodies, officer, you'd better wait until tonight or you'll find them hard to handle. Yes, well, is that all? I can certify death.' And he was out into the street before a white-faced constable called him back, and a dog began to bark.

'I was going to ask the whereabouts of Albie Jackson,' said Phryne, suppressing nausea, 'but I have a feeling that you've just found him.'

Lying broken and dead on the back verandah was an old man. Rain had soaked his hair, his shirt was torn, and a black labrador lay beside him with its head on the mutilated chest.

'Oh, Lord!' said Jack Robinson. 'The poor old bloke.'

He had seen, as had Phryne, the flat-iron burns on the chest. The face, however, was peaceful. The dog did not move, but barked and then howled. A constable who laid a hand on the corpse was promptly bitten, and jumped back.

Jack Robinson then did something that confirmed him in Phryne's high regard. He sat down on his heels and spoke directly to the dog.

'Come on, old fellow,' he said soothingly. 'I know he was your master and you loved him, but he's dead now, dog, he's dead. You have to leave him, feller. Come here, then. Come here. He's dead, mate, he doesn't need you anymore.'

Phryne felt tears prick her eyes. The dog lifted his head and stared at Jack Robinson, who held out his hand.

'Come on, then, mate. Come on.'

The black dog wavered. He got to his feet, licked the face of the corpse, and howled again. Then he walked over to Jack Robinson, pushed his nose into Jack's hand and leaned against his leg.

'Poor old bloke,' repeated Jack Robinson. 'Come on, doctor, tell us about this one.'

The doctor, keeping a wary eye on the dog, kneeled next to the dead man and pushed aside the torn shirt.

'He's been tortured,' he commented. 'With a hot iron. But he hasn't been poisoned, at least not with cyanide. I'd say he died of heart failure.'

'Natural causes.'

'If you call being tortured to death natural,' the doctor retorted. 'Now, if you have no more dead bodies on the premises, Detective Inspector, I'll be getting back to the hospital. I'll do the autopsies when you can unkink the corpses. Goodbye.' And he was gone.

'What a bedside manner,' observed Phryne. 'How his patients must love him.'

'Not particularly, Miss, but he never hears any complaints. He only deals with the dead, so he doesn't need any manners. Come on, dog,' said Jack Robinson, 'we'd better get you something to eat, eh?'

The dog, with a last look at the old man, followed him into the house.

Jack Robinson extended a forefinger to the white-faced constable. 'Go out, Jones, and buy me a leash and a couple of dishes and some dog meat,' ordered Robinson.

Phryne asked, 'What will you do with the dog?'

'I'll take him home. The kids have been asking for a dog, but the wife says that they're too much trouble. I reckon she'll have this one, though.' He smiled. 'Proper sentimental, she is. And he's a good dog,' said Robinson, as the black nose was inserted confidingly into his hand. 'He's a good old mutt.'

Robinson found two unburnt chairs in the front of the house and sat down, the dog beside him. He motioned Miss Fisher to a chair.

'So now we've got a mystery, and a murderer to find,' he observed. 'Any ideas?'

'Not at the moment. I never saw such a horrible scene, Jack, not even when I was driving an ambulance in the Great War. They told me about the tea party, though; that must have had the same effect.'

'The tea party?'

'A group of soldiers who were sitting around a little fire making tea and didn't hear the gas alert. They were all killed and, like these ones, they were struck dead as they sat, and the rescue party found them all in their places, one with a cup raised to his lips. I've seen a photograph of it.' The house stank of filth and bitter smoke. Phryne was beginning to feel queasy.

'Back in a moment,' she promised. She went into the street and was sick into a convenient bush. She then found the flask which she always kept in her car, and took it back to the policeman.

'Have a swig, Jack. It's my own whisky and contains no improper substances.'

They drank in silence. It was good whisky.

'Let's look at the facts, then. The old man reported that some-one was trying to kill him. He said that he had been shot at, and people were making threats against him, and we didn't take him seriously because he was a difficult old cuss and we get a lot of complaints from loonies. And he had the dog, too, so I thought he was safe enough. Then he said that someone wanted to buy his house, and I wrote him off as mad. Who'd want a dump like this, when there are hundreds of these houses, all the same?'

'There must have been something about this house rather than any other,' mused Phryne. 'What?'

'I better find out who used to own the place,' said Robinson, omitting to recall that such had been Phryne's advice the previous night. 'And I better organise a proper search, and soon,' he added, as the cold wind set the damaged timbers groaning, 'before the whole place comes down on our heads. Ah, here's Jones. That was quick.'

'Lady down the street has a dog, sir, and she lent me his dishes and some meat and biscuits. And I've brought some water from her place. Sir, the lady herself would like a word.'

'Good, bring her in—well done, Constable.'

The young constable, recovering from the greenish pallor of the badly shaken, blushed. He put the dishes down on the floor and filled the water dish. The dog looked at Robinson.

'Go on, then,' he said encouragingly. The dog continued to stare. It did not move, although it was obviously hungry.

'Well, you mutt, don't just sit there and drool,' said Robinson.

Phryne said, 'It's been trained not to eat before it has permis-sion. You'll have to say the right word.'

'Golly, what a case,' muttered Robinson. 'And I can't ask its late master, can I? Well, I can ask, but I won't get no answer. Go on then, Blackie! You're my guest. You're welcome.'

That was evidently the word. The dog leaped forward and buried his nose in the water dish, drinking with a great deal of splash, then wolfed down the meat and biscuits.

'That's a good dog,' observed Robinson. 'Look at him eat! How long since you last had a meal, eh, dog?'

Blackie did not reply, but licked the dish as carefully as if he was trying to remove the pattern. He came back to Robinson's side and lay down, whimpering a little, with his head on the detective inspector's highly polished boot.

'Hard to tell,' commented Phryne. 'All labradors eat like that. Look at the side of his head, Jack. He's hurt!'

Jack Robinson felt over the furry black skull, while the dog held still and licked at his hands.

'Been given a good old thump on the noggin,' he agreed. 'There's a big lump. A kick, perhaps, or a club. That explains why they didn't kill him.'

'Kill him?'

'A good dog like this wouldn't hang about while they tortured his master,' said Jack. 'He must have attacked one of them and they woodened him out, and he didn't recover until it was all over. Check for a dog bite on one of them in there, Jones, and bring in the lady, will you?'

Jones, swallowing dread, escorted into the room a thin and voluble lady so muffled in garments that one would have needed a shoe horn to get her out. She was wearing at least three cardigans in various colours and a pair of men's labouring boots.

'What has happened? Is the poor old man dead?' she asked in a shrill voice, setting all of Phryne's teeth on edge. 'Where is Mr Jackson? That young cop wouldn't tell me anything. Why there's Nubis,' she said, sighting the dog, which thumped its tail on the floor. 'He's all right, then. I thought so when the young man asked me for some dog food.'

'Nubis?' Phryne repeated.

'Something like that. That's what Mr Jackson called him.'

'Anubis?' hazarded Phryne. 'It's the name of the ancient Egyptian god of the dead. The black dog, Anubis.' The late Mr Jackson had evidently been a man of some learning.

'I don't know, I'm sure. Strange man, Mr Jackson. Come down in the world, he had. Used to be a chemist, you know, a dispensing chemist, but his wife died, and then he sort of lost interest in things. She was a nice lady, used to grow geraniums. But she died three years ago, it must be, and it just broke his heart. Wouldn't let anyone help, wouldn't talk to anyone, just stayed in the house. What has happened to him?'

'He's dead, Mrs...?'

'Greene. Dead? His heart, was it? He had a bad heart.'

'He was murdered,' said Jack Robinson gently. 'Someone killed him. We are trying to find out who did it. Were you at home last night? Did you hear anything?'

'No one could hear anything over the storm we had last night. My daughter did say that she heard a car along about midnight, when she got up to put some buckets under the holes in the roof. But I didn't hear anything until the fire brigade came, about six this morning. Murdered! What a dreadful thing!'

'Did he have any money?' asked Phryne.

Mrs Greene shook her head. 'No, not that I knew. No one ever said that he had money. But you couldn't talk to him, really. I came down a few times with a pot of soup or a cake for the poor soul and he wouldn't let me in the house. Thanked me all nice but he didn't want to be helped.'

Mrs Greene's eyes had an avid gleam, and Phryne reflected that a lone widower was fair prey for lonely local widows. She wouldn't have let Mrs Greene into the house either. What a strange man, this Albie Jackson! A man of sardonic humour, who named his dog after an Egyptian god.

'Did you know the people who used to have this house?' asked Robinson.

Mrs Greene bridled. 'Me? Know them? They were criminals. Nasty people. The man was a fence, so they said. Lots of people used to call at the house—not nice people, neither. I was very pleased when they took him to jail and she left, and then the Jacksons bought the house. She wanted a nice yard, Mrs Jackson said, to grow her geraniums in. He used to make up things, you know, cough mixtures and things, and he was ever so good with animals. He cured my Toby of distemper, and he had a poultice which could take out splinters and bring up boils beautiful. But he wasn't a doctor. If anyone was real sick, he'd always send them to a doctor. "I'm just a chemist, Mrs Greene," he said to me once when I asked him about me rheumatics. "You need to see a doctor about your leg." Pains something cruel in this weather. What are you going to do about poor Nubis, then? I'd take him except that Toby wouldn't like it.'

'I'm taking him,' said Robinson. 'Thanks for the loan of the plates, Mrs Greene, I'll return them.'

'That's all right. I hope you get whoever done it. Poor old man!'

'Jones, show the lady out.'

And Mrs Greene went, her curiosity unsatisfied and still glinting in her eyes.

With some cursing and a lot of manoeuvring, the ambulance men had taken the corpses away, and Phryne and Robinson were standing on the back verandah while three constables searched the house. Mason, asserted a shuddering Constable Jones, had a dog bite on his right forearm. Jones was not used to murder. Phryne, shivering in her parrot-patterned jumper and airman's jacket, reflected that neither was she.

'Let's reconstruct it. The three of them come to Mr Jackson's door late at night. He opens it. They jump in and grab him, flattening poor old Anubis here with that hockey stick we found by the door. They bring the old man in here and tie him up. We've found the rope—it's new washing line, which indicates that they brought it with them.'

'But they didn't bring the flat iron,' commented Phryne, crossing both arms across her chest. 'It's an old one and probably dates back to Mrs Jackson. They might have just thought they could tie him up and find what they had come to find.'

'Which was the proceeds of the bank robbery, given to the fence to hold for them, and hidden in the house.'

'Yes. They tried to just buy the house but the cranky old bloke wouldn't sell.'

'Perhaps he loved the house.' Jack Robinson wondered how anyone could, but you never really knew. 'His wife lived here, you know, and died here. And Mrs Greene said that he was fond of her.'

'Yes. Perhaps. Anyway, they can't find the gelt, either because the fence took it with him or ...'

'And they decided that he had moved it, maybe because they knew something from the fence. So, they decided that Mr Jackson knew where the money was.'

'And they tried to persuade him to tell.'

'But at some point they must have loosed him, maybe to make them a cup of tea or to get out the whisky. Just the sort of thing that the rat Mason would do—he was a nasty piece of work ...'

'And Mr Jackson poisoned the whisky with a hefty dose of cyanide from his chemist's stock, which is still in the kitchen...'

'And then he died of heart failure when they started on him again, and they flung the body out the back, where the dog was.'

'Then they sat down to have a friendly drink before they searched the house.'

'The poor old dog recovered, but he couldn't get in and so he lay there all night next to the dead man.'

'And the fire started in the parlour, where a sweep of Mason's dying arm pushed the kero lamp onto the floor, where it smashed.'

'And the fire spread slowly because the house was wet with rain coming through the roof, and it swept down the hall, away from the parlour, because the front door blew open...'

'The fire brigade came and then it was all revealed,' Phryne completed the litany. 'What a brave man! He knew they were going to kill him, or maybe he felt his heart going, and he still had enough courage and wit to poison the drink.'

'Not brave, just cranky. He wouldn't have wanted them to have their money. If he hid it, why didn't he give it to them? He didn't need it. Then they wouldn't have killed him. Just like him, to have the last laugh. If he had the money, that is.'

Phryne gazed unseeing out into the rain-swept yard where the geraniums grew tall and ragged.

'I know where it is,' she exclaimed, and ran back into the house, Robinson and Anubis at her heels. 'Where did the dog sleep?' she asked a puzzled constable, who was sorting through the contents of a cupboard which seemed to contain nothing but a thousand empty tobacco tins. He pointed to a pile of partially chewed blankets near the stove. Anubis suffered, it appeared, from night starvation.

Phryne pulled back the blankets and revealed a patch of unburnt flooring, in which a hole had been neatly cut. She pulled up the boards and dragged out a grey sack which still had the bank's identifying numbers stencilled in black.

'Anubis,' she said triumphantly, 'was the god of the dead, but also the guardian of the hidden treasure.'

The guardian of the hidden treasure wagged his tail and whined.

Detective Inspector Robinson was at home, cup of tea in hand and slippers on his feet, before his own domestic hearth, anticipating a roast of lamb for dinner and watching his children play with Blackie (as Anubis was now known). The dog showed a great tolerance for having fingers poked in his eyes, and even Mrs Robinson had wept a few tears over his fidelity to his dead master and admitted that he was a fine, gentle animal. The telephone rang, and he padded out in his slippers to answer it, swearing that if it was another murder on a night like this he would quit the police force and become a grocer.

It was not another murder. It was Phryne Fisher. 'You said that you were reading Chaucer, Jack?'

'Yes, that's right.'

'Apropos of today's events, have a look at "The Pardoner's Tale." How's Anubis?'

'Blackie's fine. The kids love him and the missus likes him too. Is that all?'

'That's all. Goodnight, Jack.'

He found the collected Chaucer and sat down before the fire, listening to the rain on the roof, and located the tale. He read the unfamiliar spelling aloud, as the three young men met an old man and asked where they could find death, for he was killing their friends. *'Death shall be dead, if we can him find,'* he translated. *'To find death, said the old man, they had but to dig under a certain tree. There they found a bushel of gold coins: two decided to kill the one, who poisoned the wine, and thus they all died.'*

> *Right so they have him slain, and that anon.*
> *And when this was done, thus spake that one*
> *'Now let us sit and drink, and make merry*
> *And afterward we will his body bury.'*
> *And with that it happened, in this case*
> *To take the bottle where the poison was*
> *And drank, and gave his fellow to drink also,*
> *For which anon they were slain both the two...*
> *Thus had these wretches their ending*
> *Thus ended were these homicides two*
> *and the false poisoner also.*

Detective Inspector Robinson read the next line and could not but agree with it: *'O cursed sin, full of cursedness! Oh traitorous homicide, o wickedness!'*

'Put aside your book, Jack,' said his wife from the door. 'Dinner's ready. Kids, come in to dinner. Yes, you can bring the dog, but wipe his paws! Was it a very bad case, Jack?' she asked, seeing how slowly and with what effort he got out of his chair.

'Yes, love.' Robinson put Chaucer down. 'It was a bad case, and I'm glad to be home,' he said, and smiled.

Carnival

Beauty provoketh thieves sooner than gold.

—William Shakespeare, *As You Like It*

Phryne Fisher, daringly elegant in a peach-and-black bloused top and a pair of palpable, scandalous trousers, mostly regretted that she had ever met Bobby Ferguson, but she had come with him because she loved all circuses and carnivals. And here it was.

The hot wind crackled through the dry grass alongside Williamstown Road. It carried not only the usual city messages—A Far Too Male Cat Has Been Here and Watch Out for the Van—but also Turkey lolly and toffee apples, animal dung, machine oil and frying grease. She sniffed an appreciative sniff.

'Oh, yes,' she said, as she headed up the dusty path towards the lights, where the wheezing of a calliope was enchanting the night. It was playing 'Daisy, Daisy, give me your answer, do', in just the wrong key. 'I love carnivals. Not your sort of place, I wouldn't have thought.'

Bobby did not reply.

What was the matter with the spoiled rotten son of a major banking house now? He complained about the car, her treasured Hispano-Suiza. He complained about her driving. No one had ever stopped Bobby from having anything he set his heart on, but no one else was going to drive Phryne's car while she had breath in her body.

She decided that a little light ignoring might cure his sulks and pressed on. She was just producing her sixpence when she heard a faint scream from behind her and was in time to see Bobby transfixed with horror as something frightful rose from the ground, giving vent to a bubbling whine like a monster from a nightmare. Phryne bore Bobby up on one shoulder and grabbed a trailing rope.

'It's only a camel,' she said soothingly. 'I rode them in Arabia. I admit that this is an unusually revolting specimen of an unattractive species. Still, I believe that there are people who love them. Hello,' she said to the woman at the gate, who still held Phryne's sixpence. 'Two tickets, please. And is this your camel?'

The woman tore off two tickets and, instead of replying, shrieked, 'Bill! Them bloody camels is out!' Then she smiled and took the tether. 'You're good with camels,' she commented in a harsh rasp. 'You in the trade, maybe? One of Wirth's dancers? Tell 'em on the merry-go-round that Mama said you was to 'ave a free go.'

'Thank you,' replied Phryne, delighted.

She passed through the gate, taking Bobby and leaving the camel, though the camel might have proved better company.

'What is the matter with you, old bean?' she asked.

'The heat. I hate the heat,' said Bobby.

'In that case you should have stayed in a nice cool hotel and drunk nice cool beer,' said Phryne. 'It's as hot as a furnace in the north, where this wind comes from.'

'And I've just realised that I've forgotten to have mother's pearl bracelet fixed. I've got it in my pocket.' Bobby, a pink young man with slicked-down hair, patted his pocket, just in case any passing thief hadn't deduced where he might have put it. 'It's very valuable. Anyone could steal it.'

'Then put it in another pocket and stop talking so loudly,' advised Phryne absently. She was looking for the carousel.

'But all these people are thieves,' protested Bobby.

A slim young man in greasy overalls paused in bolting together a collection of iron pipes and scowled. The light caught his hair. It had the same blue sheen as a cock's feather. His face was all angles, sharp and defined in the harsh electric glare.

'Nonsense,' said Phryne briskly. 'A carnival has the exact same proportion of thieves as anywhere else, and I am not excepting your bank.'

The young man gave Phryne an astonished and vulnerable smile, packed up his spanner, and vanished into the darkness between the lights.

The merry-go-round was old and a little tired. Phryne chose a rearing Lipizzaner stallion called Prancer and swung herself astride. She told the attendant about Mama and he grinned.

'Come on, Bobby!' she called.

'I'll watch you,' said Bobby, fanning himself with his straw boater.

Phryne dismissed him as the carousel creaked into life and she was off through patches of coloured and flavoured light: green and wet canvas, blue and engine oil, yellow and fairy floss, red and chips frying. She stayed on, paying a penny for the extra ride, through another set of circuits. Delicious. The moving air was almost cool.

As she descended she heard thunder. A nice drop of rain would be reviving but she hoped it would hold off for a few hours. Wet carnivals were sad.

She led Bobby along the shaky row of sideshows. 'The Wild Man from Borneo!' announced a man attired in frockcoat and someone's top hat. His voice was rich and fruity with an undertone of cigar and an overtone of port.

'The missing link!' he bellowed. 'Captured in the jungles of Malaya!'

Phryne paid and entered the booth. There was a crouched human figure, gnawing conscientiously at a haunch bone which could have come from a dinosaur. He was wearing a scanty and rather moth-eaten animal skin. His tangled hair straggled to his shoulders. He looked up at Phryne and bared his teeth. They were all filed to a point.

'Very nice,' said Phryne. 'We should introduce you to Sailor, though he might teach you bad habits.'

She was referring to the zoo's large and extremely male chimpanzee, who had been known to surprise the delicately nurtured by proving it. The wild man grinned again.

Bobby pulled at Phryne's arm. 'You don't want to see this disgusting exhibition, do you? And the next one has snakes! I hate snakes!'

Phryne thought that the Wild Man looked rather hurt. She took Bobby out of the tent.

'I do, and the next one is… ?'

'The Princess of the Amazon!' bellowed the shill, tipping his top hat to the lady. 'Brought at Great Expense from the Jungles for the Edification of the Multitudes!'

This ability to speak in capitals must have been valuable, Phryne reflected, examining her change and buying admission.

The lady might not have been royal but she was extensively blacked up and her snake was magnificent.

Phryne turned to find that Bobby had been replaced by the young mechanic. She considered that the night was suddenly improving.

'Go on, Doreen, show the lady the snake,' he encouraged.

The Amazon Princess looped a few yards of boa around her comely shoulders and moved forward. The huge blunt head of the snake rose, tongue flicking.

'My name's Alan Lee,' said the mechanic. 'This is Doreen, and that's Cleopatra.'

'Pleased to meet you all. I apologise for my escort.'

'Him? Been after Anna,' said Doreen. 'Mopes about like a sick cat. Been here every night.'

'See, Miss, we don't like strangers going after our girls,' explained the young man. He had eyes as black as ebony. It was hard to guess what he was thinking. He had shaken Phryne's hand cautiously, conscious of the grease on his own. 'The townies think they're whores. They ain't. Anna's my sister. She's going to marry Samson, our strongman. Can you take your bloke away? He might get damaged.'

'My dear Mr Lee,' said Phryne, 'Bobby isn't mine. I expect he's gone off to eat worms. I'm going to enjoy my evening. I love carnivals.'

Alan Lee smiled. 'We can tell. You want to stroke Cleopatra? Go on. She won't hurt you.'

Phryne stroked Cleopatra, who felt like a good snakeskin shoe. Not knowing the terrible thought in Phryne's mind, the snake rose a little under her hand.

'If she'd been a cat, she would have purred,' commented Alan.

The pressure to do something about Bobby was still there. Phryne sighed. 'All right, I'll try and remove Bobby—but only if you swear I can come back another night.'

His red lips parted over teeth as white as seeds. His black eyes held the promise of dark delights. If there were angels, this was a midnight one. Phryne shivered pleasantly. She gave the young man a highly combustible look and left the booth, searching for Bobby.

No great detective ability was required to locate the pink-faced pest. He was standing in the middle of the patch, next to the shooting gallery, screaming at the top of his voice, 'I've been robbed!'

'That bloody bracelet,' muttered Phryne to herself. 'I should have taken it from him. He was telegraphing "Steal This Trinket!" on all frequencies. Oh dear.' She pushed through the gathering crowd and asked crisply, 'What's the matter, Bobby?'

'Mother's pearl bracelet—it's gone!' he shouted.

'Will you shut up,' demanded Phryne. 'You're making a scene. Have you searched all your pockets?'

Around her she could sense the growing dismay of the carnival folk. This was real trouble. No one trusted carnival people. No one was likely to believe them when they swore their innocence. Everyone knew that the gypsies stole chickens and washing. And spoke a strange language and probably didn't wash and did you see the state of that woman's fingernails? Good name ruined, permits refused... This was a disaster. Phryne was incensed.

Phryne searched Bobby's pockets. No bracelet. He opened the black velvet case and showed it was empty. He was just about to bellow again when Phryne grabbed his shoulder and shook him.

'Will you stop yelling! When did you miss the bracelet?'

'I don't know. Just now. I got out some coins for the shooting gallery and found the case empty. It's gone!'

'All right, now, I'll find it, be quiet. Show's over,' she said to the gaping crowd. 'Nothing more to see. The gentleman has mislaid something. Alan, start the calliope again. Off you go,' said Phryne, and such was the force of her personality that most of the onlookers lost interest and wandered away.

The one who didn't was the policeman. 'Something been stolen, sir?' he asked, getting out his official notebook. He was a blond, blue-eyed guardian of the people. He had never trusted carnivals since he had failed to win the stuffed parrot on which he had set his heart at the age of eight and later had found out about fixed fairground guns. 'Missed something? Silly of you to bring anything valuable into a carnival! We all know what carnies are like. And they are nasty, dirty places. They wouldn't be allowed if I had my way.'

'I'm Phryne Fisher,' said Phryne, holding out her hand. She had only a few moments before that detestable oaf started writing in his notebook. She had also just caught sight, for the first time, of Samson the strongman, who must have been seven feet tall and was wheezing as though he had asthma.

'I'm a private investigator. Shall I give my good friend Detective Inspector Robinson your regards? I don't believe we need to waste your valuable time on my escort's lost property.'

She gave him a full-beam three-hundred-watt dazzling smile, which usually worked its magic on the recipient. Not this time, though. The policeman did not take her hand. He said mulishly, 'Gentleman says he's been robbed. I heard him.'

'The gentleman hasn't the brain of a peahen.'

Bobby felt that he was being ignored. 'I had it in my pocket! And there's the case, empty! What will Mother say? It's worth four hundred pounds!'

The carnies paled and the policeman stood to attention in the presence of money. Damn. Now it was official. Phryne walked away into the dark between two stalls, and Alan Lee came to her side.

'It looks bad!' he exclaimed. 'Who could have robbed him? I ain't seen any of the local dips. We always gets Samson to see 'em off. They're bad for business.'

Samson rippled a few muscles and looked down modestly. A slim, elegant girl sat on the shooting gallery bench, scowling at Bobby.

'That's Anna,' said Alan.

The shooting gallery shone. Not-very-new rifles were laid out on the counter. Targets wobbled across the back: tin ducks. On a board were the prizes—kewpie dolls, Chinese porcelain fresh from Abbotsford, glass rings and Woolworths pearls, hanging singly on hooks. Why was Bobby making this scene? Something jarred on Phryne. What thief took the jewel and left the case? Of course. This was Bobby's own doing. He had staged this scene: just take out the bracelet, distract Anna, and hang it on a hook. Then blackmail Anna: if she refused his advances, he would ruin the carnival. Simple. Phryne reflected that merchant banking really was bad for the soul.

'I'm afraid,' said Phryne, 'that even from here I can see among those trinkets a sheen only produced by irritating an oyster.'

'That's not Anna's doing,' Alan Lee protested. 'She's no thief.'

'I don't believe it either,' said Phryne. 'Now, we need a diversion.'

'What if I just break his neck?' asked Samson reasonably. 'I could do it easy. Like snapping a daffodil.'

'Thanks anyway, Samson, but not with that cop there taking notes,' replied Alan.

'Go get the Wild Man,' said Phryne. 'Er…does he speak English?'

'Tom? He's from Footscray.'

'And ask the Princess of the Amazon if Cleopatra would like an outing. Bobby,' said Phryne vengefully, 'hates snakes.'

~◦

The policeman was still taking notes. Anna Lee, frightened and disdainful, was sitting on the shooting gallery bench, affecting not to notice.

'I felt in my pocket for a penny to give a child—'

'Could the child have picked your pocket, sir?'

'It was only a small child,' said Bobby.

'Might have been a midget. You never know in a carnival…
Hell's bells!' he exclaimed. 'What's that?'

Hooting and leaping through the crowd came the Wild Man,
Alan Lee in close pursuit. Tom bounced and gibbered with
aplomb, turned a neat somersault and leaped into the shooting
gallery, where he tried to groom Anna's hair. She pushed him away
and he bounced down again, snarling now, menacing Bobby and
the policeman. They backed away. So did Phryne. She almost had
her hands on the bracelet when they turned to face her again.
Phryne cursed under her breath.

Alan Lee, stockwhip in hand, cracked it. The Wild Man uttered
a shriek and ran back to his nice safe booth with the gypsy behind
him. The crowd stirred and muttered. This was turning out to be
a more interesting evening than they had expected.

'The camels are out!' shouted Phryne, losing patience.

Both Bobby and the policeman looked away. In a second, she
had the little bundle of beads in hand. When they looked back,
Phryne Fisher had slid away into the darkness.

The constable decided to arrange a search. Phryne heard
Bobby say to Anna, 'I've got you now, girl. Me or jail,' he said.
'Now you have to come with me when I snap my fingers.'

'Snap, then,' replied Anna, voice dripping with scorn.

'By God, I will! Constable!'

The policeman was not having a good evening. Finding wit-
nesses was harder than he thought. He returned.

'I've found the bracelet!' Bobby exclaimed. Phryne thought
how unattractive he was, red with frustrated passion and dripping with sweat. 'I wondered where someone might hide it and I
thought, what about the prize board? This girl stole them,' he said,
unhooking without looking at his object. 'See? Mother's pearls!'

'No, they ain't,' said the policeman. 'They ain't worth tuppence.'

Bobby stared at the Woolworths pearls. 'Then where are Mother's pearls?' he cried.

'Here,' said Phryne Fisher, fervently hoping that it was true. She put the string into his hot hand. 'You dropped them near the carousel. You really are careless, Bobby. Now shall we just tell this nice policeman what you have really been up to?'

'No,' said Alan Lee, laying a hand on Phryne's arm. 'No trouble, lady.'

'Then we will allow him to carry on with his very useful task of keeping the world safe from carnivals,' agreed Phryne.

The disgusted constable moved away. Samson lifted Bobby off his feet by his collar with no apparent effort.

'You horrible little insect,' said Phryne dispassionately. 'Still, I suppose it is educational to find out that you can't have everything you want. And just in case you want to cause any more trouble,' she told Bobby, 'we are going to lock you up, just for a while, while I enjoy the carnival. I won't say that Doreen might leave one of her snakes in the booth,' she said, with quiet venom. 'I'll just let you find out for yourself.'

Doreen was walking through the crowd, carrying Cleopatra, who was pleased to be out of her tent. Bobby fell to his knees. Phryne took pity on him.

'Or perhaps you would prefer to give them all the money in your pockets, promise never to return, and flee the scene?'

Bobby shed three pound notes, a folded ten-pound note, seven shillings, threepence, and two farthings, and ran for his life. As he ran, Anna reached out a hand and snapped her fingers in his face.

Phryne was cool at last. Supper was over, the others had gone back to their caravans. Tom had turned out to be a cheery man who had been shipwrecked in Borneo, which gave him a new career. Doreen had inherited her snakes from her mum, who had married a grocer in Tumbarumba. Phryne had patted one snake and scotched another. A day full of incident.

The lights were out. Across the huddle of booths the rain sluiced, washing away the stains of anger and appetite and fear. Camels hooted and bubbled, surprising local owls. Alan Lee was behind her and she leaned back into his salty, soapy scent. She could feel every defined muscle in his chest.

'You could stay the night,' he suggested.

Phryne laughed and turned into his embrace, kissing the strong throat and the hollow of the collarbone. His hands slid down her sides.

'I think I might,' she said softly. 'I have always…loved…the carnival.'

The Camberwell Wonder

Mordre wol out, that see we day by day.

—Geoffrey Chaucer, *The Nun's Priest's Tale*

The constable straightened up and held out a gentleman's starched collar. It was slightly greenish from the moss it had lain in. There was a dark splotch of dried blood across the whole length of the back. He exhibited it to Detective Inspector Robinson.

'What have you got to say about this, eh, Stevie?'

The big man nodded. A glint of what might have been intelligence gleamed in his sullen eyes. He said slowly, 'I killed Mr Clarke. I killed him.'

And all the way down to Russell Street and on every subsequent enquiry, that was all he would say.

~~

It had been a disagreeable night, and Phryne Fisher fought off her escort with more force and less finesse than she usually showed. The young man was clumsy, having battered her toes to pulp while dancing with her at the Green Mill; she feared that her satin train was damaged beyond repair, and he had probably marked her dress with his hot, sweaty hands.

'Let me go or I'll break your arm,' she advised him. 'Goodnight, Mr Clarke.' She did not necessarily wait until her own door was closed before she added, 'And good riddance!'

She stalked into her parlour and flung herself down into an aquamarine easy chair.

'Dot, get me some slippers—my shoes are ruined, and my feet, too,' she exclaimed, examining her toes ruefully. 'That's the last time I do favours for people! "Take the poor boy out, Phryne, you might be able to do something with him, terribly good family, you know."' She spat indelicately into the fireplace. 'Hell and damnation, look at this satin!'

'Likely it will clean,' said Dot equably. 'How about a nice cup of warm milk?'

'Get me a small glass of green chartreuse,' requested Phryne, more civilly, for she was fond of her assistant. 'The drinks at the Moulin Vert really are frightful. But weak. You couldn't get drunk on them in a millennium. The management are foundation members of the Temperance League against Alcohol. What an evil temper I have. It's not the poor boy's fault that his father is a loony and his mother hasn't spoken to him for years.'

'What, Mr Clarke? I saw that name in the paper,' said Dot, handing over the glass.

'Oh, you must have heard of him, Dot. Old Mr Clarke, I mean. Man's got a mania for rehabilitating the retarded. Staffs his whole estate with the feeble-minded. Supposed to be a charitable man, but in my opinion he is purely cynical. If his staff are dim, they work hard, and I bet they don't get holidays and union rates. Met him once at some bazaar that Lady Rose Maillart was sponsoring, and I didn't like him. I've never trusted men with the kind of social smile that never reaches the eyes. And his wife—now called Parvati—was captured by some Indian sect and floats around in ochre robes, which clash dreadfully with her complexion, chanting mantras or sutras or whatever they are. Dreadful people. And their son just trampled my toes like the corn beneath the harrow and made a very obvious grab for my... er... attributes. Oh well, curse the lot of them. At least I'm home in one piece. What are you looking for, Dot?'

'Toad,' corrected Dot absently. 'It's a toad beneath the harrow. Here we are, Miss. Listen: "Mr Clarke the Philanthropist missing. Gardener confesses to Murder."'

'Good Lord!'

'That's about it, Miss.' Dot crossed herself. 'It says that the boy confessed freely to having murdered his master but won't say anything else. Excuse me, Miss Phryne, there's the phone, and the Butlers are out. Who could it be at this time of night?' She hurried to find out.

Phryne sipped her liqueur and scanned the newspaper for any further information. Where was the body? How had this murder been committed? She felt a pang of guilt for her dislike of the deceased. His philanthropy appeared to have been fatal.

Dot appeared in the doorway. 'Lady Rose, Miss Phryne.'

'Oh, gosh.' Phryne padded barefoot out to the phone. The tiles were icy under her feet. 'Phryne Fisher,' she said into the receiver.

'Phryne, you must come here right away!' demanded the cool, high voice. 'I have a commission for you.'

'Lady Rose, it's past midnight!'

'And what should that matter to a fine healthy gel? When I was your age I was dancing until four and breakfasting in Covent Garden at dawn on fresh strawberries! No stamina, that's what's wrong with you. Too many cocktails and cigarettes and not enough huntin'.'

'Give me a good reason why it can't wait until morning,' groaned Phryne. 'I've been dancing with the Clarke boy and it might be days before I can walk again.'

'That hobbledehoy! My dear, that was self-sacrificing of you. Tomorrow then. At nine. Sharp.'

'Sharp,' agreed Phryne, and hung up.

'What did she want, Miss?' Dot asked as she handed Phryne her slippers.

'Give me an arm up the stairs, there's a dear. I expect that it is the Clarke murder. Lady Rose knows that family very well. But what she wants me to do about it, Dot old bean, I haven't the faintest idea.'

⁓

Nine sharp found Phryne ringing the front door bell of Lady Rose's bijou Toorak residence, a small and absurd building like an iced cake. Lady Rose's maid let her in, took her coat, and confided, 'She's in a real state, Miss. Don't cross her if you can help it. I never did like that Mr Clarke. Nasty eyes. And they say he was involved in some shady dealings—import and export, you know.' Penleigh was an inveterate and poisonous gossip. 'They say that he was bringing in all sorts of odd cargoes. Through this door, Miss. And be careful.'

Warned, Phryne trod delicately. The tiny but fiery Lady Rose was sitting on her Empire sofa, embracing as much of a huge woman in a wrapper and a drab dress as she could encompass. She glared up at Phryne.

'There you are. This is Mrs Slade, my cleaner. Comes in every day for the rough scrubbing. She's been working for me for thirty years, eh, Slade?'

The large woman gave an affirmative sob.

'She has a layabout husband who is no use to anyone and a silly daughter who is a mannequin and a son called Stevie. He's twenty now, but his mind never grew up. Slade says his father dropped him on his head. He's a good boy, kind and pleasant, but he's a child.'

'And he murdered Mr Clarke,' said Phryne.

Mrs Slade gave a wail of anguish and turned up a face sodden with tears and wrinkled like an old apple. 'He'd never harm anyone—never! And he loved Mr Clarke. My Dan, he said that we'd have to put Stevie away, he was getting so big and all, so it was a blessing when Mr Clarke offered him a job. Not much pay, of course, but all found and he could come home at night.'

'But he says he killed Mr Clarke,' objected Phryne, sitting down to ease her feet. 'And they found his collar with blood on it.'

The woman's face set into stubborn lines. 'I don't believe it. Someone's been putting words into his mouth. He never done it. Not my Stevie.'

'Well, Phryne?' snapped Lady Rose.

Phryne sighed. 'I'll try, but it's going to be difficult, with a confession.'

'Everything worth doing is difficult,' said the small woman fiercely. 'Get along with you, girl, and solve the riddle. I never did like that Joshua Clarke,' she added meditatively.

'Can you take me to see the house?'

'Of course. We shall go there directly. Don't worry, Slade,' Lady Rose said, extracting herself from the sofa, 'we will get your boy back.'

Mrs Slade surveyed Phryne in her fashionable morning dress of wine-coloured wool and the Dutch-doll face with black hair swinging forward over her cheeks. She shook her head slowly. 'Thank you, Miss, I'm sure,' she muttered doubtfully. 'I'll get back to me scrubbing.'

'Come along, Phryne,' ordered Lady Rose. 'Penleigh! My coat! I'm going out.'

As Penleigh dressed her employer in a fur coat which had seen better years, Phryne said to her, 'Tell me, do you know any more about Mr Clarke's business?'

'Penleigh always knows more than she says—that's why she is so amusing,' declared Lady Rose. 'What about his business?'

'He was supposed to have got a load of watches from Hong Kong and smuggled them through customs,' said Penleigh, animated by their interest. 'And some clocks, I believe. They say he also deals in wine and tobacco, and none of it ain't paid duty.'

'Interesting,' said Lady Rose. 'But not helpful. Back directly, Penleigh. My, Phryne, what a large car, and so very red! When I was a gel, I would have been considered fast for driving in it.' She hopped into the car with delight. 'But now I'm old, I can be as fast as I like, and I do find it refreshing. Camberwell, Phryne, it's a big mansion—and he could afford it if he was dealing in smuggled wine. I wonder about that Châteauneuf-du-Pape I bought from him. How intriguing to think that it might have been illegal!'

Phryne steered the Hispano-Suiza carefully past lumbering delivery trucks and onto a broad road.

'What about Mrs Clarke?' she asked.

'Oh, quite dotty, dear, always has been. I was a gel with her older sisters, and they were all a little eccentric, but Calliope—or should I say Parvati—was definitely, well, a little touched, even when she was at school. Has enthusiasm, you know. For botany, I recall, and birdwatching, and she always threw herself bodily into her current fascination. Luckily she tires easily, and then there is a brief period of calm, then she's away with the fairies again. Poor Calliope.'

'Did they all have names like that?'

'Oh yes, there was Eudora and Euterpe and Psyche and…
now, what was the brother's name? Are we going to hit that tram?'

'No.'

'Oh, good. Xerxes, that was it. Died young, I seem to remember.'

'Of acute nomenclature,' diagnosed Phryne.

Lady Rose laughed her parrot laugh until they drew up outside a huge house. A bouncy and enthusiastic boy threw open
the massive iron gates and Phryne steered the red car through.
She tossed a penny to the boy, who grinned a Cheshire cat grin
and patted the bonnet.

'Pretty,' he yelled. 'Pretty car, pretty lady! Pretty, pretty!'

Phryne drove on. 'Are all the staff potty?' she asked, a little
shaken by the gatekeeper.

Lady Rose had not turned a hair on her well-groomed silver
head. 'No, dear, I believe that the butler and his wife, the housekeeper, are quite with us, and so is the steward.'

'Steward?'

'Yes—the head keeper, I suppose you could call him. He keeps
an eye on all of the…others. A superior man, with an eye that
could open oysters. Where shall we leave the car?'

'Here,' said Phryne. 'Next to the police car. Hello, Sergeant,'
she called to a large policeman. 'Is Jack Robinson on this case?'

'Yes, Miss Fisher,' said Sergeant Day affably. He had liked
Phryne ever since she delivered a child molester wrapped in
brown paper to the Queenscliff police station. 'And it will take
a while, too.'

'Have you found a body yet?'

'No, nothing more than the collar.'

'Has it gone to the laboratory?'

'Why should it?'

'To find out whether it's human blood. Precipitin test, you
know. You'll look very silly if it turns out to be rabbit.'

'I'll send it,' promised the sergeant. 'Inspector Robinson's inside, Miss. Are you involved?'

'Yes, I'm to restore your murderer to his mother's loving arms.'

'Good luck, Miss Fisher.'

Phryne and Lady Rose mounted steps which had been scrubbed white and were admitted to the house by a grim butler. He took their names into an inner room and a moment later escorted them wordlessly to the door.

'Miss Fisher and Lady Rose Maillart,' he announced, turned on his heel and left.

'Jack! How nice to see you!' cried Phryne, as a puzzled detective inspector rose from a couch and took her hand. There was a bundle of yellow garments on the floor.

'Oh, Calliope, do get up!' exclaimed Lady Rose irritably. 'Sit on a chair like a Christian and talk to us, or I shall lose my temper with you.'

The bundle stirred, put out a thin arm, and Phryne helped her into a chair. Mrs Clarke shook back tangled grey hair and said meekly, 'Rose, you are so forceful.'

'That's more than I could do,' murmured Jack Robinson. 'She's been sitting there all morning chanting and refusing to answer me. I reckon the whole place is loony.'

Phryne patted his arm. 'What do you want to know?'

'When she last saw her husband.'

Lady Rose took her cue. 'Well, Calliope, when did you last see Joshua?'

'In eternity there is no time...' Mrs Clarke caught the look in Lady Rose's blue eyes and stammered, 'Yesterday morning. He had a meeting with some businessmen and then he was supposed to be back for lunch but he never came. He does that, sometimes, and sometimes even if he comes I am meditating on the infinite and I don't lunch when I'm meditating on the infinite, but he always comes home to sleep and he never came, and the maid said his bed hadn't been slept in and then I called the police and they found that collar and then Stevie said...he said...'

She ran down, like a gramophone, and stared hopefully at Lady Rose.

'Was he worried about anything? Any of these business matters?' asked the policeman, and she answered, 'Oh, Joshua would never talk to me about business. He was pleased about something, though. Lately he'd been losing patience with the staff, and they do try so hard, poor things, and said he was thinking of breaking up the establishment and settling in a smaller house, and I said that I wouldn't like that, because I need space, you know, to...'

'Contemplate the infinite, we know. Really, Calliope, you are the silliest creature I ever met! Was he intending to leave you?'

'Leave me?' The vague eyes, half closed, were shocked into opening wide. 'How could he? This is my house, Rose, and he hasn't any money—at least, I don't know what money he has, but it can't be much because he's always asking me to sign cheques for more, but he seemed happier lately...yes, happier. He sang in the bath.'

'What did he sing?' asked Phryne, without any clear idea of why she was asking. Jack Robinson gave her a censorious look.

'French songs.' Calliope Clarke hummed in a surprisingly tuneful voice, then sang the words, *'Je donnerais Versailles, Paris et Saint- Denis, le tours de Notre-Dame et... et...'*

Phryne finished the song. *'Et le clocher de mon pays.* That's "Auprès de ma blonde." Did he usually sing?'

'Oh, no, no, not for years...' Calliope's attention, engaged like a faulty gear, was slipping.

Lady Rose shook her. 'The nice policeman wants to ask some more questions, Calliope.'

'Nothing more, madam, just permission to search the house.'

'Of course.' Calliope sat down on the floor again, crossed her legs and began to chant.

Jack Robinson led the way into the hall.

'Dear, dear, she's pottier than ever,' sighed Lady Rose. 'You go and search, Phryne, and I'll sit with her a little. Perhaps some tea.'

The hard-faced man was at her elbow. 'Tea, Lady Rose? I shall order it immediately.'

'Thank you.' Lady Rose went back into the drawing room and Phryne detained the man.

'Are you the butler?'

'No, Miss, the steward. The butler is indisposed.'

'Take us to Mr Clarke's rooms, please.'

'If I could give the order for tea first? Annie!' He tinkled a little bell and a very clean maid ran to him. 'Tea, Annie, for Mrs Clarke and a visitor, and be careful with the tray, mind! Now, Mr Clarke's rooms are this way.'

Very well-appointed rooms, too. Leather-bound books covered the walls, the desk was a massive slab of walnut, and the carpet both Persian and precious. It was all in perfect order and smelled of beeswax.

'This room has been cleaned,' accused Jack Robinson. The steward nodded.

Phryne poked about then asked suddenly, 'What was in the wastepaper basket?'

'I'm sure I don't know, Miss.'

'Where is your rubbish put?'

'In the bin, Miss. Burnables in the incinerator.'

'Show me,' demanded Phryne.

The steward glanced at Detective Inspector Robinson for his cue, and the policeman nodded. Resignedly, the steward led the way through the hidden region of the house, into a cold, scrubbed passage lined with American cloth and out the back door into the kitchen garden. There, Phryne picked her way through a wilderness of pea sticks and fallow asparagus beds until she was led to a brick incinerator.

'Take off the lid,' she requested, and delved inside, sneezing as ashes crept into her nose. She emerged a moment later to ask, 'Did Mr Clarke smoke cigars?' and received an affirmative. Bits of paper were in both hands when she came into view again, and she sorted them rapidly. Brochures and shipping lists, a partly destroyed book, and a mass of paper which looked as if it had been torn from a notebook, covered in figures in a neat, cramped hand.

'Good. Go and get me a bag, will you? That sack will do.'

The bemused steward assisted Miss Fisher in transferring the waste paper into a sugar sack. He noticed that she retained one scrap in her hand as she ran back to the house, leaving him to toil behind with the sack.

'Jack, where are you? Come on, we have to hurry. I've got some things to confirm, but you must go forth and do battle with the heathen. Quick, there's no time to lose, it's eleven already!'

Jack Robinson, who had found nothing out of the ordinary in the study, seized Miss Fisher by the elbows, judging her hysterical, but she twisted free.

'I'm fine, Jack, really, take this paper, see? The pencil mark. In the second column. Now get down there, and I'll see you at Russell Street—hurry!'

Jack was still staring at the scrap of paper in his hand when he heard the front door slam behind Lady Rose, Phryne Fisher, and the sugar bag. Then he ran after her towards his car, calling for Sergeant Day and all the horsepower at his disposal.

Lady Rose sorted through the papers as Phryne drove at an electrifying pace straight down Canterbury Road.

'His business certainly seems to have been smuggling, dear, as Penleigh suggested—she knows everything, that woman. These columns of figures are accruing—a bank account, perhaps. The shipping list numbers agree with this list, and I expect that these are numbers of watches, or weights of tobacco, and this is certainly wine. Nothing else is measured in litres. He has been running a thriving business.'

'What's the last figure on the accruing column?' asked Phryne, flicking the big car past a dray and waving at the cursing driver.

Lady Rose held out the list. (She refused to wear glasses.) 'Sixty-four thousand nine hundred and eleven pounds, three shillings and fourpence. Where are we going?'

'To your house to pick up Mrs Slade. Can you read the title of that wad of print?'

'Torn out of a book, evidently. It's rather tattered, but if this piece fits in there… Yes, it's from a book called *Famous Historical Puzzles* and the chapter heading is "The Camden…" No, that bit is missing. What is this all about, Phryne?'

'See if you can find the missing scrap.'

Lady Rose rummaged. 'Fancy, it had slipped down onto the floor. Yes, there, and to think I was never good at jigsaw puzzles when I was a gel! "The Camden Wonder." Would you like to tell me what is happening?'

'"The Camden Wonder" has always been a favourite puzzle of mine,' said Phryne. 'I knew the answer to the riddle as soon as I saw that torn book. Imagine. It is just after the Civil War in England. A certain gentleman, who has had shady dealings with both sides, vanishes one night. All that is found of him is a torn shirt, stained with blood, and one shoe. A nice touch, that. The steward of his house confesses out of the blue that he, his mother, and his brother murdered the gentleman. Both mother and brother deny it fiercely, beg their relative to come to his senses, but it goes to trial. The gentleman has been gone for a year. Then the steward changes his story, tries to withdraw his confession, says that he doesn't know what happened to the gentleman. Here we are—can you go and get Mrs Slade? I'll continue the story on the way.'

Lady Rose was only gone for a moment before she returned, dragging the tear-stained Mrs Slade with her and cramming her into the car as though she was stuffing a cushion.

'We are going to Russell Street, Mrs Slade, and if Jack Robinson has behaved like his namesake I think you shall have your son back today. To continue'—Phryne addressed Lady Rose—'the steward withdrew his confession, but they were all tried anyway.'

'What, without the body? I thought that you had to have a body.'

'Do you think so too, Mrs Slade?'

The big woman nodded. 'Stands to reason. Got to have a corpse. Have they found Mr Clarke, Miss?'

'I hope so. So you both think that you cannot be tried for murder without the body?'

Lady Rose and Mrs Slade nodded.

'Right. Russell Street. All change. Wait for me,' said Phryne, dropping them at the door of the police headquarters, 'I have to put the car away.'

With magnificent assurance, Phryne parked the Hispano-Suiza in the street next to a sign that said 'Chief Inspector's Vehicle Only' before ushering her companions into the police station.

'We want to see Stevie Slade. Detective Inspector Robinson has given me leave,' said Phryne to the duty policeman.

They were conducted to a small room where Mrs Slade's huge offspring was sitting on a chair, a hulking lump of misery. His eyes brightened when he saw his mother.

'Oh, Mum! Are they gonna let me out?'

'I don't know, son, I'm sure. Talk to the lady.' Mrs Slade dropped into another chair.

Phryne surveyed Stevie Slade. He was huge, at least six foot four, with a gentle, foolish smile on his turnip head. He was favouring one arm. 'Show me your arm, Stevie,' Phryne said quietly. There was a long cut on the forearm. Phryne was suddenly so angry that it was an effort to speak.

'Mr Clarke is your friend, isn't he, Stevie?'

Stevie nodded.

'But Mr Clarke cut your arm, didn't he?'

Another nod.

'What did he say, Stevie? That it was a joke he was playing on Mrs Clarke?'

'Joke,' agreed Stevie, grinning widely. 'Joke.'

'So he was going to vanish, and you were to confess to having killed him, and you wouldn't be in any trouble because there has to be a body for anyone to be convicted of murder?'

Stevie nodded again, his eyes widening at the lady's perspicacity.

'But you wouldn't hurt him, would you, Stevie? Even though he cut your arm to bloody his collar?'

'Didn't hurt much,' said Stevie. 'I asked Mum about the body, and she said that Mr Clarke was right.'

'My God, he did ask me,' said Mrs Slade, clutching the collar of her wrapper. 'He did ask me, the innocent!'

'But the joke's over now, Stevie,' said Phryne, sick with disgust. 'Mr Clarke wants you to tell the truth, now.'

'Joke's over?' Stevie repeated. They all nodded.

'I didn't like saying it, Mum, because it was a lie, and you always said liars would go to hell,' said Stevie Slade at last, and his mother dived across the cell to cradle his head against her breast.

'You stay here, Mrs Slade,' said Phryne through her teeth. 'By the sound of that shouting, I should say that Jack Robinson has caught his man, and I want to meet him.'

She left the cell, told the policeman at the door that he no longer had a murderer to guard, and strode down the corridor towards a fair-sized argument. A strident male voice dominated. Lady Rose scuttled at Phryne's heels, agog with curiosity.

'You have no right to drag me off my boat just before sailing!' objected a small, furious gentleman in overcoat and hat. 'It's outrageous. Do you know who I am?'

'You are Joshua Clarke,' said Phryne Fisher, in a voice which would have frozen nitrogen. 'And you are a murderer.'

This silenced Mr Clarke.

'Jack, this gentleman had a joke with his poor retarded gardener. The boy was to say that he had killed Mr Clarke, and everyone knows that you can't be tried for murder without a body, so he was in no danger. He was so fond of the gentleman that he allowed him to cut his arm with a razor to provide human blood for the clue of the collar. Then Mr Clarke would pop up and say "April Fool" and everyone would laugh. But Mr Clarke wasn't going to pop up. Mr Clarke was heading for France with all of his ill-gotten gains and as much of her estate as he could convince his poor silly wife to give him.'

'And in pleasant company, too,' Jack Robinson added. 'A Miss Gladys Worth. Typist. Or so she says. He didn't tell her about his wife. She's creating something awful at the front desk.'

'There was one thing he didn't tell Stevie, either,' spat Phryne. 'You can be tried for murder without a body. In "The Camden Wonder" the three were hanged, and the gentleman came back after three years and found all his accomplices neatly removed to heavenly judgement. You intended Stevie Slade to be hanged, Mr Clarke, and that's attempted murder, isn't it, Detective Inspector?'

'Oh yes, it's attempted murder all right. And your law is correct,

Miss Fisher. No need for a corpus if there's enough circumstantial evidence and a confession. Now, sir, don't make a fuss. Just you come this way and we'll find you a nice cell. Sign Slade out, will you, Sergeant Day? He can go home. Sorry he's been troubled. No charges.'

'It was a joke!' protested Mr Clarke, turning a sweating face to Phryne and attempting a light laugh. 'Just a harmless little joke, that's all!'

'You bastard,' said Phryne. 'You malicious, smug, hypocritical bastard. How long have you been hatching this plot? When did you start milking your wife's estate? And when did you decide that poor Stevie Slade was expendable? I hope they hang you,' she concluded.

'It was a joke!' Mr Clarke struggled with the constable, who was escorting him towards the custody sergeant to be booked in. 'How dare you speak to me like that!'

Lady Rose laid a warning hand on Phryne's arm. Stevie Slade was coming down the corridor, his mother in tow, having been released. Catching sight of his erstwhile master, Stevie laughed massively and called, 'Joke's over, Mr Clarke! Good joke, but joke's over, Mr Clarke!'

His laughter followed Mr Clarke all the way to his cell.

'Good joke, Mr Clarke,' said Phryne with unconcealed venom. 'Good joke, Mr Clarke, but it's over.'

Come, Sable Night

But in her heart a cold December

—Thomas Morley, *April is in My Mistress' Face*

1928 was a good year for madrigals.

The Honourable Miss Phryne Fisher surveyed the crowd of singers, drawn from the Glee Club and the Women's Choir, as they moved through patches of sunlight in her sea-green parlour, shoes clicking on the polished boards. It was a summer's day, still cool enough to make the sunshine welcome, and they were worth looking at. So was Phryne, in a golden afternoon dress with silk embroidered bees, her bobbed hair as shiny as embroidery floss. She had invited the Madrigal Choir to her bijou residence for their rehearsal. She provided the refreshments and they provided the music—and the scandal.

Phryne watched the distribution of champagne cup and listened to the low voice of the large bass who stood behind her. Claude Greenhill, engaging, calm and the best-informed gossip in the Western world, was providing a situation report. Phryne's neat black head came up to his first waistcoat button.

'Lawrence has done something outrageous,' commented Claude dispassionately. Phryne watched the tall, blond, athletic scion of the Newhouse-Gore fortune as he divided his attention between two adoring young women.

'Lawrence is always outrageous,' she replied. 'He treats the Women's Choir as a harem, always has—and his success, I have to say, is remarkable. I don't know how Diane stands him.'

'She doesn't have to endure him anymore,' whispered Claude.

'Oh? Come to her senses, has she? I wouldn't have thought it—she seemed quite besotted with him. He does have a clean-cut, Captain of the Boats charm, you have to admit.'

Diane Hart was sitting by the window. The light set her long red hair aflame and bronzed her grass-green dress. A bunch of red roses lay on her lap, and she was staring at Lawrence with an expression Phryne could not read.

'I admit the charm, but this is going too far,' said Claude, taking a gulp of champagne cup. 'He's dumped Diane and taken up with Violet.'

'Oh dear,' said Phryne lamely. Violet was Diane's younger sister, mouse to her bright scarlet. 'How do you know?'

'Diane spent most of last night telling me about it.' Claude made a gesture which mimed wringing out the shoulder of his white shirt. 'I suppose that they can transfer the wedding plans to the sister. The funeral baked meats, that sort of thing.'

'The dress won't fit,' said Phryne. 'Lord, lord. Any more gossip, Claude?'

'Oh, yes. Poor Alexandra is devastated. She's always been Button B in that ménage, and now she's pipped at the post. Violet looks sweet enough, but she's got a will of adamant. Our Lawrence won't be dropping in to Alexandra's house for tea and sympathy anymore. And she really did love him.'

Phryne noticed Alexandra. She had plaited her long black hair into a punitive queue and was on her third cocktail. Her dark eyes were shadowed with grief.

'Damn Lawrence, why will he do it?' said Phryne suddenly. 'He's rich enough to buy all the companionship he needs. Must he reap the Women's Choir like wheat?'

'He's not as bad as Victor,' said Claude.

'This is true. Victor is a rakehell, a Casanova, a totally unreliable cold hungry bastard,' agreed Phryne. 'But he lays all his marked cards on the table. No young woman, however self-deluded, could think that Victor really liked or appreciated her.'

'There's one who does,' said Claude, angling his chin to indicate a drooping figure leafing through a photograph album. Jane, who had been a fiery proponent of Free Love, with all her fire gone and a suspicious bulge at her waist.

Victor caught Phryne looking at her and advanced with a plate of cheese straws, expostulating, 'Miss Fisher, you shouldn't believe all you hear.'

'Oh?' Phryne disliked Victor's practised smile even more than usual. He was slim and dark and moved like a dancer. His eyes were blue and knowing. 'Why shouldn't I?'

'You know Causeless Claude—gossips like an old woman.'

Phryne grinned. 'I know Claude, Victor, and I know you.'

His smile faded.

Claude leaned over her and collected a handful of cheese straws. He was opening his mouth to speak when Lawrence clapped his hands and bellowed, 'I've got an announcement to make.'

Silence fell. He was the centre of attention, where he always felt he ought to be. He took the hand of the girl standing next to him and said, 'Violet has agreed to be my wife. Congratulate me!'

There was some scattered applause. Violet looked up at the blond Adonis with such an expression of perfect trust that Phryne's mouth dried. He patted her shoulder.

'Champagne,' said Victor. He produced an opened bottle of Moët and two glasses. 'To the bride and groom!' he said, and watched as Lawrence and Violet, laughing, drank.

'You're all invited to sing at the wedding,' said Lawrence, grinning.

The assembled choristers toasted them. Talk broke out in an excited babble. Alexandra looked crushed and bit the end of her plait.

Diane, now sitting by the fireplace, approached the happy couple and thrust her bouquet of red roses into Lawrence's hands. 'I hope you'll be very happy,' she murmured.

'That's good of you, old girl. No hard feelings?' Phryne heard Lawrence ask in a condescending tone, as she and Claude came up to add their congratulations.

'None,' said Diane in a tight voice.

Phryne marvelled that Lawrence seemed to instantly accept her statement. After all, it had only been six months since the same man had announced that Diane was going to marry him, and with the same panache as he showed now. Lawrence's fingers closed around the stems as he leaned to kiss his fiancée's sister on the cheek.

'Ouch,' he said, shaking his hand. 'These roses have thorns!' he told Phryne, insulted that they should dare to prick him.

Phryne took the flowers and handed them to a waitress, saying, 'Put these in water, will you?'

'Time to start singing.' Arthur Dauphin, the chorus master, decided to intervene before anyone said anything they might later regret. 'Claude's got the music. This is the order in which we will sing the madrigals. Don't shuffle them. Nothing worse than a choir which rustles. All right, come along, please, ladies and gentlemen.'

Phryne watched the inchoate gathering resolve itself into

groups of sopranos, altos, tenors, and basses. Sleek Arthur raised his hands and they began to sing warm-up exercises. Collaring a glass of the champagne, Phryne sat down out of the way and surveyed the choir. They were very young, mostly good-looking, and although they were shaken and excited by Lawrence's announcement, they were relatively disciplined and professional. Even Alexandra had shelved her broken heart. Diane among the sopranos drew in a deep breath. Claude among the basses was concentrating on low notes while Lawrence was mopping his brow, possibly in relief at having escaped a scene. Victor among the tenors was ogling an alto on whom he had his eye. She was blushing.

They opened their music and began: *'Now is the month of Maying, when merry lads are playing.'*

'Tenors, you are flat. That's a major third,' said Arthur, brushing back his hair. 'Sopranos, pay attention. Timing is of the essence in madrigals. All right. Now, the next song, "Fyer, fyer." Crisply, now.'

They completed the song with only minimal grumbling from the conductor: *'Ay me, ay me, I sit and cry me, and call for help alas! But none comes nigh me.'*

'Sopranos, that was an interesting interpretation, but I prefer Thomas Morley's version. Let's get on. Page four, please.'

'Come, sable night,' they sang, so sadly that Phryne was moved. *'Put on thy mourning stole... and only Amyntas wastes his heart in wailing. In wailing...'* the carefully pitched voices rose in exquisite harmony... *'in wailing...'* Arthur's hand flicked at the basses. Their voices rose. *'In wail—'*

With excellent timing, Lawrence Newhouse-Gore's voice hit the top note, stuck, and failed. In failing, he fell, sprawled among the surprised choir.

A stockingless medical student called Anne bent over the prone figure, felt for a pulse, and shot a look at Phryne.

'He's dead,' she told her hostess quietly.

'Lawrence!' screamed Alexandra. She clawed for the body and was held back in the firm embrace of three sympathetic friends. Diane did not move a muscle. Victor, into the sudden silence, laughed. Claude raised both eyebrows. Everyone else stood astonished, at a loss for a response.

Arthur's was possibly uncharitable. 'Damn, the concert's in two weeks.'

This was the signal for the choir to start reacting. Phryne watched them carefully. Those who usually screamed and cried duly screamed and cried and were comforted by those who usually comforted. Claude had wrapped his arms around an alto half his height who was snuffling into his chest. Violet had retreated from the body, shocked into blankness, and someone had found her a chair and a drink. Her sister Diane did not come to her side. In fact, she did not even turn to look at the fallen man.

Phryne took charge. 'Well, we'd better call a doctor—no offence, Anne dear. Claude, Jack, can you lift him?' Claude and Jack, another large bass, disengaged their petitioners, bent to heave up the long form of Lawrence Newhouse-Gore and laid him on the couch. Phryne and Anne inspected him.

The face was dusky with blood and swollen, and his lips were blue. He was definitely dead. Phryne untied her golden scarf and covered his face.

'Arthur, I think you should move the choir into the drawing room,' said Phryne. 'There's nothing to be done for you now, Lawrence,' she said to the inert corpse. 'I think we'd better keep singing.'

'Take your music, everyone,' ordered Arthur, gathering up the reins. 'Come along. We mustn't give way,' he added, ushering the last soprano out of the room.

Phryne, sitting by the body, heard them begin the next

madrigal, raggedly and out of tune. *'Oyez! Has any found a lad? Take him quick before he flieth.'* But by the time they came to the next song they had recovered most of their skill. *'Sleep fleshly birth… thy doleful obit keeping.'*

Summoned away from his Sunday dinner, a cross local doctor was announced. Dr McAdam had been looking forward to roast lamb and minted peas and had promised his wife he would not be called away. He was elderly and displeased. But he examined the dead man expertly and quickly.

'Anaphylactic shock,' he said crisply. 'He was allergic to something. Very allergic. What did he have to eat or drink?'

'Er… well, some egg and mustard cress sandwiches, some caviar, a glass or two of champagne… I don't really know,' Phryne replied.

'Strawberries?' snapped the doctor.

'Yes, there were strawberries.'

'Well, that's it then. I'll certify death.' He scribbled busily. 'These are the undertakers I use, though doubtless his people will make their own arrangements. Coroner will have to sit on him, of course. Pity, really. He's very young. Good afternoon, Miss Fisher.'

He bustled off to his interrupted dinner. Phryne made a telephone call to the young man's bereaved parents and resumed her place by the body. Anne came in and sat down with her.

'The doctor said he died of anaphylactic shock,' Phryne told her. 'What's that?'

'Oh, was that it?' asked the young woman. 'Yes, that explains the cyanosis. No one knows how it works, but some people are so sensitive to some foods—strawberries are one of them, mustard, but it can be anything—that their whole body reacts. Their throat swells up, their lungs fill with fluid, and they suffocate.'

'But Lawrence must have known that he was allergic—he wouldn't have eaten whatever it was,' protested Phryne.

'It can sneak up on you. Like bee stings. One bee sting just creates a swelling, the next makes you really ill, and the third can kill. What are you going to do about the body?'

'I've called his parents. They told me to order an undertaker so I've done that. And I thought it was going to be such a relaxing day. You're very cool, Anne.'

'If I started to get worried about every corpse I saw, I'd be a wreck. And it's not as though I liked Lawrence. Sorry, old chum,' said the medical student, laying Phryne's scarf back over the puffed and horrible face.

Next door, the choir was singing: *'Weep, weep, mine eyes, a thousand deaths I die.'*

Phryne asked, 'Could someone have given him the substance— ground up, so that he wouldn't recognise it?'

'It's possible.'

'Can you go and cut Victor out of the crowd for me, Anne? And Claude.'

'All right.' Anne seemed not much interested. Phryne wondered if this callousness was real or affected. Anne had been mentioned as one of Lawrence's many conquests.

Phryne contemplated death. Here was a beautiful young man who had every reason to assume that the world would continue to conform to his desires, through a suitable marriage and the production of pattern children to an honourable career until a replete old age. And he was dead, faster than she could snap her fingers. Snatched out of the world. Phryne lifted the cooling hand and laid it on the immaculate breast.

Victor and Claude came out of the drawing room, closing the door on *'Death do thy worst, I care not.'*

'I say, Phryne,' Victor began excitedly, 'is old Lawrence really dead?'

'He's really dead and I'm wondering if you really killed him,' replied Miss Fisher.

Victor went as pale as his screen idol's tan would allow. 'What do you mean?' he demanded.

'Apparently he died of a violent allergy to some substance,' said Phryne firmly. 'That bottle of champagne, Victor—where did you open it?'

'Just outside the room. I wanted it to be ready and I didn't want the pop to be heard before he made his announcement.'

'Unconvincing,' said Phryne, pulling the palpitating tenor down to sit between her and Claude.

The bass nodded. 'Very unconvincing.'

'What did you put in that otherwise unexceptionable wine, Victor?' Victor looked into green eyes as cold as jade and faltered.

'Nothing, nothing, I swear.'

'Why don't I believe you? How well did you know Lawrence?'

'We were old friends, used to go out together, you know that.' Victor was perspiring freely.

'Used to go out together? Or stay in together?'

'I don't know what you're suggesting,' bridled Victor.

Claude shook his head sadly. 'Yes, you do. Not a new suggestion, either. Not that we mind. Some of Miss Fisher's best friends are practitioners of the love that dare not speak its name. Come on, Vic, this is serious. Was Lawrence your lover?'

'How dare you!' Victor blustered.

Both pairs of eyes considered him, grey and green.

He collapsed. 'Yes, yes, once or twice. He didn't really like me, though. How did you know?'

'I always suspect young men who make such a show of their manliness. You protest too much, Victor. Now, did you know that Lawrence was allergic to some kind of food? What was it?'

'I have no idea—he ate what he liked, always.' Victor squirmed, then said, 'He was allergic to bee stings, though. He must have been stung, that's it; no one killed him, it was an accident. I'm glad he's dead. He had a letter of mine. He wanted me…he wanted me to…'

'Tell us,' said Phryne, grasping the shaking hands.

Victor gasped, 'He wanted me to marry Diane. Take her off his hands, make her a good husband. She likes me well enough, but I couldn't—I couldn't…'

He burst into tears, leaning his forehead on Phryne's bosom. She held him for a moment, then pushed him gently away. Not even out of pity could she really bear Victor this close. He stank of Californian Poppy and fear.

'There, there, now blow your nose and sit up. Go and wash your face, Victor. The bathroom's through there.'

'Do you think he did it?' asked the bass, seriously, when Victor had left the room.

Phryne shrugged. 'We'll know if he comes back. He's scared enough to bolt. That's why I am giving him the chance.'

'He might be faking. And we still don't know why he opened the bottle outside the room.'

The choir had begun on the next madrigal, *'Adieu sweet Amaryllis, for since to part your will is…'* when Victor returned, mopped up and red-eyed.

'There's something I want you to do, Victor,' Phryne told him.

'Yes, anything.' Victor was eager to please this woman who was in possession of knowledge which could ruin him.

'Jane. She's in a bad way. I want you to resolve her future, Victor. Settle quite a lot of money on her. I'm not asking you to marry her,' said Phryne, gently but inexorably. 'But you must take care of her. And abandon all this philandering with women. Go and find someone you can love.'

Victor straightened. For a moment his customary sneer visited his lips. Then it fled and he said brokenly, 'As you wish, Miss Fisher.'

Claude lit Miss Fisher's gasper and his own. Phryne sent Victor into the rehearsal to find Violet and Alexandra.

They came out together, holding hands. Alexandra was half embracing Violet, who looked exquisitely uncomfortable. Phryne asked, 'Did you know that Lawrence was allergic to something?' Both heads, dark and mouse, shook. They looked at her solemnly, like two good children unfairly battered by fate. The fact of Lawrence's death had not sunk in. They were still shocked and numb. Phryne wanted to talk to them before they woke to a world without Lawrence in it and recognised their loss. She had never had much patience with hysterics.

'He would have told me,' said Violet. 'He told me everything.'

'I thought the same,' said Alexandra. 'When he was with me we sometimes talked all night.'

'Diane might know,' said Violet. 'She's—she's not happy about all this, about him and me. I don't know how much she loved him, you know. She never said. But Lawrie said...he said she could go to Paris. She's always wanted to go to the Sorbonne; it's been her dream ever since we were children. She's so clever. She ought to have been a man. Mother said—oh God, I have to tell Mother, we have to cancel the wedding, all the arrangements... Oh, Lawrence...'

Alexandra bore up Violet's drooping weight and said, 'We neither of us know anything, Phryne. I'd better take Violet home.'

'Not yet. Go back into the rehearsal. You needn't sing—sit down on the couch with this cognac and have a drink or three. You're doing well, Alexandra. I'm proud of you.' Phryne smiled into the tear-wet eyes. Alexandra murmured something, hoisted Violet, and went back into the drawing room, where the choir was beginning on the penultimate madrigal, 'Hark All Ye Lovely Saints Above.' Phryne listened: *'Diana hath agreed with love, his fiery weapon to remove.'*

'Well, it doesn't look like they knew about it,' commented Claude Greenhill, butting out his cigarette.

'No, Claude dear, but you did,' said Phryne, suddenly enlightened. She seized Claude by the earlobe and led him, protesting, into the alcove where a view of the assembled choristers could be had.

'Phryne, what's this all about?' he said, doing 'outraged innocence' quite well.

'You're the librarian, aren't you?' she demanded, dragging his face down to hers. His grey eyes were watering with pain and he smelled of wine and tobacco smoke, musky and attractive.

'Ouch, yes!'

'So you arranged the music in the order in which it would be sung,' she continued, keeping hold of the offending lobe.

'Damn it, Miss Fisher,' he protested, then grunted, 'I did.'

'Stay still unless you want to go through life in a mono-aural state. So you were responsible for "Now is the Month of Maying," "Fyer, Fyer," "Come, Sable Night," "Oyez," "Sleep Fleshly Birth," "Weep, weep, Mine Eyes," "Adieu, Sweet Amaryllis," and "Hark All Ye Lovely."'

'Well actually, Morley, Ward, Tomkins, Ramsey, Wilbye, and Weelkes were, but—ouch!... I put them in that order, yes.'

'To spell out a message to the hearer. One particular hearer, I suspect.'

She released him and he straightened up, rubbing his ear. 'What message?' he bluffed.

'The one that identified the murderer. You knew this was going to happen, Claude. Why didn't you prevent it?'

'No, I didn't know.' He was offended. 'I didn't think that she'd do it. She's been breathing fire and brimstone about it, screaming that she'd kill him. So I...challenged her, perhaps. Any of the choir who were paying attention could have noticed it. I thought I'd shock her out of it.'

'But you didn't.'

'No, it appears not.'

'Merry lads are playing. And call for help. Put on thy mourning stole. Oyez, has any found a lad; take him quick before he flieth. Thy doleful obit keeping. A thousand deaths I die. Death do thy worst, I care not. Adieu, sweet Amaryllis and Diana hath agreed with love his fiery weapon to remove. She must have known he was allergic to bee stings. She pressed a bunch of roses into his hand. One of the thorns pricked him. You can see it—the whole hand has swelled. She was furious at being jilted and ... oh Lord, I wonder if he left her any money?'

The large bass was pale. 'Yes, he changed his will when he was going to marry her. He's worth a fortune.'

'Wills made in expectation of marriage are vitiated if the marriage does not take place,' said Phryne.

'Yes, but does she know that? He borrowed her Sorbonne money, you know. Short on his allowance—he always was. But she never got it back.'

'You know, I'm beginning to feel that he had it coming to him,' sighed Phryne. 'All she had to do was to smear that rose thorn with bee venom—which only requires one to dissect a bee—and it's pretty, Claude, a really pretty plan. The problem with most poisons is making sure that the right person gets the bit of cake or whatever. In this case, if that thorn had pricked anyone else they wouldn't have been killed.'

'What are we going to do?'

'We haven't any proof. The bee venom, if it was there, would have been washed off when the roses were put in the vase.' She lifted the bunch and scrutinised the stems. They seemed quite clean. 'Nice roses. She must have bought them specially.'

Phryne looked through the little window at the choir. Diane Hart was standing among the sopranos, pitching her voice carefully and without strain, to judge by her expression. A faint smile lingered around her mouth.

'It's a good idea, generally, not to offend women with that shade of Titian hair,' mused Phryne. 'What do you think of your part in all of this, Claude?'

'I rather wish I hadn't done it,' admitted the bass.

'Hmm.' Phryne leaned back against Claude. He was superlatively comfortable to lean against and Phryne could understand the popularity of his shoulder among the distraught. Equally, there was a sharp mind and a sense of moral outrage which made Claude a dangerous enemy. There was more behind the arrangement of songs than just an attempt to shock Diane Hart.

'We can't prove any of this, Claude. In fact, I almost wish that you hadn't known about it. I'm no good at ethics. Lawrence made a complete blackguard of himself and to some extent invited revenge—you might almost feel that someone had to get him sometime. But I wish it hadn't been here in my house. Gosh, I sound like Lady Macbeth. Well, if Diane killed him, I fear that she is going to go free. I expect she'll get her Sorbonne money back out of the estate. She's got away with a near-perfect murder.'

'We could tell the police,' said Claude distastefully.

'And they'd laugh in our face. Besides, do we want to tell anyone? Damn it, Claude, I hate dilemmas.'

'There's nothing to be done,' he insisted. 'There'll be an inquest, maybe it will come out there.'

'Not a chance. Drat.' Phryne lit another cigarette and threw herself back against the bass hard enough to make him sway and grab her.

The choir were concluding 'The Silver Swan.'

'Farewell, all joys, oh death, come close my eyes. More geese than swans now live, more fools than wise.'

'Miss Fisher…' gasped Claude. 'Phryne, look!'

Phryne turned in his embrace to follow the pointing finger. Her eyes widened comically, then she started to laugh. Claude joined in after a moment, and they reeled, clasped in a close embrace, slipping down onto the Persian rug where they laughed until they cried.

Drunkenly, unsteadily, out of the velvety heart of Diane's red roses, a bee was crawling.

The Boxer

She was pinch' d and pull' d, she said
And he by friar's lanthorn led,
Tells how the drudging goblin sweat
To earn his cream-bowl duly set…

—John Milton, *L'Allegro*

'Miss Fisher, I want you to find my granddaughter.'

It was a cold winter's day in St Kilda, and Mrs Ragnell was wrapped up so tightly in furs and a sense of personal grievance that she resembled a polar bear with a hangover. This awful woman was sitting in Phryne's parlour, drinking tea from a bone china cup and making unpleasing slurping noises. It was a parlour which at most times exuded comfort. An *art décoratif* mirror and statue (a nude bronze nymph), vases stocked with winter flowers on a mahogany mantelpiece, a blazing wood fire, comfortable arm-chairs and sofas, and a splendid Chinese sculpted carpet (supplied by the Lin family) generally made this a room designed for elegance, comfort, and civilised conversation. Phryne was currently experiencing none of the above.

Mr Butler hovered nearby, one eyebrow raised interrogatively, silently asking if further refreshments should be offered. Phryne gave him the briefest of head shakes and eyed Mrs Ragnell curiously as Mr B disappeared back into the kitchen. Her visitor would be under fifty, but deep lines were scored across her face, at the corners of her wide, disagreeable mouth and between her eyebrows. This argued either myopia or habitual bad temper. Phryne was prepared to wager a modest amount on the latter. The strong, determined jaw could have been used for ramming triremes.

'Mrs Ragnell, this photograph you have given me is a useful beginning, but when did she go missing? Where was she last seen? And what is her full name?'

Her visitor snorted, plainly feeling that Phryne should be able to produce the lost girl by willpower unaided. 'Christina Elliott Forrest,' she vouchsafed after a dragging moment. 'She is eight years old, and she lives at my house. Here is my address.' She leaned forward with some difficulty, handed Phryne a visiting card, and subsided back into the chair, which creaked ominously under her considerable girth. It bore, amid some watercolour swirls, the legend *Mrs Florence Ragnell, 19 Samuels Rd, St Kilda Tel 4967.*

Phryne looked up expectantly.

The slate-blue eyes narrowed. 'We last saw her a couple of weeks ago. She ran out of the front door to play in the street, and we have not seen her since.'

Phryne gaped inwardly. 'I assume you reported her disappearance to the police?'

'Police!' Mrs Ragnell shook her head in scorn. 'What use are they? They are insolent jacks-in-office utterly incapable of tying their own shoelaces without a map and compass! And so I have come to you. You are reputed to be so clever at this sort of thing.'

Mrs Ragnell's mouth parted in what she clearly hoped was an ingratiating smile.

'I see. And what about the child's mother? Does she live with you also?'

She shook her head. 'Ellie ran away some years ago, poor girl. Such a tragedy.'

'I see. And what was Christina wearing when last you saw her?'

The top lip buried itself inside the lower in a look of mulish obstinacy. 'I…I don't remember now. Normal clothes, I expect. A dress and her red overcoat. And her galoshes.'

Phryne stood up, indicating that the interview was over. Mrs Ragnell lurched to her feet and looked Phryne straight in the eye. 'Such a dear sweet girl,' she crooned, in a voice of pure marzipan. 'You will find her for me, Miss Fisher?'

'I will do my best. Good day, Mrs Ragnell.'

What an unpleasant individual, Phryne mused. (She would normally have asked Dot for her views, but her companion was away visiting an ailing aunt with chicken soup, lemon-and-honey drinks, and relentless sympathy.) Something here did not add up. Mrs Ragnell had lost a granddaughter, declined to report it to the police, and waited a whole fortnight before reporting the child missing. On top of this, she casually volunteered the information that she had lost a daughter as well. She seemed uncommonly careless.

Phryne put on her deep blue overcoat—velvet and silk, with gold frogging on hems, collar, and cuffs—and called for Mr Butler to bring the Hispano-Suiza around to the front of the house. Her first stop would be City South police station, where, she knew, Hugh Collins would be making his indefatigable contribution to policing in the sovereign state of Victoria. And Hugh might be able to shed some light on this curious disappearance.

‑‑‑◯

'Yes, Miss Fisher, I do remember Mrs Ragnell.'

The desk sergeant knew Phryne, and thought of her as expensive trouble. If Detective Sergeant Collins was happy to see her, that was fine with him; and Phryne was permitted—most unusually—to pass into Hugh's shared office, where they sat at the plain deal table. She gave Hugh a look of concentrated sympathy. 'I expect she made your lives thoroughly wearisome.'

'Well, Miss, I wouldn't go so far as that.'

'I'm sure you wouldn't, Hugh. Your professional reticence does you great credit. I would, however. Since she didn't see fit to report to you her granddaughter's disappearance, in what circumstances did you make her acquaintance?'

Confronted with this question, Hugh Collins found himself at odds with himself. On the one hand, police officers were not supposed to proffer opinions on members of the public to other members of the public. On the other, both he and Detective Inspector Robinson liked and trusted Phryne. Add to this the fact that he had intensely disliked Mrs Ragnell on sight, and he decided that candour was not only warranted but essential.

'She lost a pearl necklace and barrelled in here demanding that we search for it.'

'And you didn't?'

'Well, no. We asked her if she had reason to believe it had been stolen, and she said that it must have been because she couldn't find it anywhere.'

'And you told her not to waste police time on lost property, and asked her to fill in a form with a description of the necklace and we'll let you know if it turns up?'

'Yes, that was about it. She was very unhappy with us and went off in a huff.'

'I see. And do you know anything about her missing granddaughter?'

Hugh grimaced. 'Miss, it's possible you might find her among the working girls.'

Phryne frowned. 'That seems very unlikely to me, Hugh, and I hope it isn't true. Christina is only eight years old. Why would you believe that?'

'Because her mother is a working girl—though we haven't seen her around much of late.'

'That's what happened to the runaway daughter! So Ellie might have taken Christina away with her.' Phryne lowered her voice. 'How do you go with working girls, at this station?'

Hugh shrugged. 'Unless there are complaints, we let them be, Miss. And nobody here's on the take, just so you know.'

'Well, I do know where the girls are wont to gather. In the absence of any other clues, I may as well ask them what they know.'

Hugh's eyebrows lifted. 'Be careful, Miss.'

'I don't think I've got anything to fear from working girls, Hugh. Thanks for the tip.' Phryne wrapped her fur coat around her and departed.

The working girls were to be found on a certain cobbled street off the main thoroughfare in South Melbourne. They were, as Phryne had expected, guarded in their speech and not inclined to share secrets with anyone. One of them told Phryne where to go and what she could do with herself when she got there and another offered her a long waxed match. Phryne declined both the instruction and the match, handed over a penny and passed on. She had her eye on a likely source on the corner of the street: younger than the rest and with an unlined face. Phryne lit a cigarette in her long black holder and inhaled deeply. She contrived to suggest that she was going nowhere in a hurry; that she was not here to evangelise anyone; and that expensive cigarettes might be included in any conversation. Presently the girl approached, and Phryne held out her gold cigarette case. 'Care for a gasper?'

The girl accepted a cigarette and a light from Phryne and looked her over. A pale, fine-boned face with intelligent green eyes and a small, determined mouth. Her black hair was cut short and her street attire—most notably the silk and velvet winter coat in blue and gold—was dazzling beyond the reckoning of these mean streets. The girl looked at her with frank curiosity. 'Miss, I can't place you at all,' she said. 'You don't look like one o' them God-botherers. And I doubt you're looking for trade. I saw Dulcie give you the bum's rush and you didn't seem to care at all. So what *do* you want?' Phryne showed the girl the photograph supplied by Mrs Ragnell.

'I'm looking for Christina. Have you seen her?'

The girl's features instantly set into a flat mask. 'I'm sorry; I can't help you there. Gone missing, has she?'

Phryne looked the girl full in the face. I see, she mused. You aren't saying you haven't seen her, are you? Just that you can't help me. Curiouser and curiouser. 'Yes, she has. You don't know a woman called Ellie, do you?'

The girl's face froze still further. Phryne decided that a degree of candour would be required. 'I am a private detective.' She handed over her business card and the girl stared at it. 'You may have heard of me. I don't intend to find anyone who doesn't want to be found, but I am beginning to suspect foul play and I would appreciate as many answers as you feel you can give me. If you can't tell me about Christina, please tell me anything you know about Ellie.'

The girl looked up. 'Ellie was ... one of us, but she disappeared a few weeks ago. There's been a few who've gone missing. We don't know what to think and, well, we're scared, Miss.' She stared at the card again. 'Look, I'm sorry, Miss Fisher. I can't tell you anything more. Thanks for the smoke.' With that, the girl disappeared around the corner.

Phryne lit another gasper and considered her next move. A visit to her sister would seem to be in order. Eliza and Lady Alice Harborough—now plain Miss Alice Beaconsfield to all she met on these fatal shores—lived in a small flat on Beaconsfield Parade, quite near Phryne's house, and devoted themselves to good works among the poor. They might know something about Ellie, and possibly even Christina.

~~⌇~~

Eliza was delighted to see her sister. Her philanthropic work seemed to have improved both her spirits and her temper, and she hugged Phryne impulsively. 'Come in and have some tea!'

'Yes thanks. I'd love a chat. Her Ladyship not home?'

Eliza's face split into a grin. 'She's gone to see a member of the government to give him a hard time. Come and sit in the kitchen, then.'

Her sister's flat was in a building made of brick and bluestone, and its interior was small, unpretentious, and filled with books and notepads. It was scrupulously clean and tidy otherwise, however. There seemed to be a lot of G.B. Shaw, and Beatrice and Sidney Webb's massive tomes were also in evidence, bristling with bookmarks. Eliza and Alice were committed Fabians, and the Webbs and Shaw were the high priests and chief prophets of gradualist socialism. Eliza made a pot of tea and offered Phryne a cup, which she sipped without enthusiasm.

'What is Alice seeing the government about?' Phryne enquired, putting down her cup.

'Working girls. We know it's unlikely we'll get prostitution legalised: there're so many cops on the take that the police are dead against legalisation. It's all just part of—'

Phryne, smiling, raised her right hand.

Eliza paused mid-harangue. 'Sorry, Phryne,' she said. 'I mustn't treat my own sister like a public meeting. Anyway, you know all this, don't you?'

'I do. And it's funny you mentioned the working girls, because that's what I've come to talk to you about.'

Eliza leaned forward over the table, all attention. 'Any in particular?'

'You know the girls who solicit in South Melbourne?'

'Yes, I do. The local cops don't bother them much, because they're honest—the cops, I mean—and they've got too much else to worry about. Why do you want to know?'

'I'm interested in a woman called Ellie who disappeared a few weeks ago.'

Eliza sat back in her chair and frowned. 'Disappeared? That doesn't sound right. She caught pneumonia and was taken to a private hospital run by a friend of ours, Dr James. He looks after the girls when they're sick, and he does it for free. He's independently wealthy, you see—but he's a good man and very strong in The Cause.'

'I see.' Phryne thought about this. 'Did you know Ellie had a daughter? She's eight, apparently, and she's missing too.'

'No, I didn't. But you must be talking about a different Ellie. The girl Dr James is caring for is no more than twenty. She can't possibly have an eight-year-old child.'

'No, I suppose not.'

They chatted of this and that, retreating to the back garden to smoke, since Her Ladyship did not approve of smoking and would not allow it in the house. By the time Phryne took her leave it was late afternoon and the winter dusk was beginning to close in. It was a long shot, but her detective instincts silently urged her to return to the South Melbourne beat.

Two of the women on the grimy footpath squared their shoulders, preparing to repel boarders, but presently went into a brief huddle. Their aggressive poses relaxed and they waved her through. Phryne turned a corner and saw a small child in a grey overcoat holding a long package. A man approached her and she handed something over. Phryne caught a glimpse of a penny piece, which disappeared into the child's coat pocket.

Phryne approached. When she was a few yards away, the child turned a pair of bright blue eyes on her. A long cardboard packet was thrust out in front of her. 'Matches, Miss? Guaranteed waterproof, only a penny.'

Phryne presented her with a penny. 'Thank you,' she said. 'I hope this is red phosphorus and not white?'

The child clasped her hands around the box. 'Yes, Miss. You use sandpaper to make it light. White phosphorus is very danger-ous!' she announced with the air of one imparting state secrets.

'It is indeed. My name's Phryne. What's yours?'

The child looked carefully at her. Her hair was blonde and framed a face filled with optimism and wariness in equal measure. Eventually a decision was reached. 'Christina.'

'I thought it might be. Aren't you a bit young to be out on the streets alone?'

She shook her head with emphasis. 'No, because I've got Bear. Mummy gave me to Bear, and he looks after me. And the ladies won't let bad men come near me either.'

'May I see Bear?' Phryne enquired.

Again the blonde head shook.

'No. Bear doesn't want to see you.'

Phryne did some fast thinking. Clearly this was the missing child, but it was equally plain that Christina was under the protection of the street women. Until Phryne knew far more, there was no point in attempting to persuade Christina to go anywhere. The child's unearthly self-possession declared that there was a lot going on here beneath the surface.

'Well, it's very pleasant to meet you, Christina. If I need another match tomorrow, will you be here then?'

The girl gave her a look of shattering directness. 'Yes.'

'And will Bear be here tomorrow?'

'Maybe.'

'All right. See you then, Christina.'

Phryne turned her back on Christina and left the narrow street. The skin between her shoulder blades was itching uncontrollably, which could only mean that unseen eyes were watching her every move. She returned to the Hispano-Suiza and drove home in deep thought.

~~~

Next morning, Phryne went into the city to visit the Registrar of Births, Deaths, and Marriages in Lonsdale Street. Everything about Phryne's conversation with the child had been unnerving. Most alarming of all was the statement that 'Mummy gave me to Bear.' Teddy bears did not generally have custody of children, and unless this particular Bear were possessed of supernatural powers it was probable he was a man. But what manner of man was he, to accept runaway children? Perhaps the Bear was Christina's father. Mrs Ragnell had not volunteered anything at all about Christina's parentage. Maybe the father had been what was euphemistically known as an unsuitable match. The only

way to find any answers, in this miasma of mystery and conceal-
ment, was to see for herself what the city's records might show.

She left the building at two thirty in a silent, fuming rage. The
black letters on the yellowing pages danced in front of her eyes.
It had taken her hours to find out the missing pieces, but there
they all were. On 1 March 1908 Florence May Ragnell, aged
twenty, had given birth to May Elliott Ragnell. The father was
unknown. And on 5 June 1921 May Elliott Ragnell had given
birth to Christina Elliott Forrest, father unknown. She wondered
where the Forrest had come into the picture, since the girl was
clearly illegitimate—like her mother, who had been debauched
by a person or persons unknown at the all-too-tender age of
twelve. The final entry had been May Elliott Ragnell, died 14
April 1929. Cause of death: Pneumonia. Certified by Dr Henry
James. Whereupon, recalling that her informant of the day before
had expressed concern over a number of disappearances among
her colleagues, Phryne's thumbs had pricked and she went on
searching among the more recent deaths. And there they were.
Jane Lawrence, milliner, aged twenty; Florence Gorey, seamstress,
aged twenty-seven; Mildred Smith, milliner, aged thirty. And in
each case, the annotation: *Cause of Death: Pneumonia. Certified
by Dr Henry James.*

There being no better plan on offer, Phryne waited until
almost five before she left the house again and returned to the
footpath in South Melbourne. And there was Christina, holding
her cardboard box of matches. She did not seem at all surprised
to see Phryne. 'Bear told me you'd be back,' she announced.

'And here I am,' Phryne answered, handing over another penny.
'May I see Bear now?'

The girl looked at the gunmetal sky for a moment, then nodded. She pocketed the penny and handed over another match.
'All right. Come with me.'

The child skipped along the cobbles, turned at the next corner, and beckoned. Phryne followed slowly, unsure as to whether or not she was walking into a trap. But the street turned out to be a quiet cul-de-sac entirely innocent of menace. Christina pushed open the front gate to a small but well-tended cottage. A golden light shone out through a small gap in the curtains. 'Bear says you should wait here.' She had, it seemed, her own key to the front door. She let herself in and shut it behind her.

Phryne waited for she knew not what in the utterly silent street. Presently the door opened again and a looming figure walked down the narrow path towards her. Two massive ebony hands laid themselves on the gate, and she found herself looking up the mountainous slopes of a giant. He must have been six foot seven at least, and nearly as broad across his mighty chest and shoulders. Phryne was staring at a blue button well below the collar of a check shirt.

'Hello there,' the man announced. The accent was distinctive to say the least: a gentle Southern drawl from the formerly Confederate States of America. 'Might I know your name?'

Phryne handed him her business card. The giant read it then nodded.

'Come in, Miss Fisher. My wife will make you tea.'

Phryne prided herself on never being at a loss, but she could do little but await further revelations. She followed as she was bidden into the parlour, and sat herself in a chair. She gave her host a winning smile. 'Well, sir, you know my name. Might I know yours?'

In one corner of the room was an oversize chair which presumably had been built to order from a decommissioned sailing ship. The man sat himself in it and extended his hands on the thick wooden armrests. 'I am Bear, Miss Fisher. And Christina is my adoptive daughter.'

Phryne's mouth opened in surprise. 'Oh. I see. As you can imagine, there are those who would contest that statement. I am retained by Mrs Ragnell, who would rather like her granddaughter back. *Is* Christina her granddaughter, do you think?'

'Yes, ma'am—in blood, she is. Now, I'm not goin' to use harsh language about that lady, but she is not a good woman, Miss Fisher.'

'That may well be the case, Mr Bear.' Phryne paused for a moment. 'I'm sorry, but do you have another name?'

Bear folded his hands across his Herculean chest and shook his head. 'Bear is good enough for me, Miss. I was the Black Bear once, out of Montgomery, Alabama. I was a tent boxer and there ain't nobody that ever beat me. I was part of a travelling circus, which I will decline to name, and the owner of that circus set to thinkin' he owned me. Now I know you will say we was all emancipated in 1865, but there sure are a lot of white folks back home who hain't quite cottoned on to that. I have been showed off as a circus freak right across the United States. I kept my thoughts to myself until we landed here in Melbourne, where I jumped ship.' He grinned again, showing perfect white teeth in a red mouth which had, Phryne considered, considerable gentleness in it. 'The boss, he complained somewhat, but I told him that the great Lord Mansfield had made a judgement. *The air of England is too pure for any slave to breathe! The first breath he takes is as a free man!* And I figured that the laws of Britain hold true here as well.'

'And was your boss happy with this piece of jurisprudence?'

'He was not, but there weren't nothing he could do. I walked free, and he paid me what he owed me. He did not want to, but I was very persuasive.'

Phryne laughed. 'I am very sure you were, Bear. Now may I ask: what do you want with Christina?'

Bear had just opened his mouth to speak when Mrs Bear

entered with a silver tea set and two cups of white tea, a sugar bowl, and a plate of shortbread. Phryne watched her with interest. She was small and slim, well dressed in a black trouser suit, and her sharp, thin face was vibrant with goodwill. 'Here you are, dear.'

She returned Phryne's scrutiny. 'I've heard about you, Miss Fisher. Chrissie told me you'd come looking for her. But you'll do right by us, won't you?' She inclined her face, which Bear held with exquisite gentleness and kissed on the cheek.

'Now don't you fear, Rosie. I'm sure Miss Fisher won't do nothin' rash.'

When Rosie had left the room again, Bear gave Phryne a penetrating look. 'Rosie can't have children of her own,' he explained. 'She used to be a working girl, and that can be something of a problem if you want to bear children thereafter. But she met me, and I married her, and I bought this house for us with my circus wages. I'm proud of my Rosie. She's a good woman, and that's why the working girls keep an eye out for Christina. They know 'bout her, and they know 'bout Mrs Ragnell.'

'And Ellie? Christina's mother?' Phryne prompted.

The easy smile vanished, replaced by a stern, suspicious look.

'Miss Fisher, what do you know of her?'

'More than you might think.' Phryne leaned forward in her chair, sipped her tea and looked Bear straight in the face. 'Would I be right in supposing that Mrs Ragnell has similar plans for Christina?'

The expression on the man's face told Phryne she had guessed right.

'Miss Fisher, have you met a man called Forrest?'

'I have not had that dubious pleasure. And please, Bear, I urge you to restrain yourself—for Christina's sake. By the way, why is she selling matches in the street?'

'She believes that everyone should earn an honest living, Miss

Fisher. Rosie works in a shop now. And I'—he leaned back in his chair, all too conscious of his gigantic strength—'I am employed to keep order in certain public houses. Christina declared that she wanted to work too. And so we let her sell matches when she is not in school. No harm will come to her in this neighbourhood.'

Phryne stood up. 'Thank you for your time, Bear. I intend to tell Mrs Ragnell that her granddaughter cannot be found.'

Bear stood up also, his head slightly bent so it did not brush the low ceiling. 'Why thank you, ma'am. This has been a pleasure.'

Phryne returned to her car in thoughtful silence. She would need to telephone Dr MacMillan. Then there were two more visits to make tomorrow and then the case would be finished. One visit would be very unpleasant; the other less so.

～ら

'Miss Fisher!' Mrs Ragnell greeted Phryne with enthusiasm and ushered her into the sitting room. 'You have news?'

Phryne surveyed her ghastly surrounds—all chintz wallpaper and gimcrack furniture—and stared with disfavour at a loathsome object sitting in an armchair adjacent to Mrs Ragnell. He was large, portly, and wearing evening dress. He rose properly, made the most perfunctory of bows, and settled back in his seat. He had the sort of moustache that looked as though a caterpillar was making its way across his lip preparatory to disappearing up one nostril. His weak, ingratiating expression and watery blue eyes made Phryne want to hit him in the face with a half-brick.

Mrs Ragnell caught Phryne's look and clasped her hands together. 'This is Mr Forrest. Such a comfort to a poor old woman alone in the world.'

'The pleasure is all yours, Mr Forrest,' Phryne ventured.

Both faces gave a look of clouded puzzlement.

'Mrs Ragnell, I am sorry to say that your daughter Ellie is, alas, deceased, and Christina has emigrated to Queensland. She has left instructions to the effect that she has found a happy home and that no correspondence will be entered into.'

Phryne scrutinised both faces with the utmost care. While they were decidedly weather-beaten, the matching expressions were exactly those of children whose ice creams have melted and fallen out of their cones onto the footpath. Christina was more adult than the two of them together. Suddenly, Mrs Ragnell's features rearranged themselves into what she plainly imagined was moral outrage.

'Really! This is outrageous! The child is far too young to know what's best for her, Miss Fisher!'

'And you do?' Phryne enquired, raking both of them with a freezing stare. 'After all, you took such good care of Ellie, did you not?'

'Oh.' Mrs Ragnell began to speak further, but her voice trailed away into incoherent nothings. Elliott Forrest beamed at Phryne as if he expected another ice cream would manifest itself.

Phryne continued remorselessly. 'I regret that I have had to expend considerable sums in order to discover these facts. My fee will be thirty shillings. Cash.'

Mrs Ragnell looked to Forrest, who disinterred a greasy leather wallet from the unwholesome recesses of his costume and handed over three ten-shilling notes.

Phryne stowed them in her handbag and gave an airy wave. 'Sorry, must dash. People to see and all that.'

She let herself out into the street and took a deep breath. Well, that was the fun bit.

Phryne drove to Dr James's hospital, filled with foreboding. He turned out to be a pleasant young man with a face far too lined for his thirtyish years. He received her in his private surgery and shook her hand, offering a smile of unutterable weariness.

'Miss Fisher, is it? How may I help you?'

'Dr James, you are in a great deal of trouble. I am hoping that *I* can help *you*.'

Phryne watched as the meagre colour in his pallid features drained away. He shook his head in silent despair. Finally he spoke, as if expecting to hear the angel blowing the Last Trump. 'Is this about one of my, er, female patients?' he murmured.

'You've lost four working girls this month, Dr James. You've been helping them out of their misery, haven't you? You look on their wretchedness and you think: how much pain can humankind endure? Now, Ellie never had much of a chance in life. I know her story. Sold off at twelve by her mother to a degenerate lecher; ran away from home onto the streets of South Melbourne. She caught syphilis, did she?'

James shook his head. 'Just gonorrhoea—which isn't much better. We don't have enough medicines to cure them properly. And there isn't enough morphia in all the world to cure their sorrows.'

Phryne leaned forward and lifted the drooping chin with her right forefinger. 'All the same, you cannot keep euthanasing them. Four deaths this month? That's too many! This is getting to be a bad habit.'

'I know.' If Dr James had been any lower in his seat he would have curled into a fetal ball.

'Dr James, look at me.'

He did so, raising dead grey eyes to hers.

'You are quite, quite mad. Later this afternoon, Dr Elizabeth MacMillan is coming here to assess you. I expect she will find you unfit to plead to the fourfold murders you have committed. I gather you have private means? Use them, Dr James! You may have the run of the best sanatorium Melbourne has to offer. One thing you are not going to do any more is play God with street girls. You are a good and worthy man who has fallen into a chasm of despair. Now do exactly as I tell you and you will not be hanged. Do you understand me?'

The man shook his head, put both hands to his face and began to weep.

Phryne allowed him ten seconds' grief then slapped him hard across the face. 'Come on!' she urged. 'Play up, and play the game. Grammar expects no less.'

He blinked at her. 'Grammar? How did you know that?'

'I made enquiries. It's what I do, you know. Now, do you know what *you* have to do?'

This time he slapped his own cheeks. Such neat hands, too. His white coat hung sadly from shrunken shoulders. 'Yes, I think so.' He looked Phryne in the eye. 'I think you're right, you know. I am mad, aren't I?'

'Mad as a spoon. Good luck!'

As Phryne left the hospital, she allowed herself a smile. No, that wasn't fun. But returning again to Christina's happy home and handing over Elliott Forrest's thirty bob to Bear and Rosie— now that was going to be visitation of pure joy.

A Matter of Style

With store of ladies, whose bright eyes
Rain influence, and judge the prize
Of wit, or arms, while both contend
To win her grace, whom all commend.

—John Milton, *L'Allegro*

On a bright winter's morning, the Hon. Phryne Fisher repaired, as was her fortnightly wont, to the Salon de Paris in Port Melbourne for a trim. She liked Madame Latour and spoke French to her. Madame ran a fine French-style salon and was more patient with her snobbish clients than Phryne would have been. She parked the Hispano-Suiza directly outside Salon de Paris and entered with considerable perplexity. In the general course of events the salon was a place of quiet contemplation. It smelled of comfort, quiet efficiency, and unguents. Brushes, combs, and scissors were flourished. American oilcloth flooring was swept at least twice an hour. Conversation was pleasantly fitful, discreetly gossipy, and carried out at a steady mezzo piano above the whirring hum of the hair-styling machines. They looked menacing. Phryne had never regretted cutting her own hair short, long ago.

The Salon de Paris this Thursday morning was anything but quiet. And at the centre of events was Mrs Daphne Ballard, orating on the subject of Items Missing as though she were addressing the multitudes from Hyde Park Corner. She was by no means the only orator—Mrs Jones was quietly complaining about a missing necklet, while Mrs Jenkins was bemoaning a missing hairclip in a muted alto continuo—but Mrs Ballard was the undisputed soloist in the dolorous ensemble.

Phryne pursed her lips in vexation. Most of Mme Latour's clients were respectable housewives who came for their monthly brush with Gallic exoticism as Madame spoke Paris-accented English to them, with a sprinkling of French phrases carefully pruned of grammatical complexity. The customers were generally pleasant enough, and could be relied upon to deal gently with Madame's hard-working staff—all except for Mrs Ballard. She was the wife of the local Member of Parliament: a shy, meek-tempered man with a stammer who kept his public utterances mercifully brief in consequence. His wife had sufficient temper for them both, with enough left over for a trade union rally and a bar-room brawl. One of the girls had once called her Mrs Bollard to her face. Doubtless a slip of the tongue, but a splendidly apposite one: Mrs Ballard was cylindrical in shape, with a fiercely proud head like a bad-tempered torpedo. And today she was giving of her best.

'Utterly disgraceful I call it. Last week Miss Garland's opal ear-ring went missing. As if that were not sufficient, today my best silk scarf has been stolen right under my nose by one of your thieving girls! It cost me ten pounds at Georges, you know. What are you going to do about it, Mme Latour—if that really is your name?'

'*Calmez-vous, Madame, je vous en prie.*' Mme Latour was a slight woman with cropped black hair just like Phryne's. She was leaning against one of the styling machines and visibly taking her own advice as best she could. 'Perhaps it has fallen to the floor and been swept up with the *cheveux*? I will institute enquiries immediately.'

The supporting chorus had by now fallen silent. Still relishing being the centre of attention, Mrs Ballard stood with both hands on her hips. 'See that you do. I will give you twenty-four hours to recover it. I shall return here tomorrow at this hour. I expect you then to return my scarf and Miss Garland's earring…' She paused for a moment, suddenly cognisant that she was not alone in bereavement today. She waved a dismissive hand at both Mrs Jones and Mrs Jenkins. 'And everything else that has gone missing in this den of thievery! Twenty-four hours, Madame, and if the Items Missing are not returned I intend to call the police and lay a complaint against you and your shop. Good day to you.' And out she swept, in the highest dudgeon Port Melbourne had seen since the police strike.

Phryne looked around the room. Two women sat under the whirring headpieces, looking uncomfortable and embarrassed. Another sat in a high chair reading a newspaper while her hair was being clipped, utterly oblivious to all around her. One of the assistants was staring at the still-vibrating front door with an expression of loathing. Jean the manicurist stood motionless, leaning against the side wall as white and frozen as vanilla ice cream.

Mme Latour gave Phryne an emphatic, if martyred, look, and Phryne moved to her side. 'Madame? A word in private, if you will?'

Mme Latour's eyes fixed upon Phryne with a sudden surge of hope. 'Carry on, *mesdames*, if you would be so good,' she implored her customers and staff, and gestured with her small, beringed hand.

Phryne followed the Frenchwoman into her private sanctuary. It was a tiny office with a small table, two chairs, a telephone, and a stout wooden door, which Madame shut with finality and leaned against.

'*Quelle cochon!*' Madame muttered. 'Oh, Miss Fisher, what am I to do?'

'Please sit down and tell me everything,' Phryne encouraged. 'Although you can leave out Mrs Ballard. I heard it all. They probably heard her on number four dock.'

Madame explained that Edna had been in charge of Mrs Jones's styling, while Elsie had been ministering to Mrs Jenkins.

'What about Miss Garland and her opal earring?'

Madame took out a lace handkerchief and dabbed her eyes with it. 'Oh, Miss Fisher! Miss Garland left on Friday in a good humour, but rang later to ask if we had seen her earring because she had missed it.'

'One moment. Did she have any hair dressings applied?'

Madame leaned back in her chair and considered. 'I am not sure. But I remember that it was Jean who attended on her. I will call her in, perhaps?'

'Please do.'

Madame exited the room and returned a moment later with Jean, who stood to attention with her hands clasped tight.

'Jean, I want you to tell Miss Fisher about Miss Garland last Friday.'

Jean opened her mouth to speak but nothing emerged.

'No one's accusing you of anything,' Phryne said reassuringly. 'I just want to know whether you applied any liquid dressing to Miss Garland's hair.'

Jean's narrow shoulders relaxed somewhat. 'Oh. Yes, I believe I did. Why? Is it important?'

Phryne inclined her head. 'Well, yes it is, Jean. If you did, you would have asked her to take off her earring, because opals are a fruit of the desert sands and cannot abide moisture. Did you do that?'

Jean nodded. 'Yes, I did. She also took off her rings for the manicure. Then I trimmed her hair and put some dressing on it. Before that I took her earring out—she only had the one, on her left ear—and put it on the side table with her rings.'

'And you gave back her rings when you'd finished? What about the earring?'

Jean screwed up her face and closed her eyes. 'Yes. I saw the rings on her hands again. And the earring? I put it back, I'm sure. Though perhaps I didn't fasten it properly.'

'So it could have fallen out on her way home?' Phryne prompted.

'Yes! Yes, it could have done. Madame, I am so sorry. Please don't give me the sack! I'll be more careful, I promise.'

'It is no doubt as you say, Jean,' interposed Madame. 'Very well, you may go.'

Jean rushed out of the room, all but collapsing with relief.

Madame looked at Phryne. 'And the scarf? Do you have any ideas, Miss Fisher?'

Phryne nodded. 'Let me be sure first, but yes, I believe so. Was Mrs Ballard wearing her scarf when she arrived?'

'I can swear to it. It was a hideous thing. Turquoise and apricot together? *Non!* It was a horror. And it cannot have left the salon, since no one has departed since she arrived. Must we search my girls? I said it might have been swept away on the floor, but it is truly *impossible.*'

'I see. Did she sit under one of the machines?'

'*Mais oui,* Miss Fisher.'

'Please show me which one.'

To a suddenly enthralled and silent audience, Phryne was conducted to the machine—now safely inert—and reached into its gaping maw. She withdrew her hand and held the missing scarf aloft triumphantly. Hands joined in spontaneous applause, and Phryne grinned at Madame. '*Voilà!*' she announced, and presented the turquoise-and-orange monstrosity to Madame with the slightest of bows.

'Wait just a minute.' Phryne rummaged further inside a second machine and brought out a silver-ish necklet and a hairclip. She handed the hairclip to Mrs Jenkins and the necklet to Mrs Jones, and gestured to a brass pin attached to Mrs Ballard's scarf. 'Madame, I think there may be some loose magnets inside these machines. You might think about getting them seen to.'

With that, Phryne relaxed into one of the chairs while Elsie attended to her trim. Phryne was watching the clock and watching Jean, who returned her a nervous look. Phryne locked eyes with her and inclined her head towards the shop door. Jean nodded, tight-lipped.

After Phryne left the shop, she loitered in Bay Street, ostensibly window-shopping. Presently Jean was standing beside her outside a florist's. The girl was trembling. 'Jean, are you on your lunch break?'

'Yes, Miss.'

'There's a decent teashop over there. Let's eat some lunch. And then you are going to tell me all about it.'

Jean's murmur of acquiescence would not have drowned out the alighting of a butterfly. Phryne took the girl into the shop, where she ordered chicken sandwiches and a pot of tea. The girl ate in terrorised silence until Phryne set down her teacup.

'All right, Jean. I have not denounced you. Not yet. Instead I took you to lunch. And in return, you are going to tell me exactly what you did with Miss Garland's earring. It was a good story you told, but I don't believe a word of it. You gave her back her rings, and when she didn't ask for her earring back you slipped it into your purse and took it home. Where is it now, Jean? Please tell me you still have it.'

Jean shook her head. She began to rock from side to side, and her slender hands were clutching at nothing.

Phryne reached out and gripped both hands tight. 'Jean, we have very little time. Tell me now, and perhaps we can fix this. If you just sit there trembling like a she-oak in a winter gale I can't do anything to help you. I don't believe you wanted the earring for yourself. Did someone else put you up to stealing it?'

This got a reaction. The girl swallowed, shook her head, and silent tears rolled down her thin cheeks. 'It's Matt, my boyfriend,' she whimpered.

Phryne nodded. 'And Matt is always down on his luck. He lost his job, and he told you there must be lots of chances in a salon to walk off with unattended jewellery. And he said if you really loved him you'd do it, and you did.'

This brought a silent, tearful nod.

'Where is Miss Garland's earring now, Jean?'

Jean folded her hands before her breast and looked more stricken than ever. 'He pawned it!' she whispered.

Phryne thought for a moment. 'All right, Jean. Here is what you are going to do. This afternoon, straight after work, you are going to see Matt and demand that he give you the pawn ticket. Warn him that he'll be going to jail if he doesn't do as you say.'

The girl was trembling all over. 'Oh, Miss, I couldn't! It's just ...' She looked positively frightened at the prospect and it occurred to Phryne that the boyfriend might well be violent as well as shiftless and stupid.

In a softer tone she said, 'In that case, tell me where Matt lives and I will see for myself what can be done.'

Jean took a deep breath. 'He lives at twenty-one Hodges Street in South Melbourne.'

Phryne took out her notebook and wrote down the address. 'And what is Matt's last name?'

'Strong. And he really is strong, Miss—plus he's got a temper on him. Please be careful!'

'Oh, believe me, I shall be.' Phryne grinned at the girl, whose face began to clear. If it was not exactly the breaking of dawn in her eye, it was certainly the glimmer of the morning star of hope.

Number 21 Hodges Street turned out to be a rundown boarding house. Weeds grew plentifully all over the sprawling garden. Three rosebushes, badly pruned, had given up their attempts to add some colour to the dreary ambience.

Through the open front door of the house Phryne could see a middle-aged woman in a grey smock mopping the hallway. She glared up at Phryne. 'Yair? Whadder ya want, missus?'

'I am looking for Matt Strong. Is he at home?'

The woman plucked a cigarette end from behind her ear, lit it, and took a feverish pull on it. 'Youse can bloody have 'im, for all I care. Bloody useless lump that 'e is. You'll find 'im out the back in the shed, prob'ly. I ain't even askin' what 'e does there.' Beady, slate-grey eyes glared at Phryne. 'Go on! Don't bloody well mind me!'

Phryne walked down the dingy corridor. Faint groaning noises emerged from behind closed doors. She ignored them and thrust open the back door in time to see a strapping lad of twenty or so sauntering up the brick pathway. He saw Phryne and stopped dead in his tracks.

'Hello, Matt,' she began. 'I just wanted to let you know that the police are on their way, and your only chance of avoiding six months' hard labour is to give me that pawn ticket right now.'

What a specimen, she thought with disgust. Slack mouth, unshaven chin, grimy blue shirt, repellent brown trousers, old boots with the heels gone, and withal an aroma of greasy self-regard unsupported by the faintest vestige of merit. Leaning against the clothesline, he crossed his muscular arms. 'Dunno what you're talkin' about, lady,' he drawled.

Phryne gave him a winning smile. 'The pawn ticket for the opal earring which you persuaded your girlfriend to steal from her workplace. It's in your pocket, isn't it? It's unlikely you'd leave anything in your room in a squalid boarding house like this. Hand it over, Matthew, or the prison doors will slam on your sorry carcass and real hard men will belt the stuffing out of you night and day, just for fun. Got that?'

After searching his visitor's face in vain for any sign of mercy, Matt reached into his trouser pocket and handed over the pawn ticket, which Phryne slipped into her purse.

'Thank you, Matthew.' Phryne inclined her chin towards him. 'And just so you know, if you ever go anywhere near Jean again, I will hunt you down with a blunt knife and carve my initials in your liver. Good day!'

Mrs Ballard's triumphal progress to the Salon de Paris concluded at precisely eleven a.m. She swept into the shop with a pale, embarrassed girl in her train and beheld Madame Latour with an eye that would have transfixed a charging bison. 'Well, Madame? What have you to say to us?'

Madame smiled softly. Her eye swept around her four other customers, who appeared to be smirking, and proceeded to her office door, which creaked open. Phryne emerged, walked up to one of the machines, reached her hand inside the works and produced the scarf and the opal earring. They shone in her upturned hand.

'These machines are still in their infancy, you see,' she explained. 'Doubtless one day someone will invent a hairdressing cone which does not imbibe customers' personal belongings. Until that day, you would be well advised to doff them before entrusting yourself to the wonders of modern hairdressing. And you would be even better advised to be far more cautious about strewing wild accusations as though you were feeding the ducks on Albert Park Lake, Mrs Bollard!'

Mrs Ballard inflated like a balloon. 'My name is *Ballard*, Miss Fisher. And my husband is a Member of Parl—'

'And he will scarcely thank you for causing him public embarrassment. I can just see the headlines in *The Hawklet*, can't you, Mrs Bollard?'

Mrs Ballard's swelling features turned bright crimson. 'You wouldn't dare!'

'Would I not? You seem very confident.'

Mrs Ballard drew in a giant breath, as if stoking a furnace full of coal. 'Well!' she steamed. 'I shall certainly not darken the doors of this establishment again, let me tell you.'

Madame Latour stepped forward, took the scarf from Phryne and handed it to her now-deflating guest. '*Quel dommage*, Madame. But I shall moderate my grief. *Au revoir!*'

Seeing no alternative, Mrs Ballard exited the building, and there was a general exhaling and a relaxation of tension. Miss Garland walked over to Phryne. She was smiling. 'My thanks, Miss Fisher. And my apologies, Madame. And to you all. Good morning.'

Phryne handed over the earring and Miss Garland made her more graceful departure.

'*Mille remerciements*, Miss Fisher.' Madame allowed herself a taut smile. 'If you would care to join me in my office for a small moment?'

'*Certainement.*'

When the door was shut and both were seated, Madame looked Phryne over. 'Miss Fisher, you are miraculous. How did you contrive it?'

'I was fortunate, Madame.'

'Such a foolish girl, that Jean. Please tell me that she has shown the door to her *cochon* of a boy?'

'I believe I have frightened him off. You will not dismiss her, I hope?'

'No. Not if the boyfriend stays away from her. She is a good girl at heart and she has learned her lesson. I hope it did not cost you much?'

'Ten bob at the pawn shop.' Phryne grinned. 'It was worth every penny to be able to give that vile Bollard a telling-off. And I hope you will not lose custom?'

Madame chuckled. 'Now that she does not return to my salon, I shall gain more customers, I think. I weary of social climbers. The respectable middle class is what I want here.'

'*Toujours la bourgeoisie, vraiment.* Madame? Since we are in private, may I ask you a personal question?'

The small, pointed chin jutted downwards. 'So long as the answer does not leave this room, yes.'

'Madame Latour, are you really from Paris?'

Madame's lips parted in joyous mischief. 'To you only I tell this, Miss Fisher, trusting in your discretion.' She glanced at the door. 'My name is Maisie Field, Miss Fisher. I have never been closer to France than Moonee Ponds. If I attempt it, I might be able to reproduce the vowels of North Port, where I was born. But what would you? Better I do not, lest they emerge unbidden. To my customers I am Madame Latour from Paris, for who would come to the Salon de Maisie Field?'

'I see. Madame—for so I shall call you always—your French is very good.'

'For Maisie from North Port, perhaps.'

'Wherever did you learn it?'

'Night school. I did Intermediate French at high school but that does not go far, so I attended the Alliance Française in the evenings. M. Dupont was an exacting teacher, but he pronounced me passable.'

'Indeed. Well, Madame, your secret is secure. I am delighted to have assisted you.'

Maisie Field rose and shook Phryne's hand. *'Bon d'accord.'*

The Chocolate Factory

And ever against eating cares
Lap me in soft Lydian airs,
Married to immortal verse
Such as the meeting soul may pierce…

—John Milton, *L'Allegro*

Phryne sat in her front parlour, arrayed in a crimson peignoir, looking down at a sleeping Ember, who was curled up in blissful content on her lap. She inhaled the autumn breeze which wandered through her open window, bringing the scents of salt, seaweed, and languor. Seated at an easel on the other side of the fireplace, a thin young woman was putting the final touches to her portrait. The painter wore the obligatory cap, from which a few stray black hairs had escaped their confines. She was wrapped in the customary artist's smock—an austere grey—which had far fewer daubs of paint on it than was usual. Stroking Ember's blissfully purring charcoal head, Phryne watched Miss Carson. Neat was what she was. Her thin lips pursed from time to time, her slate-grey eyes flickered back and forth, and her brush dipped into the globs of paint on her palette with all the precision of a sparrow picking up crumbs from the ground.

'I think that will do,' Miss Carson declared. 'Would you like to have a squiz?'

Phryne rose and proceeded to the canvas.

Miss Carson gave her a quick grin. 'What do you think?'

Phryne admired. She saw herself in her peignoir, smiling complacently and looking down at her sleeping black kitten. Phryne's gold-framed mirror was strategically placed so that it was a double portrait. A second Phryne and Ember looked out from within the glass. The surrounding background was a sage-green which did not reflect her own jazz-coloured walls. Miss Carson pointed with a paint-stained finger. 'I thought your actual wallpaper would be too distracting, Phryne.'

'I see. It's beautiful. I hope Madame likes it.' Phryne had agreed to sit at the urging of her friend Mme Charpentier, who intended to make a print of the painting to use for the box of her new chocolate assortment. 'I think she's calling this collection Dark Lady, which I suppose I am. I hope she's paying you for this?'

Miss Carson took off her smock, folded it, and deposited it into her capacious satchel. 'Of course. She said she'll invite you over as soon as the first box comes off the production line. Now, where did I put the rose madder?'

～◦

That had been two months ago. As it happened there was no need for Phryne to make the crossing to Footscray. On a dark winter's evening a car pulled up outside Phryne's house. A uniformed lad opened the front gate and knocked on the door. Mr Butler inclined an interrogative head. 'Yes?'

'Miss Phryne Fisher?'

'This is her residence. How may I assist you, young sir?'

'Package for her.'

Overawed by Mr B's magisterial presence the lad handed him a large cardboard box and fled back to the security of the car.

Phryne opened the box, to an excited audience of Ruth, Jane, and Ember. Within was a cloud of shredded paper. 'Cats don't eat chocolate. But you may have this instead.' She put the rustling box on the floor and Ember dived in headlong and began to burrow and shred. Phryne held aloft a dark red carton. On the front was the portrait, with the words *Dark Lady* in an ornate serif font. She placed it on the table and opened it. 'Girls, you may have one each. Choose carefully.'

Ruth and Jane stared at the contents then pored over the underside of the lid, which gave a map of the flavours. Not that this was strictly necessary, since the attar of roses were carved into rose shapes and the strawberry, orange, and apricot crèmes were equally eponymous. Even the coffee crèmes were carved into the semblance of a tiny coffee pot. Jane chose apricot and Ruth rose. Phryne selected coffee. They nibbled, tasted, inhaled, and exulted. 'Well, girls, what do you think?'

'Miss Phryne, that is amazing.' Ruth's pink tongue slowly circumnavigated her lips, determined to sweep up every last fragment. Jane seemed to have gone into a fruit-flavoured trance. Phryne replaced the lid with some determination.

Ruth nudged her sister. 'Look, it's Miss Phryne and Ember!'

Jolted awake, Jane examined the design. 'The wallpaper is all wrong, but I believe that is this very room! Miss Phryne, did you have your portrait painted here?'

'I did. While you girls were at school.'

'Why didn't you tell us?' Ruth stared at the picture in admiration.

'I didn't know whether I was going to like it,' Phryne admitted.

'Miss Carson I only know distantly. But Madame Charpentier, who is the maker of these astonishing chocolates, is a friend, and so I agreed to sit for the portrait.'

'Are you going to buy it?'

Phryne raised her eyebrows. 'I already have a portrait.'

Ruth's and Jane's eyes locked for a moment, and Ruth suppressed a giggle. The painting in question was of Phryne without clothes. Both girls had admired it several times when Phryne was absent.

'I trust the chocolates met with your approval?'

'It was astonishing!' Ruth exclaimed.

'When may we have another one, Miss Phryne?' Jane asked.

Phryne smiled. 'Not until tomorrow—we must make them last.' She picked up the empty cardboard box in which the chocolates had been delivered. To her surprise, it rattled. 'That's odd,' she said, and reached inside the shredded packing paper. 'Well, now. Look here.' She handed a small box to Ruth. This one was plain white cardboard and had sustained a number of sabre cuts during Ember's in-depth investigation. 'It seems that this one must be for you girls.'

Ruth looked at Phryne wide-eyed. 'Are you sure, Miss?'

'Yes, I am. I hope that is satisfactory?'

Jane exchanged a look with her sister and opened the box. 'I believe these are nougats, Miss. Nougat!' She rolled the word around her tongue and pronounced it good.

Ruth looked over her shoulder, poked one with an experimental forefinger and grinned. 'There are four of them, Miss Phryne, but they're all soft.'

'Nougat is supposed to be soft,' Phryne assured her.

The girls trooped off to their bedroom to be alone with their treasure. Phryne considered that if the box survived the night, she would be very surprised.

Later that night, Phryne offered one chocolate each to Mr and Mrs Butler, one to Tinker, and had one more herself. The Butlers quietly glowed and thanked her. Tinker ate his with relish, pronounced it 'Grouse, Miss' and thanked her also. Then she retreated to her room. The carton had contained twenty heavenly masterpieces. Since there were now only thirteen left—an inauspicious number—she allowed herself one more. The attar of roses was the sort of chocolate angels would nibble in heaven. And the carving was so intricate. The machine tools must have cost a fortune. Madame Charpentier was from Belgium, where they understood what chocolate should be like, but she was by no means wealthy. Phryne hoped she had not got in over her head with this project of hers. Still, Phryne considered, it was probably wise to set sail for the very pinnacle of the market. The mass-market chocolatiers (Cadbury, Fry, and Rowntree) were unassailable, but there was always room at the top.

～

The telephone rang at ten the following morning. Phryne, barely out of bed, heard Mr Butler speaking in his grave butlerine voice. There was a pause, and presently a respectful knock at her bedroom door.

'Miss Fisher, it is the chocolate maker, wanting to know if the delivery arrived safely.'

Phryne, to whom conversation was anathema at so early an hour, replied, 'Tell Madame thank you, and I will call her back.' She sipped at her espresso and heard Mr B's quiet, determined footfall on the stairs and his reassuring voice on the phone. She looked out through her window at the waves rolling in to the beach.

There was another knock on the door, and Phryne looked at it dagger-eyed. 'Yes?'

'It's me, Miss.' That was Dot's voice, and Phryne relaxed.

'Come in.' She was always at home to Dot. Her companion bustled in and hovered irresolute on the carpet. 'All right, Dot. Something's got in among you. What is it?'

Dot held out her hand. There was one of the nougats, still in its wrapper. 'Miss, I think there's something wrong with these nougats. The girls felt sick this morning and wanted to stay home from school.'

'And have they?'

'No, Miss. There's nothing really wrong with them—they don't have temperatures and their insides seem to be all right—so I packed them off and told them not to make such a fuss.'

'So they did eat the rest? I thought they might. What do they think is wrong?'

'Ruth said they tasted funny, and Jane said they'd better leave the last one as evidence.'

Phryne laid the offending morsel on her dressing table and carefully unwrapped it. She bent down and sniffed. 'That's odd. This smells of mustard. What do you think?'

Dot leaned over, sniffed, turned her face away, and sneezed loudly. Phryne handed over one of her silk handkerchiefs and Dot wiped her nose with it. 'Yes, Miss. There's mustard powder there all right.'

'I doubt it will catch on as a flavour. This isn't good, Dot. Especially for Mme Charpentier.'

Phryne took up her letter opener and made a few incisions. She cut away the surface from one end of the nougat then cut the remains in half. She put one in her mouth and considered. 'Dot, try the other piece. It's all right. It tastes good to me. But I'd like a second opinion.'

Dot popped the other piece into her mouth. 'There's still a faint tang of mustard, Miss.'

'Indeed there is, but only a trace, which tells us two things: first, that the mustard powder was added recently, probably no later than yesterday, and second'—she looked at Dot meaningfully—'this is deliberate sabotage.'

'But who would want to do such a thing?' Dot cried. 'It's a crime!'

'Well yes, Dot. I rather think it is. And we are going to find out who—and why.'

Phryne asked Mr Butler for the chocolatier's telephone number, and broke the news to Madame, who was predictably both outraged and terrified. 'Phryne, this is *trop fort*! I sent crates to Myer and Georges this morning. Should I recall them?'

Phryne cogitated furiously for a moment. 'No. Not yet. It would be terrible for your business if you had to do that. We need to find out if it's just the nougats. And the Dark Lady chocolates were wonderful, with not even a suspicion of mustard powder.'

Madame was not comforted by Phryne's tribute. 'But it is impossible! Mustard has no place in chocolate! *Nous sommes trahis!* Please, can you help?'

Phryne sighed. 'I'll see you in an hour.'

〜〜⌒

The factory was in a back street in Footscray, just across the Maribyrnong River. Though small, it was big enough for its purpose. Madame was similarly petite: a dark-haired woman in middle age, with a sharp, angular face and gold teeth peeping out between her lips when she spoke. She was distrait, but business-like.

'Phryne, I must show you over the process and perhaps you will be able to discern where the treachery took place.'

Phryne watched as sugar, chocolate, and water were boiled in vats. ('As you may know, chocolate is naturally very bitter and must be sweetened,' the chocolate maker explained.) Flavours and unguents were added, then the couverture was assembled: the chocolate was melted, cooled, then heated again, rolled and laid in its intricately carved moulds. The crème filling was ladled into the moulds, and the upper mould was slammed down onto the top to remove air bubbles.

'One moment,' said Phryne. 'Who does all this?'

'Only myself. It is very intricate and I trust no one to do it properly.'

'Can anyone else walk in here?'

The chocolate maker shook her head. 'I keep this room locked and I have the only key.'

'Madame, I need to interview everyone who works here. Do you have a private office?'

'*Bien sûr*. I shall take you there.'

The tiny office was sparsely furnished with only a desk, a chair behind the desk and one in front, a small spirit stove, and a coffee pot. Two wire baskets on the desk announced themselves as In and Out and the telephone stood upright on its receiver. There was a lingering aroma of coffee.

Phryne took the seat behind the desk and, at a timid knock on the door, called, 'Come in!'

'Miss Fisher? I'm Helen.' A small girl of perhaps seventeen sat herself in the opposite chair and folded her hands in her lap. She wore a white cap, from which a few strands of blonde hair escaped. Her body was covered by her grey work overall. Inasmuch as anything could be seen of her, Phryne deduced that she would be decidedly pretty out of uniform.

'Hello, Helen. Have you heard the news?'

'About the nougat, Miss? Yes. Madame was beside herself.'

'Now, how many people work here?'

'Janet and I do the packing, but Madame makes all the chocolates herself and nobody else is allowed in there.'

'Do you think somebody has got in there, even so?'

The girl thought about this. 'I don't think it would be possible, Miss. Madame never leaves the door unlocked.'

Phryne stared at the ceiling for a moment. 'Helen, you do realise that if today's deliveries to those big shops are found to have mustard in them, then Madame will go out of business and you'll all lose your jobs?'

The girl nodded, her expression worried. 'Yes, Miss. We want this mystery solved as much as you do.'

'All right. Can you please send in Janet?'

Janet turned out to be a plain, freckled girl with a long, single black plait, which she shook out from her cap and held on to with her right hand. Her eyes were bright blue and she looked Phryne straight in the eye.

'Miss Fisher, I just want to say it wasn't Helen or me that messed up the chocolate nougat.'

'I'm glad to hear it, Janet, since unless I can solve this mystery today then you're all going to lose your jobs. You know that?'

The girl nodded fiercely.

'Tell me about the small boxes,' Phryne prompted. 'Like the one sent to my house with nougat in it.'

'Was it a small, plain box?' Janet asked.

'Yes, it was. Is that significant?'

'Madame gives us a pack of four chocolates to take home every night.' Her thin lips spread in a smile. 'It's the best thing about this job, I can tell you. But mine were all nougat. I don't like nougat, so I gave them back to Madame and she gave me them rose ones instead. They were great.'

'And what did Madame do with the nougats?'

'I saw her put them in the parcel to be delivered to you.'

'I see.' Phryne thought this over. 'So the mustard-laced nougats were meant for you originally. Can you think of any reason why someone would want to spoil your chocolates?'

A trace of a frown crossed the girl's face, then she said, 'No, Miss. It makes no sense.' She closed her mouth with a snap.

'Janet? Call me suspicious-minded, but I think you're holding out on me. Don't.'

Janet sighed. 'Miss, have you met the delivery boys, Harry and Charlie?'

'No. Tell me about them.'

'Charlie's a bit older—maybe twenty-one?—and he's a bit fresh with us girls. He makes rude comments.'

'Suggestive remarks?'

'Yes. But I slap him down. Helen just blushes and ignores him. She's polite. I'm not.'

'Good for you, Janet. And Harry?'

'Harry's real sweet on Helen. He's quiet. Never says boo to a goose.'

'And how does Helen feel about Harry?'

Janet shook her head. 'I told him he didn't have a hope.'

'Really?'

'No chance, Miss,' the girl said with certainty.

'I see. Can you please send the boys in now?'

Charlie swaggered in first, took one look at Phryne and whistled. 'Cor, missus, ain't you a corker? Yer too old fer me but.' He leaned against the wall and folded his arms in an attitude of greasy nonchalance. Phryne lowered her eyebrows.

'Charlie, isn't it?' she purred, with Antarctic courtesy. 'Please let me assure you that the only thing you're likely to get from me is a matching set of black eyes and a broken ankle. That's if you're intending to get fresh, which of course you aren't, are you, Charlie?'

Charlie blinked, unfolded his arms, and stared at her. 'Er, no, Miss.'

'Good. Now, Charlie, tell me about your relations with the packing room girls. Take your time, and do please endeavour to keep it clean.'

A vacant expression of utter puzzlement descended like a fog over Charlie's visage. 'What, them sheilas? Nothin' to tell, Miss. We pass the time of day, that's all. Helen's a real looker, but there's nothin' doin' there. She's a good girl. And Janet's okay. Gives as good as she gets, you know?'

'Very well. That will be all. Please send in Harry.'

Charlie exited the room, looking confused but relieved.

Two minutes later, Phryne was seated opposite a white-faced, shivering young man who looked as though he had been stampeded by a herd of elephants.

'Harry, you were wasting your time,' she told him. 'It was a stupid idea anyway. Helen wants a self-confident young man with prospects; she's not interested in a tongue-tied imbecile like you. And when Janet told you this, you decided to punish her by giving her mustard-flavoured nougats! Is that correct?'

No words emerged, but Harry managed a terrified nod.

'And you couldn't even get that right! Janet doesn't like nougat, so she swapped them for something else, and Madame slipped the mustard-laced nougats into the delivery for me. Did you tamper with anything else? Tell me right now, or heaven help you!'

The trembling youth squealed in anguish, 'No, Miss! It was just that one box, I swear!'

Phryne gave a grave nod. 'Harry, you are a nitwit.'

The wretched youth nodded. '*Squeak.*'

'The only good thing about this ridiculous episode is that at least Madame's business is safe and Helen won't lose her job—unlike you. I'm afraid you will have to leave, Harry. Anyone who would pull a preposterous stunt like this is unsafe at any speed. In a special act of mercy, Madame has promised me that she will not be calling the police.'

'Squeak?'

The poor boy was now so flattened that Phryne's wrath subsided. She reached into her purse and drew out a pound note. 'Harry, take this. Don't spend it all at once. And please learn some sense.'

Harry drew himself into something approaching rectilinearity and rediscovered his voice. 'Thank you, Miss.'

As Harry slipped out the door into the rest of his ignoble life, Phryne looked down into her lap. Two more boxes of chocolates nestled there, courtesy of a grateful Madame Charpentier. At ten and sixpence a box, Phryne felt adequately recompensed for her interrupted morning. And Lin Chung would be visiting that very evening. The Dark Lady would have a little something extra with which to entertain him ...

The Bells of St Paul's

Sometimes with secure delight
The upland hamlets will invite,
When the merry bells ring round
And the jocund rebecks sound...

—John Milton, *L'Allegro*

The bells of St Paul's began to ring in the middle distance as the Hon. Miss Phryne Fisher and her companion Miss Dorothy Williams leaned back in their exquisitely padded chairs and sighed. High tea at the Windsor was everything it ought to have been. The tea was Earl Grey and marinated to perfection; the sandwiches imaginatively variegated; the cakes light, flavoursome and pneumatic; and the champagne enthusiastic, brut and from the altogether superior cellars of the Widow Clicquot. The savouries were superb: each morsel of pie, quiche, and meatball was appropriately spiced, garnished, and encased in pastries of delicate toothsomeness that did not simply melt in the mouth but, rather, insinuated their way into the tastebuds like a lissom foreign agent diffusing exotic perfumes.

Dot, as she frequently did, admired the brazen effrontery of her employer's Erté gown (slate blue with black ruffs at the wrists and hem) and Phryne gazed with affection at Dot. It was a silent battle betwixt them. Dot preferred plain, reticent, economical attire, while her employer always wished to push the boundaries and make her undeniably attractive companion shine a little brighter than the latter might wish. Today's autumn-brown dress—custom-built by Mavis Ripper—was the latest in a series of mutually acceptable compromises. Miss Ripper was something of an anomaly in Melbourne: a couturier who ignored the fashions of Europe and blazed a solitary trail of independent creation. Both Dot and Phryne wished her every kind of luck.

Presently Phryne opened her eyes wide, and reached for her chain-mail and chamois purse. It was rather larger than was customary for ladies, owing to the unorthodox items it contained, including a pearl-handled .22 Beretta pistol. Dot experienced a momentary terror that Miss Phryne might be about to shoot out the lights in the Windsor's tearoom but subsided into her chair when her employer produced instead her notebook and gold pencil. She began to scribble feverishly. Then she put the pencil down and lifted her head, listening to the distant bells. Dot opened her mouth to speak, but Phryne shook her head in warning. As far as Dot could tell, the bells chimed their stately way through their endless permutations in a perfectly mundane fashion. She had no idea why this particular carillon should have so aroused her mercurial employer. Finally, she sensed that it would be in order to intrude herself.

'Miss Phryne, what's wrong with the bells? They ring them every day.'

'Indeed, Dot,' her employer agreed, 'but there's something different about today's ring. They're doing a standard quarter-peal,

I expect, but at the beginning I heard the same bell strike twice in a row. Now I am no expert in change ringing, but I do know—wait!' She held up a warning finger.

As Dot listened, she heard the same note strike twice. Then different bells sounded, and another rang three times more. Phryne continued to scribble, turning over a page in furious haste. A waiter hovered near them, plainly wishing to hint to the gracious ladies that afternoon tea was now officially at an end; the other guests had already folded their tents and departed. On the other hand, the Hon. Miss Phryne Fisher was on a rather exclusive list of Exalted Personages to Be Indulged At Almost All Costs, and finding his honoured guest engaged in furious ratiocination, he melted away into the mahogany background. As he did so, he caught the eye of the attendant maître d', who gave him an emphatic nod of approval.

Phryne laid down her pencil and grinned at her companion. 'Dot, I believe we have a mystery on our hands. And if I guess correctly, our message will be repeated at least once more. Whoever is the intended recipient of this conundrum will probably require three turns to decipher it.'

Dot looked, as ever on such occasions, both apprehensive and excited. 'Is it a code, Miss Phryne?'

'I believe it is. I think I have the gist of the message, but at present it makes no sense. However, we shall see.' She continued to listen intently. 'Nearly all of this peal sounds like their usual thing: Stedman's or Grandsire or whatever it is. But they are sending somebody a secret message. They've done it twice. And that I find profoundly intriguing. Don't you?'

'Yes, Miss. If it's a secret message, then all the ringers must be in on it.'

Phryne folded her hands on the arctic white tablecloth and nodded. 'Exactly. And the recipient must be a bell ringer also, or else a musician who can recognise notes without difficulty. But either my ears are all wrong, or some of these notes are higher than one would expect. If I had perfect pitch, I would know. Alas, like almost all of humanity, I don't.' She paused. 'Keep listening, Dot. As soon as we hear the same bell strike twice or more, I am going to write it down again, and see if it matches.'

Dot's knowledge of music was limited to singing hymns in her Catholic church, but she knew that every note had its own letter and that they took in the first seven letters of the alphabet. But how could you make a message using only seven letters? Even the word *abracadabra* needed an *r*. Dot closed her eyes, and began to run through all the words she could think of. *Ada bagged a beaded beef*? No, that was just silly. She had got as far as *Fed, Bea begged a cabbage* when she gave up. She would have to leave the decipherment to her employer.

Time passed. The maître d' began to look at his watch with increasing ostentation. The other tables were cleared by silent minions in black and white. And still the Hon. Miss Phryne Fisher listened to the bells. Dot began to fret, seeing the unmistakable signs of welcome being, if not entirely worn out, at least rendered threadbare.

At last the pattern emerged again. Phryne scribbled in her pad, checked it against the previous pages, and grinned triumphantly. The bells ceased their clamour and she rose, shouldering her purse. Dot rose also. As they passed the door, Phryne gave the maître d' a winning smile and handed him a ten-shilling note. '*Mille remerciements*, Jean-Pierre.'

'*À la bonheur*,' mused Jean-Pierre, pocketing the tip. Doubtless the English milady had been performing acts of detection, as was her way. The offence was considerable but the reparation more than ample.

The journey homewards in Phryne's Hispano-Suiza was no more sprightly than usual and Dot contrived to survive it, as was her wont, by keeping her eyes shut and praying unobtrusively. When they were safely settled in Phryne's parlour, Dot looked expectantly at her employer, who smiled. Dot recognised the symptoms of detection: heightened colour, lips slightly open, and a certain frisson of tension around the shoulders.

'Dot, I think I have it. It's hard to tell, because I read somewhere that there are twelve bells, or thirteen, or something like that, instead of the usual eight. But I think this was it.' She selected a brand-new sheet of paper from her escritoire and wrote in block capitals. 'What do you think, Dot?' On the page was written BEDDDEAFFFFFFBBDGGBBGBFFF. And underneath was inscribed BERE AT MIDNIGBT. 'I think the repeated notes mean that you start again, so that the DDD is really R, and so on.'

Dot stared at it and shook her head. 'They wouldn't be drinking beer in a church, surely?' She was innately suspicious of Protestants but this seemed a little excessive, even for them. 'Are you sure about the B's, Miss? If they were H's it would mean "here at midnight".'

'Yes, that's what I thought. But... wait. Where's that booklet now? I was looking at it last Sunday.' Phryne sprang to her feet and began to rummage in a pile of books, without visible success. Dot glided to the bookcase and drew out a slim hardcover book labelled *The Bells of St Paul's*. She dimpled as she handed it over, and Phryne's face lit up like a Christmas shop window.

'What would I do without you, Dot? Yes, here it is. Aha!' Phryne riffled through it and planted an accusatory finger on page 4. 'See here? Twelve bells, tuned in C sharp. I thought the notes were higher than usual. Our cryptographer knows that in

German *B* proper is actually *B* flat, and they use *H* for *B* natural. And our mysterious messengers have pruned away all the sharps, and left us a gorgeous puzzle.'

'If you say so, Miss.' To Dot, the nuances of musical theory were like abstract German philosophy: she was glad it was there, but she was more than happy to leave it to others. 'Maybe they just used *B* instead of *H* because you would only have to ring the bell once instead of twice?'

'That's a very good point, Dot. They were taking a big risk, even so. And we are going to attend at midnight and find out why they are doing it. I wonder... Surely it can't be Russian spies? They used a bell code like this during the war. It's harder in Cyrillic, of course.'

'Miss Phryne, are you sure we should?' Minding One's Own Business had been drilled into Dot as a child, frequently at the end of a cane.

Phryne's face sparked with mischief. 'Of course, Dot. Since they were so very public about their message, it would be a shame to miss out on the fun. Wake me at eleven, and we shall find out who is meeting whom in the dead of night at St Paul's, and why.'

Flinders Street late at night was more Gothic than Dot felt comfortable with. The cathedral towered over them: dark, forbidding, and alien. One or two eldritch figures hurried past them, but otherwise the streets were deserted. Had it not been for the ghostly streetlamps and the faintly illumined sandstone edifice of Flinders Street Station, it would have been as dark as the interior of an Egyptian pyramid. Though well wrapped against the late autumn chill, Dot shivered anyway. The distant clock face of the town hall registered twenty minutes before midnight.

'Well, Dot, it would seem that the dread portals are not open to visitors at this hour. But I believe there is a side entrance and thither we shall repair.'

Phryne led the way along Flinders Street and turned down a short cobblestone alley. Her flat boots clicked decisively, proclaiming to anybody passing that she did not care if she were overheard. Dot's own footfall was lighter. She hoped there would be no trouble about this.

At the end of the alley, under a pallid lamp, stood the slight figure of a girl. Phryne noted the glint of spectacles, short, brown hair, and an air of quiet authority. Phryne extended a gloved hand. 'Good evening. I'm Phryne Fisher. It's a cold night for whatever you're doing here, isn't it?'

To Dot's complete astonishment, the young woman began to laugh. 'Dear me, the famous detective. To what do we owe the pleasure?'

'I hope you're not here to steal the silver candlesticks. And who might you be, anyway?'

'I can't say it's any of your business, Miss Fisher.'

'True, but I could say I suspect a crime is being committed and call a policeman. I have a whistle in my bag.' Phryne grinned archly in the pale luminescence. 'So let's just assume we've said all that and get to the nub of it, shall we? Are you one of the bell ringers?'

The girl laughed again. 'Did you work it all out? I thought nobody would notice.'

'It was the repeated notes that gave you away. Do you know,' Phryne continued, 'I rather suspect an elopement? But why? Surely they don't keep you all chained up in the vestry and only let you out to ring bells? Come on, young lady, I haven't got all night—out with it!'

The pointed chin jutted for a moment, sizing Phryne up in the looming darkness. 'All right, I'll tell you. My name is Frieda von Mises, and I ring bells here. The Dean doesn't like to have women ringing, but he had no choice after he gave Michael the sack. Nobody else would take Michael's place and—'

Phryne held up a gloved hand to pause the recitation. 'Why did the Dean dismiss him?'

'He got disgustingly drunk at a party, and when the Dean arrived to pick up his daughter he found Michael throwing up in the rhododendrons. There had been an Understanding between Rose and Michael. The Dean wasn't all that happy about it but he tolerated the courtship of his daughter until then.'

'And after that?'

'He forbade him to come anywhere near the cathedral or his daughter. And just to make sure, Rose is confined to quarters.'

'So you sent the message to Michael, telling him to meet her at midnight? It seems a melodramatic solution to a straightforward problem.'

'It was the only solution. The problem is that none of us knows where Michael lives and we think his real name is something different.'

'Why so?'

Frieda shook her head. 'We've seen letters addressed to him as Windermere, or Grasmere, something like that. Something in the Lake District. Now they might be letters he's keeping for a friend, but I doubt it. And he never talks about his childhood or schooldays. As you doubtless know, most young men never shut up about them.'

Phryne smiled. 'And yet, despite these suspicions, you are helping the Dean's daughter to elope with him?'

'Why not? Miss Fisher, when you have got drunk with some-one several times over you really do know them to their marrow. Michael's a big puppy. And he adores Rose.'

'I see. Well, I've met the Dean and I agree he's something of an Obadiah Slope. The sort of man who makes you want to wash your hands every three minutes. Very well, then.'

An outbreak of clumping boots erupted down the laneway and a large, shambling figure lurched to a halt. 'Frieda! Is everything all right? Why did—I say, who the devil are these people?' He indicated Phryne. Dot had backed herself unobtrusively against the church wall, but she was taking it all in.

Phryne turned towards the newcomer. From her purse she produced a small torch and scanned the pale anxious face from side to side.

'Toby Windermere! What on earth are you doing here in Australia?'

'Good God, Phryne! Is that you? What the devil are *you* doing here?'

'Existing beautifully, as ever, Toby. But you haven't answered my question.' Phryne turned to the wicket gate, which had now creaked open, and an aureole of angelic blonde hair atop a slight body announced the arrival of, in all probability, the eloping daughter.

'Everybody, this is Toby, Viscount Windermere. And he shall now expound the mystery of how he comes to be ringing bells at the ends of the earth and courting a dean's daughter under an assumed name.'

The blonde girl looked up, her face a mixture of eagerness, concern, and perplexity. She set down the valise she was holding and folded her arms. 'Michael? What's all this about? Are you really a viscount? Why didn't you tell me?'

The noble lord looked downcast, as though someone had thrown a stick over a picket fence just too high for him to leap over. 'Rose, I'm so sorry. I didn't want to say it because you'd think I was terribly rich and I'm not really. Pater—the earl, you know—has gone and lost the family fortune, so I came out here to make some money.'

'And have you?' Phryne wanted to know.

'Yes, rather. I've made quite a bit, actually. Business isn't so hard. I found I was pretty good at it, even though everyone knows I'm a bit of a duffer in most things.'

'And what made you come and ring bells, Mich—Toby?' Rose enquired.

He blushed. 'I love ringing bells! I used to ring every Sunday at our parish church, so when I arrived in Melbourne I decided to ring them here too. And I met you. And I love you, Rose, and I want to get married.'

Rose stared at him for so long that he began to squirm. 'So when were you going to tell me I was to become Lady Windermere?'

'Sounds a bit off, doesn't it? I mean, that play of Wilde's, everyone wanting to know where your fan was and all that. But one day you'll be the Countess of Grasmere and that won't be as bad. Look, I can renounce the title if you'd like.'

Rose moved forward and kissed him. 'That won't be necessary.' He wrapped his arms around her and held her tight.

∽

'Rose, dear, you really are careless.'

Everybody in the now excessively tenanted laneway whirled around. There, in the open doorway, a faded woman was looking with considerable affection at the blonde girl. The latter all but fainted, but her intended's strong arms held her up. 'Mother? What are you … ?'

Mrs Dean was holding out a large manila envelope. 'Rose, if you really are going to elope, you ought to take your passport with you and not leave it behind. You will also find I have taken the liberty of enclosing two steamer tickets. You may want to stay with my people in Bournemouth, if you can stand it. Hampshire isn't so bad.' She stared straight at Toby. 'Not if you really are in love. And of course you'll be married by then, won't you? I believe ship's captains are allowed to do it.'

In the spreading pool of silence, Mrs Dean turned to Frieda. 'I take it the bell code was your idea? I should have guessed you were up to something.'

For once, Frieda's self-possession faltered. 'How did you know about that?'

A wry look appeared on the Dean's wife's face. 'I wanted to ring bells too. I know how it's done. But Henry wouldn't let me.'

Phryne had been staring open-mouthed for what she considered quite long enough. 'Are you saying that you cracked the code too?' she asked Mrs Dean. 'And you don't mind about the elopement?'

'No, Miss Fisher, I don't mind. Oh yes, I know who you are. I didn't know this one was a lord, but if eight more or less God-fearing bell ringers are prepared to vouch for him, he's good enough for my daughter. Now go, both of you,' she urged the affianced couple. 'Before Henry starts sleepwalking and spoils the fun!'

When the lovers were safely fled away, the four remaining women gave each other long, searching looks in the gloom. And then, all at once, they began to laugh.

GLOSSARY

American cloth: early form of linoleum.

Art silk: artificial silk which brought silk stockings within a working-class budget.

Ballyragged: harassed, pestered.

Bijou: French for jewel; dainty and precious.

Blighter: reprehensible person.

Californian Poppy: a hair oil.

Cloche: a close-fitting felt hat, globular in shape.

Corker/corking: wonderful.

Dip: a pickpocket.

Docket: a criminal record.

Épergne: large silver or china bowl which obstructs table conversation. Usually filled with flowers.

Erté: one of Phryne's favourite fashion designers, and designer for the Ballets Russes.

Famille Rose: ancient Chinese porcelain.

Flapper: originally a schoolgirl with her hair in a braid down her back; later a fashionable woman with short skirts, short hair, and no corset.

Flat stony motherless: entirely without capital of any kind.

Floris: very lovely brand of fragrances, cosmetics, and hair tonic, still in operation in Soho.

Free love (1928 style): living together without marriage.

Gees: horses.

Gelt: money (from the Yiddish).

Gen: information.

Grouse: somewhere between 'good' and 'wonderful.'

Gussied-up: dressed for a party.

Hellenic beverage: Phryne's very strong Greek coffee.

Jacks: police.

Knut: a dandy.

Mash: brew the tea.

Mozz: to 'put the mozz' on someone/thing is to put a curse on it.

Natural: a 'natural' is a child with some congenital cognition fault; also used as emphasis, 'a natural-born bastard.'

Out of the top drawer: from the best families.

Plackets: petticoat pockets, separate from the garment, or the slits in skirts made so that they could be reached.

Poitou: a French fashion designer.

Queue (in relation to hair): a long plait.

Rakehell: a bibulous and loose-living gentleman.

Raree show: a carnival or sideshow.

Scotch, to: to frustrate or foil.

Shill: a person who hangs around a carnival sideshow and draws in customers.

Silvertail: a rich person.

Sly grog: illegal sales of alcohol outside drinking hours.

Spooning: kissing and caressing.

Sugar sack: calico sacks, used for clothing the poor.

Thimble-rigger: offers a game with three cups and a ball which you cannot win.

Three-card trick: also known as 'find the lady,' the object is to guess which card is the queen. See 'thimble-rigger' for your chances of success.

Tickety boo: excellent.

Turkey lolly: spun sugar or fairy floss.

Two-bob watch: not a reliable source of information.

Valenciennes: very good Belgian lace.

Voluntary (of an organ): a piece played as the organist wishes.

Wet arse and no fish: an unsuccessful venture.

Withdrawing room: a parlour in a hotel.

Zinc: the counter in a French bistro.

If you've enjoyed these short adventures of Miss Phryne Fisher,
read on for an excerpt from Kerry Greenwood's
latest full-length Phryne novel,

Death in Daylesford,

now available from Poisoned Pen Press.

Chapter One

The Sons of Mary seldom bother, for they have
  inherited that good part;
But the Sons of Martha favour their Mother of the
  careful soul and the troubled heart.
And because she lost her temper once, and because
  she was rude to the Lord her Guest,
Her Sons must wait upon Mary's Sons, world
  without end, reprieve, or rest.

—Rudyard Kipling, *The Sons of Martha*

It was a lazy, late summer's morning in St Kilda. The early sun
was no longer the copper-coloured furnace of January, and
instead of beating at the window with bronze gongs and ham-
mers was knocking respectfully at the shutters, asking leave for
admittance. Without, the tide was gently turning, lapping over
the mid-ochre sands of the beach and promising light refreshment for anyone wanting a matitudinal paddle. Last night's
windstorm had blown itself out, and through the open window
drifted a cool, damp sensation of overnight rain.

Phryne Fisher rose from her bed, wrapped a turquoise satin dressing-gown around her impossibly elegant person, tied the cord, and tiptoed towards the bathroom, where a malachite bath-tub and unlimited hot water awaited her. Pausing at the door, she turned and raked her boudoir with a long, ever so slightly greedy and thoroughly complacent look. She admired the wickedly crimson satin bedsheets. The hand-painted silk bedspread (the Book of Hours of Marie de France, now wantonly disordered, with its scenes of medieval life carelessly strewn over the aquamarine Chinese carpet). The half-empty crystal decanter (with matching balloon glasses, both empty) whose contents had been imported at absurd expense from the sunny vineyards of Armagnac. The outstretched paws and arched back of the sleeping cat Ember, jet-black and sleek with good living. And the jet-black eyebrows and perfect features of Lin Chung, who arched his golden back and burrowed further down between the sheets. She admired his bare, muscular shoulder, smiled with a thrill of retrospective delight, and entered the bathroom.

From her extensive collection of bath salts, Phryne chose the china pot labelled *Gardenia* and emptied a goodly pile into the shaped malachite tub. She opened both brass taps and watched as the twin torrents of water swirled and effervesced. A warm, fragrant aroma of English Country Garden caressed her nostrils. Phryne slipped out of her gown and lowered herself into the water. She surveyed her slender body with a certain level of satisfaction, her imagination still ravished by the previous night's passion. A woman on the brink of thirty always nurtured secret suspicions of fading charms—even someone with Phryne's armour-plated self-esteem. Yet, judging by her lover's awed reactions and responses, it would seem that this was far from being the case. Lin himself was utterly unchanged by marriage. So many businessmen let themselves go; their waistlines expanded along with their incomes.

Lin's copper-coloured body was as smooth and strong as a teen-age boy's. The only sign of change she had observed was a small knot of ebony hair in the centre of his delectable chest, with the merest suggestion of a line of down heading due southwards. Her tongue had given this matter some considerable exploration the previous evening.

Phryne grinned, and began to soap her person. *I'm well and truly on the shelf now, and the world can watch me not care,* she told herself. How fortunate that her idiotic father had shown the fore-sight to dismiss her from his baronial presence some years ago, otherwise she would have been visited with a plague of suitors of varying degrees of loathsomeness. For the English nobility, an unmarried daughter of twenty-nine was a matter of some uneasiness, somewhere on the continuum between Unsuitable Entanglements and Failure to Ride to Hounds. Her father's threat to cut her off with a shilling for gross disobedience had been rendered toothless when, upon obtaining her majority, Phryne had calmly removed her assets from her father's rapacious fingers. To compound his sense of disgrace, his other daughter Eliza had combined the twin horrors of Socialism and Unnatural Vice.

Phryne's opinion of her father had not been improved by this attitude. Socialism was frequently affected in noble families, and lesbianism could easily be forgiven in polite society given that Eliza's Chosen had been of impeccably noble birth. Once you were in Debrett's, unnatural vice was magically transmuted into Passionate Friendship, which had been socially acceptable ever since Lady Eleanor Butler and the Hon. Sarah Ponsonby had set up house together as the Ladies of Llangollen. Even the Duke of Wellington had visited them. Although that said less than it might, since the Iron Duke was renowned for not giving even one hoot for popular prejudice. Nevertheless, Father had broken off all contact with both daughters, and all his attention, such as it was, had been lavished on his son and heir Thos. Of whom the best that could be said was that the future Baron of Richmond-upon-Thames would be a worthy heir to the present one. Neither the present nor future lords would ever visit either Phryne or Eliza. Phryne felt she could moderate her grief.

She sank down deeper into the smooth embrace of the steaming waters. It was so much easier dealing with the Chinese. Lin's wife Camellia was a typical exemplar of Chinese womanhood: small of body and voice, discreet, self-assured, and possessing a will of pure adamant. The greeting she gave Phryne whenever they chanced to meet was gracious, polite, and filled with iron Confucian certainty. *You are my husband's honoured concubine and I trust you implicitly. You may walk through Chinatown in perfect security. Anyone who offers you offence may expect consequences of considerable severity, up to and including a small battleaxe to the back of the head. I, on the other hand, am Lin's First Lady. I have my position, and you have yours. We understand each other perfectly.*

Phryne sat up in the bath and listened. Noises Off appeared to be happening. Since Dot was unlikely to outrage her maidenly modesty by attempting to bring her employer breakfast in bed when Phryne was Entertaining, this must mean that Lin himself was doing the honours, with the assistance of Mr and Mrs Butler. She climbed out of the bath, dried herself off with two towels of spotless white cotton, and wrapped herself anew in her turquoise silk robe. 'Do I smell eggs and bacon, Lin?' she enquired, opening the bedroom door.

Lin Chung pushed a prodigiously laden tea trolley into the centre of the boudoir and gestured to the two cushioned seats. 'Eggs, bacon, and all the accoutrements of an English breakfast,' he announced. 'I believe there are roast tomatoes, sautéed mushrooms, and sausages made from absurdly pampered pigs. There is also toast, Earl Grey tea, marmalade, and strawberry jam. Will the Silver Lady join me at breakfast?'

Phryne lifted the lids of the chafing dishes one by one and inhaled deeply. 'I was scarcely expecting such luxury. How did you manage to get the trolley upstairs? Was Cantonese magic involved at all?'

Lin folded his hands in an imitation of a stage Chinaman. 'Ah! The East is filled with mysteries.'

Phryne gently pushed him down into one of the chairs. 'Well, yes, Lin, otherwise why would it be called the Mysterious East? But how—oh, of course, I forgot: the dumb waiter.'

Mr Butler had of late come down with a serious outburst of Home Handyman and had installed a dumb waiter where one of Phryne's wardrobes had been. Phryne had been about to object in the strongest terms when she recollected that Mr Butler was, it must be admitted, getting on in years and that, moreover, the day would inevitably come when Dot would finally achieve holy matrimony with Hugh Collins and might not be available to attend upon Phryne. Yet refreshments must be conveyed to the lady of the House in her first-floor bedroom. So, the dumb waiter had been installed, skilfully concealed behind a Chinese silk screen when not in use.

For some time, conversation gave place to unbridled gluttony. It was not Phryne's habit to eat breakfast at all, beyond a French roll and a morning coffee, but erotic adventures awoke her hunger for other forms of bodily delights. As Phryne closed the lids on the devastated remains of the hot dishes and looked with devotion at her beautiful lover, he reached out his right hand and closed it around her left. 'Phryne? May I ask you something?'

'Ask me anything, and I shall answer.'

'Yesterday I saw Bert and Cec driving their cab, and as their fare debouched right in front of me, I enquired after their health.'

'As one does.' Phryne buttered herself another piece of toast and smeared it with marmalade. 'And how did they respond?'

'Cec looked inscrutable and muttered something, and Bert gave it as his opinion that he was a menace to shipping. What does this mean?'

Phryne clasped his hand tighter and raised it to her lips. 'It means he is in robust spirits. Your English is perfect Oxford, but I presume Australian argot did not feature in the curriculum at Balliol College.'

'No, it didn't. Is this like a bald man must always be called Curly?'

'And a red-haired man is always Bluey. It's similar, but … not quite the same.' Phryne pondered for a long moment how Lin Chung had got along with the rowdy undergraduates, deciding there were several reasons why he would have flourished there. Balliol was one of the more intellectual seats of learning at Oxford. His imperturbable calm would have unnerved most of the bullies. And the whiff of serious money would have inspired automatic respect.

As she nodded to herself, Phryne became aware that Lin was studying her closely.

'You are perhaps wondering how I fared at Balliol, being so blatantly Oriental?'

'I was,' Phryne confessed.

'It was largely trouble-free. Don't forget I had Li Pen with me. Having one's own servant in college lent a certain cachet. And …' He paused and allowed himself a complacent smile of recollection.

'And Li Pen was also available to chastise the rowdier elements under the influence of excessive alcohol?' Phryne suggested.

'He was. It is his duty and pleasure to serve.'

'I trust no one was seriously injured?'

'He inserted three of them into an ornamental fountain.

They suffered nothing worse than bruises, both to the person and personality.'

'Youthful high spirits?'

'That was indeed the official verdict.'

'I see. Lin?' Phryne leaned back seductively. 'How soon must you depart?'

He gazed with appreciation at a glimpse of perfect ivory breast beginning to escape from her robe. 'I have a meeting at noon.'

Phryne glanced at her bedroom clock: a modest walnut arrangement standing on the mantelpiece. 'It's only nine thirty. Plenty of time.' She leaned closer to Lin. 'Tomorrow I am departing for the countryside.'

'And which district will be favoured by your august presence?'

'Daylesford. I have received an unusual request, and I am minded to investigate. Do you know of the place?'

'A little. They are building a new lake there. And, unfortunately, the market gardens of the local Chinese will be submerged by it. There has been a great deal of talk about it in the *Daylesford Advocate*. Everybody wants the lake, but nobody wants a rather expensive road diversion. But no one has spared a thought for the market gardeners.'

'That is very careless of them. Perhaps I should intervene on their behalf. Or perhaps the Lin family...?' She allowed the sentence to hang delicately in the air. Lin leaned back in his chair and retied his crimson dressing gown around his delectable body.

'There is no need, Phryne. Measures have already been taken. The gardeners are being moved to Maldon and elsewhere. The land did not actually belong to our people; it was theirs by grace and favour, and now it is being resumed by the local community. I will send someone around with copies of the newspaper from my files, if you like?'

'That would be most helpful. Lin, do you happen to have files on every town in Victoria?'

He laughed aloud. 'Only those where my people are involved, directly or indirectly—which is perhaps more than you would think. Only thus can we maintain our honoured position here.'

Honoured position! But at least there had been no massacres of the Chinese in Victoria, thanks to Constable Thomas Cooke of the Castlemaine police station, representing in his lonely self the awesome majesty of Queen Victoria and her laws. But fear, loathing, ill-will, and general xenophobia there had most certainly been, and it had not yet abated. Still, divining that Lin would like the subject changed, and quickly, she returned to the subject of her own forthcoming visit to the region.

She stood up, reached into her purse, and unfolded a letter, handing it to him. Lin perused the following with raised eyebrows.

The Spa
Hepburn Springs
23 February 1929

Dear Miss Fisher,

I write to you at the recommendation of Dr Elizabeth MacMillan, who has visited here on occasion. I know that you served with distinction in the war, and you will be aware that all too many of our brave survivors suffer from shell shock. The Army and the Ministry offer them little sympathy, and even less help. They are not shirkers or cowards, but men who have endured more than flesh and blood can manage. At my spa, I am attempting to provide my patients with the rest, recuperation, and care they so badly need. I

would like to invite you to see my establishment for yourself,
after which I hope you may see your way clear to supporting
my endeavours. Would you care to join me for dinner this
coming Friday?

Yours sincerely,
Herbert Spencer (Capt., ret'd)

'What do you make of that?'

Lin slipped one hand inside his dressing-gown and ran his hand over his chest. Phryne suppressed the erotic thrill that surged through her body. Any information this admirably well-informed man could supply beforehand might be vital. 'The first thing I should mention is that Hepburn Springs is not Daylesford. While the two communities are contiguous, they have quite different characters. Hepburn Springs is further into the mountain forest.'

'How far away from Daylesford?'

'They are about three miles apart, town centre to town centre. Though there are houses all along the road connecting them.'

'And the spa?'

'It was once a place of secret women's rituals among the local Aboriginal tribes, who were, naturally, comprehensively dispossessed last century. The spa is said to have extraordinary healing properties. And now this Captain Spencer is using it for shell-shock victims? Intriguing. Your Captain sounds like a kind and generous man.'

'Indeed. And how is Daylesford so different?'

'Hepburn Springs is a place of quiet refinement. Daylesford, which is far larger and more spacious, is rather more boisterous. And it possesses a remarkable curiosity.' Phryne raised an eyebrow. Lin matched her by raising both of his own, with matching grin. 'There is a licensed premises called the Temperance Hotel.'

'That does appear to be one of the less successful advertising decisions in history,' Phryne remarked.

'So one would think, at first glance. However, the pub does serve wine, beer, and cider; only spirits are forbidden. This appears to be a compromise widely acceptable in the local community.'

How very Australian! Vociferous arguments in favour of temperance would be made so long as drunken husbands staggered home from the local pub ready to take out their incoherent frustration with the world on their long-suffering wives and children. But while it was possible to get rolling drunk on beer alone, it required a good deal more focus to attain the condition of violent drunkenness; thus, while many Australians had agitated for total prohibition (which had worked so well in America), a substantial body of opinion held that such a compromise was both achievable and prudent.

Phryne smiled at her lover. 'I would be intrigued to visit this place. Perhaps, when I have seen Captain Spencer, I should pay a visit to Daylesford as well. Do any of the other pubs serve spirits?'

Lin chuckled. 'They do. But married patrons are severely discouraged—by their wives—from visiting such places, whereas a few drinks at the Temperance Hotel is something the women of Daylesford can accommodate for their hard-working husbands. Also—' Lin paused, and smiled the smile of a fallen angel '—apparently one of the barmaids is a famous beauty. Her hand in marriage is comprehensively sought.'

'But not yet attained?'

'Not thus far. And I imagine that the rivalry between her suitors sells many a drink on the premises.'

'No doubt. You mentioned wine and cider as well as beer. The wine is because of the Swiss Italians, I expect. Do they make it locally?'

Lin nodded.

'But cider? It is hardly a common drink.'

'This would be the local Cornish influence.'

'Lin, you are a minefield of information.' She squeezed his hand. 'It is now almost ten. You said that you have a meeting at noon?'

'I do, Silver Lady, and I must depart a half hour before.'

'But until then?' She leaned forward, allowing the front of her gown to fall open.

Lin's almond eyes flickered over Phryne's breasts for a moment. 'Until then, I would be pleased to accompany you once more among the chrysanthemums. If it be your will?'

Phryne reached out and took his face between her hands. Her mouth opened, and she traced the tip of her tongue around his lips. 'It is indeed my will.'

Lin's hand closed around her left breast, and Phryne stood up, reaching for the cord of his dressing-gown. She began to chant a poem she had recently discovered. It was called 'Butterflies in Love with Flowers,' and she hoped that Lin might know it, even though it was originally written in Mandarin, and his family spoke Cantonese.

'I would rather drink to intoxication.
One should sing when one has wine in hand,
But drinking to escape offers no reprieve.
I do not mind that my clothes are getting looser.
My lover is worthy of desire.'

Lin's strong arms pulled her body close as their garments fell unregarded onto the carpet. 'Come, little flower, the butterfly is impatient,' he whispered, and he carried her, without effort, back to bed.

ABOUT THE AUTHOR

Kerry Greenwood is the author of more than fifty novels, a book of short stories, and six nonfiction works and the editor of two collections of crime writing. Her beloved Phryne Fisher series has become a successful ABC TV series, *Miss Fisher's Murder Mysteries*, which sold around the world. She is also the author of the contemporary crime series featuring Corinna Chapman, baker and reluctant investigator. The most recent Corinna Chapman novel was *The Spotted Dog*. In addition, Kerry is the author of several books for young adults and the Delphic Women series. When not writing, Kerry has been an advocate in magistrates' courts for the Legal Aid Commission and, in the 2020 Australia Day Honours, was awarded the Medal of the Order of Australia (OAM) for services to literature. She is not married, has no children, is the co-warden of a Found Cats' Home, and lives with an accredited wizard. In her spare time, she stares blankly out the window.